Unnatural Selection

Hailey tried to hang on to her composure, but it was tough when Rick was so obviously undressing her in his mind.

'Did you like what you saw?' she asked.

'You and Cade put on quite a show. Not really appropriate for a family park, though. I could arrest both of you for indecent exposure, and possibly for corrupting minors.'

'*You* could arrest me?' Hailey laughed. 'What are you, a cop?'

'County sheriff.'

'You're kidding. Aren't you?'

Rick looked her straight in the eye. 'Nope. It's an elected position. Of course, we don't have a lot of crime in this county, so it's only a part-time post.'

'Then I guess you're only authorised to give me a part-time sentence.'

'You seem to think you deserve to be punished,' Rick said. 'You must have a guilty conscience.'

Hailey trailed the toe of her sneaker along the ground. 'I guess do have a lot to feel guilty about.'

'Such as?'

'Voyeurism, for one thing. Sexual acts in public places, for another. Then there's sex in public places with men who are engaged to be married.'

'What do you think your punishment should be?'

Hailey tipped her head to one side as she considered his question. 'You're the one with the legal background. Why don't you choose?'

By the same Author:

Hard Blue Midnight
Switching Hands

Unnatural Selection
Alaine Hood

BLACK LACE

Black Lace books contain sexual fantasies.
In real life, always practise safe sex.

First published in 2005 by
Black Lace
Thames Wharf Studios
Rainville Road
London W6 9HA

Design by Smith & Gilmour, London
Printed and bound by Mackays of Chatham PLC

ISBN 0 352 33963 2

Contents

1 Diving into the Gene Pool

It was easy to get into the Amazon on a Thursday night. All you needed were a pair of hotpants, a mane of wild blonde hair and a ballbusting attitude. Hailey planned to use all three of those assets to get past the bouncer, who was checking IDs and, more importantly, looks. Sexual selection in action, right at the front door, weeding out the fashion victims and the hopelessly unhip.

'I'm doing field work. The owner always lets me in for free,' she said, when he demanded a ten-dollar cover charge. The bouncer eyed her skeptically. She wasn't famous, her clothes were strictly thrift store and, though she qualified as a knockout, she wasn't all that young. 'Please,' she begged. 'It's in the interest of science. Sexual evolution is happening in there, even as we speak.'

While the bouncer was mulling this over, Hailey squeaked past him and headed straight for the pounding heart of the club. She didn't have to be a student of evolutionary biology to see which way her species was heading at the Amazon Room – if you didn't look hot, you had no chance of reproductive success here. The club was a resurrected martini bar, the type of joint that used to serve bleeding porterhouse steaks and caustic cocktails back in the fifties. Now it was a retro jazz club, still serving hunks of rare red meat and potent drinks, but the steaks were carefully trimmed, and three cocktails would cost you a week's wages.

Here we go, she thought. Head-first into the gene pool.

Hips pumping to the loud Cuban jazz, Hailey stalked towards the bar in her three-inch stiletto heels. The drums beat in time to the throb of her blood. High on expectation, she felt her adrenaline soar. There was always something new at the Amazon Room, some sexual treasure that she'd never heard of, read about or imagined.

Before Hailey had ordered her first drink, she'd been waylaid by a thin bald man in a black turtleneck who claimed to be a director (the business card he handed her said that he made industrial instruction films), a male–female couple who invited her into a three-way rhumba and a kid so young she could swear she'd been his babysitter at one time. She could smell the mousse on the boy's hair, which was ruffled up like a bird's crest in mating season. He wore a collar of gold chains around his neck, an oversized red T-shirt and twice as much cologne as Hailey.

This was what she loved about the Amazon Room; the males put out more effort than the females. That's how it worked in the wild.

'You wanna?' he asked, so drunk that he was almost – but not quite – cute.

Hailey didn't need to ask what he 'wanna'ed'.

'Forget it, honey. I'm here to watch,' she said. She went to the bar and ordered the drink special of the night, a splash of booze in a balloon glass. The bartender called it a Côte d'Azur, but it looked more like a puddle of window cleaner topped with a plastic hibiscus.

'Eight-fifty,' the bartender said.

'Eight-fifty? Are you serious? At that rate, this will be my only drink of the night.' Hailey lived on a grad-school stipend, a minuscule teaching salary and a part-time bike-messenger job. Her retro glamour was strictly second-hand; she borrowed her clothes from a friend whose mother used to earn grocery money performing acrobatics with her male neighbours in the afternoons.

The bartender shrugged. His haughty gaze panned across Hailey's breasts, which were threatening to leap out of her sequinned tube top. 'Don't blame me. The owner jacks up the drink prices. Keeps out the riff-raff.'

He was a beautiful little bitch, lean and sleek. Much prettier than Hailey, or most of the other women she knew. Obviously he wasn't going to cut her any slack.

'Hey, riff-raff keeps the species going.' Hailey opened her plastic purse, pulled out a ten-dollar bill and deposited it on the counter. 'Keep the change,' she snapped.

A male hand, wearing a pinkie ring with a chunky ruby, scooped up the ten-dollar bill and gave it back to Hailey.

'Gorgeous women don't pay those prices,' said the hand's owner. 'You know better, Chaz.'

The boy pouted. 'I thought we only had to give free drinks to women on ladies' night.'

'For Hailey, every night is ladies' night. You charge her again, and you can look for another job.'

'Thanks, Marco.'

Hailey turned around to hug her friend. In her towering heels she had to stoop down to put her arms around the club owner's short, stocky body, but getting an armful of Marco was worth the effort. What he lacked in looks, he made up for in brains and muscle mass, and the more you got to know his twisted sexual imagination, the more you realised that he was worth ten movie stars in bed. Hailey had never fucked a movie star – or Marco, for that matter – but she knew which one she'd rather take to a desert island.

'How do you like my new duds?' Marco asked, stepping back to model for her.

If those drink prices allowed him to buy gorgeous suits like the one he was wearing, Hailey almost didn't mind paying. The suit was a delicious shade of crème brulée, which set off Marco's dusky complexion and dark, pomaded curls to perfection. The double-breasted suit hung on his sculpted body as if the tailor had sewn every stitch with visions of a naked Marco filling his head.

'You look good enough to eat,' said Hailey with a leer.

'To steal a quote from you, it's all in the interest of science. Speaking of which, I have a new specimen for you to check out. This one's going to knock you out of your hotpants.'

Hailey's pulse sped up instantly. She grabbed her drink and followed Marco through the club, past the booths where girls with plunging necklines and gardenias in their hair sat next to rappers wearing baseball caps and multiple piercings – members of a band that was in town for a concert. The Amazon Room was hot this week, but few of its clientele, even the glam-trash superstars, ever made it into the private rooms behind the club.

Hailey had been following Marco for years, from the first club he worked in as a bartender, to the first restaurant he managed, all the way to his latest brainchild, the Amazon Room. Because she'd been such a loyal customer, she was always the first to see each addition to his personal collection.

'You've never seen anything like this.' Marco's eyes glowed. 'This baby is going to be the jewel of my collection.'

'That's what you said about the last one,' Hailey reminded him, but her heart was beating faster when he opened the door to his private rooms. Stepping inside, Hailey breathed a sigh of pleasure as the perfectly humidified, near-tropical air engulfed her. When he shut the door, the sound-proofed walls blocked out the cacophony of the club. Hailey couldn't hear anything but the gurgle of water from the filtered aquarium and the hiss of a humidifier.

This room was Marco's private pet shop, a paradise that he installed for himself wherever he went. Gems of moisture glistened on the heart-shaped leaves of his exotic plants, their waxy foliage so dark that the green bordered on black. In the glass tanks that lined the walls lived reptiles whose DNA could be traced back to the dinosaurs: a lizard with a lacy ruff, a blue iguana with its incandescent hide and Hailey's favourite, a creamy yellow python. The human species was barely born compared to some of these ancient beauties.

'So what have you got to show me, Marco?'

'Relax. Enjoy your drink. You're always running around and checking your watch, like some kind of yuppie,' Marco scolded. 'Sit down.'

Hailey obeyed, curling up on a pile of Moroccan pillows that edged the walls. Marco had always had a gift for kitsch. The décor in this room came straight off the set of a 1940s B-movie.

'That's only because I wasted so much time being the wild child in my twenties, Marco. I partied my way out of college . . . how many times was it?' Hailey took a sip of her cocktail. Like all of Marco's specialties, it looked like a sissy drink, but it had a high-octane kick that would knock her on her ass if she wasn't careful.

'Only twice,' Marco said. 'What does it matter, anyway? You got through it. Now you're becoming my beautiful scientist. When you finish your thesis, I'll have to add you to my collection.'

'Marco, as much as I love you, I'll never be one of your pets. I'm not a collectable kind of girl.'

'So you say. But you can't tell me you wouldn't enjoy being pampered, spoiled, handled like a precious jungle orchid . . .'

'Till you got tired of me and buzzed off to the next flower.'

'I'd never get tired of a beauty like you.'

'Give me a break. I'm no beauty, not compared to the stunners you chase after.'

That was true; she wasn't even close to Marco's type. The women he hunted were so rare and unusual that you could only find them on the black market; while Hailey qualified as a babe, she was strictly homegrown produce. Her big hazel eyes were her best feature; light gold that bordered on yellow, they caught attention wherever she went. Her legs came in a close second, but they were getting battered these days from the spills she took on her bike. Her nose was snubbed, and she had to daub it with concealer when she wanted to hide the freckles. She dyed her hair an impossible shade of blonde called Sunset Boulevard, but her natural colour was dishwater.

Hailey had always been a tomboy, every guy's best buddy, the girl who was invited to climb up into the tree house or tag along to go skinny-dipping at the rock quarry, even though no other female was allowed. She was good at sports, and she never cried when she biffed on her skateboard. Best of all, she knew more about bugs, birds and frogs – and how they reproduced – than anyone else.

'Maybe you're not a jungle orchid,' Marco admitted. 'More like a tiger lily.'

'Well, my stems are getting badly damaged. Check this out. I took a spill and landed on a broken bottle.'

She peeled up the hem of her pants leg to show him the latest scar in her battle to earn a living on her bike: a four-inch laceration, neatly sutured, running just below her kneecap.

Marco frowned. 'You shouldn't be doing that job. It's a job for street punks, not for grown-up women.'

'Oh, please. That's such chauvinistic crap. I can kick any of the guys' butts and, unlike them, I don't have a problem stopping traffic when I need to. And who're you calling "mature", anyway? I haven't even hit 35.'

'There's nothing wrong with maturity. Age enhances a woman's beauty, like an heirloom diamond.'

He sat down next to Hailey and fixed her with his hottest bedroom gaze. Marco had the eyes of an actor; they could 'smoulder like coals' or 'weep passionate tears' on demand, while he was thinking of nothing deeper than a cold beer and a hamburger.

'That's way too cheesy, even for you,' Hailey snorted. 'The only reason I followed you into your lair was to see your latest prize, so let's start the show.'

Marco unfolded his legs and leaped up with the grace of a dancer. Hailey had to give her friend credit – he could be the most hardcore flirt on earth, but he was classy enough to know when to quit.

'Fine. If you won't be one of my pets, you'll have to watch *me* enjoy them.'

Marco disappeared behind a mini-grove of palm trees. Hailey lay back, took another sip of her drink, and admired Marco's reptiles. As beautiful as they were, her heart belonged to the family Felidae. Cats were Hailey's passion. Big or small, she adored them all, but her favourites were the large exotics: tigers, leopards, panthers. Hailey's thesis advisor kept encouraging her to move away from cats and their mating habits – in fact, he said, she'd be better off leaving the zoological realm altogether and getting into molecular biology. If she went into genetics or immunology, she might have hopes of getting a grant. Mammals – at least the furry, four-legged ones – weren't high on anyone's research agenda these days.

But Hailey couldn't help it; she loved cats, and she wanted to spend her career studying the way they'd evolved. She didn't want to be like her father, who had given up his goal of being an airplane pilot for a desk job in aeronautical engineering. She didn't want to be like her mother, who had spent 27 years ignoring her husband's affairs, while trying to hide her own. Hailey's frustrated, disappointed parents had taught her two important lessons. First, she should never compromise when it came to her dreams. Second, she would never find happiness in a monogamous relationship.

'Hailey, let me introduce you to my latest discovery.'

Marco was back. Hailey sat up in expectation. He'd taken off his jacket and shirt and was naked to the waist. Hailey almost choked on her cocktail. Wrapped around Marco's shoulders like a mink stole was a tiny, exquisite brunette, wearing nothing that she hadn't been born with, except for a pair of gold rings through her little brown nipples. The girl couldn't have been a day over nineteen, which was young even for a cradle-robber like Marco. Her dark hair was cut short, like a pelt, emphasising her enormous eyes. Those knowing eyes made Hailey think twice about how old she was;

the big brown orbs looked like they'd seen a lot more than cartoons and bubble-gum rock concerts.

'Hailey, I'd like you to meet Ilena,' said Marco. The proud pet-owner knelt down (not an easy thing to do with a naked woman wrapped around his shoulders) and let his captive go free. 'Until two weeks ago, she was flying through the air as a trapeze artist. I helped her escape from the circus. Actually, they sold her to me.'

'I'm sure she's got a whole repertoire of tricks,' Hailey said.

'Ilena's a natural performer. She couldn't wait to do her act for you tonight. Isn't that right, little pet?'

Ilena smirked. Hailey didn't expect her to talk. Someone that amazing didn't need to. Hailey believed Marco's story about the circus; whatever this girl had been doing for most of her short life, it had involved intensive physical training. You could see years of self-discipline in her perfect posture, her clearly etched muscles. Even though she was relaxed, you could sense a simmering tension in her thighs, as if she might spring off her feet into a back flip at any moment. Hailey knew of only one other species that was so power-packed for motion, and that species was equipped with fur, claws and a tail.

The girl's breasts rode high atop her ribcage, and in spite of the jungle heat in the room, her dark nipples jutted out as if someone had teased them with a popsicle. The gold hoops twinkled against her olive skin. Her pitch-black pubic hair was thick and bushy – a nice move on Marco's part, letting her grow wild down there instead of shaving her pubes into a sexless pencil line – and the stretch of skin between her mound and navel was tattooed with an elaborate arabesque.

'What do you think?' Marco asked.

'Uh –'

Before Hailey could form a comment, Marco spun the girl's nimble body and bent her backwards over his arm. She curved into the backbend so fluidly that Hailey decided she must have some kind of genetic disorder; she'd been born with rubber in her joints instead of cartilage.

Supporting Ilena with one arm, Marco began to caress his pet, his hand starting at her throat, then moving slowly between her breasts and along the arc of her belly, skimming her thighs, and stopping at her ankles. Then, just when Hailey remembered that she was supposed to breathe, his hand made the journey in reverse. This time he lingered on her pussy, back-brushing the wiry curls with his fingers and tugging her lips. He made circles on her muscular abdomen with his palm. He rubbed her breasts at a gentle pace, moving faster and faster until the girl's arm and leg muscles quivered, and sparks were practically flying off her nipples. Hailey could swear she heard a purr rumbling in Ilena's throat.

Perfect abs. Perfect tits. Sonar-sensitive nipples. Hailey didn't know if she were more aroused or envious at this point. Marco loved to taunt her with his women, because he knew that no matter how much she claimed to have a scientific interest in his choice of mates, she really got off on watching what he did to them.

This is just another form of research, Hailey told herself sternly.

Yeah, right. She was wet, probably as wet as Trapeze Girl over there and, in her excitement, she'd gnawed every trace of candy-apple lip gloss off her mouth. Marco caught her eye and smiled. See what you're missing? his lips taunted. He helped his gasping pet stand upright, then, as if he hadn't tortured Hailey enough, he stood up and smacked Ilena's apple-firm bottom several times, until the girl whimpered. Hailey felt her own flesh tingle in response.

The smacks were Ilena's sign to perform her next acrobatic manoeuvre. Extending her hands, she lifted herself into an effortless handstand. Her arms trembled only a little as she held herself upside down. Hailey was in awe. Her own arms would have buckled long ago, but that was natural in a 34-year-old woman who spent too much time in nightclubs and not enough at the gym.

'Full split, Ilena,' Marco ordered.

Very deliberately, with her dainty feet arched and her toes pointed, the trapeze artist spread her legs; wider, impossibly wider, until her body formed a T. Marco knelt down again and bracketed her body with his thighs. He was no slouch in the muscle department himself; his abdomen and arms were a rock-hard testimony to the hours he clocked on the weight bench, and Hailey could see the outline of his quads through the fabric of his trousers. Gripping one of Ilena's thighs in each hand, he grinned at Hailey over the glistening cleft of her fruit.

'You know what's next, don't you?'

Hailey nodded. She was way beyond speech at this point. It was all she could do not to reach for her own pussy as she watched Marco lower his head into the shadow between the girl's thighs. His tongue swam back and forth along her notch, making moist noises like a fish twisting through the water. The burbles and sighs of the humidifier added to the sexy chorus of sounds. Together Marco and his lover formed an exotic hybrid creature: the girl with her legs spread like wings, Marco with his arms wrapped around her thighs. Soon Ilena's arms were shaking from the sensation of being licked, and she couldn't hold herself up on her hands any more.

'Let me down,' Ilena begged, in a choked whimper.

So the girl could talk, after all. Marco pulled her legs together, and she rolled unsteadily onto the floor, then lay on her back, parted her legs and let out a hoarse, imploring moan. Her back was already arching, nipples pointing skywards. Marco positioned himself between her thighs, took hold of her nipple rings and tugged just enough to elicit a yelp.

'My pet likes a little pain, doesn't she?' he murmured.

Hailey didn't need to be told that the girl liked what Marco was doing. Ilena's big brown eyes were closed, and her head moved back and forth, as if she'd been hypnotised. The growl coming from her throat was continuous now, as she pumped her hips up and down in a fuck-me rhythm.

Hailey realised that her own hips were thrusting at the same pace, and her inner muscles were getting tighter by the second. Her right hand had taken on a life of its own and was stroking the crease where her thigh met her outer lips, but she was too aroused to care. Marco had given some great performances for Hailey, but he'd never gotten her so turned on before. The track lights cast shadows on his biceps as he lowered his arm to slide his fingers into his lover's sex. She wanted more than his fingers inside her, but Hailey knew that Marco wouldn't give her anything more, not while he had an audience.

Marco turned to fix his eyes on Hailey. A cluster of black curls fell over his forehead, which was pearled with sweat. His eyes had real heat in them this time, not just the Don Juan pseudo-passion that he could turn on or off at will. Hailey knew what he wanted. He sat back from Ilena so that he could unbuckle his leather belt. Hailey could see the ridge of his hard-on through his elegant trousers, forming a 45-degree angle against his torso.

Whoa boy, here we go, she thought. In all the years they'd been friends, Marco had never let her see the full length of his cock, but if that organ were as thick and powerful as the rest of him . . .

It was all that, and more. Hailey had heard rumours about Marco's penis, mostly from male bartenders like the vicious twerp outside, but she'd always believed they were exaggerated. A waiter had once told her that the club owner was 'hung like King Kong', and Hailey had laughed it off as a joke. Now she saw that the waiter wasn't all that far off base. Marco's erection jutted away from his body like a branch of a small tree. He was uncut and, as he watched Hailey's reaction to him, he slowly stroked the sleeve of skin.

'See what you're missing?' he teased, pulling a condom out of his pocket and cloaking himself. 'All this could be yours.'

But Ilena wasn't going to let Hailey have him. In one lightning-quick motion, she wrapped her steely thighs around Marco's torso and pulled him down – on her and into her. Marco wasn't about to let the baby beast have her way with him, though; he insisted on fucking her at a killingly slow pace, his strong arms holding him above her while his pelvis rocked back and forth. Hailey could hear the air hissing through his clenched teeth as he fought for, and won, control. Marco and Ilena were so absorbed in each other that they didn't notice Hailey sliding her hand under the waistband of her hotpants. She nestled back into the pillows, spread her legs, and fingered herself in time to Marco's thrusting.

Ilena moaned, thrashed, begged. Hailey sympathised. It must be hell to have such a big rod of muscle gliding back and forth inside you, when what you really wanted was to be hammered into the fourth dimension. Hailey longed for a sample of that cock herself, but she made do with her fingers. Her lips were brimming with juices, and her clit throbbed at a tempo all its own. She was beginning to think that Marco was never going to give his pet or Hailey any release that night, when he suddenly grabbed Ilena's wrists, lowered his body and took her in earnest. The lovers' hips moved together like a fabulous flesh machine, up and down, until Ilena screamed. Marco kissed her open mouth, then threw back his head and groaned as he came, too.

Hailey hit her own silent peak, arching back into the Moroccan pillows. Intense ... unbelievably intense. Marco could wrench the most amazing orgasms out of her, even though he'd never touched her sexually. Her shudders died down as Marco and his pet relaxed into a moist tangle of arms and legs. Ilena smiled at Hailey, her eyelids drooping with post-come bliss.

'I'm going to be with this beauty forever,' Marco said, giving his pet's sleek thigh a proprietary caress. 'This is the last woman I'll ever make love to, for the rest of my life.'

'Whatever you say, Marco.'

Hailey cared too much about her friend to remind him that he said the same thing every time. She expected nothing less. Emotionally, Marco was a romantic who fell hard for all of his women. But sexually, he was a rover, a seed-sower, the perfect example of the drive to sprinkle his genes throughout the human pool. When it came to sex, Marco was the poster boy for population genetics.

After Marco had taken Ilena back to her room, he invited Hailey to stay for a free steak. She was tempted. Marco always hired the best cooks in town, and this one was a genius with beef. But she was giving her freshman class their biology final tomorrow, and she had to be in class for the last day of the spring semester. Fortunately, all she'd have to do was prop herself up at her desk and watch her students take the test, but she had to make sure she could crawl out of bed when her alarm went off at 7 a.m.

Hailey kissed Marco goodnight, wished him luck on his new romance and caught a cab outside the Amazon Room. Just as the cab was pulling up in front of the duplex that she shared with two other grad students, Hailey's pager went off. She peered at the pager's electronic display and saw the unmistakable digits of Mercury Couriers.

'Oh, no!' she cried. 'No way!'

'Ignore it,' the cab driver suggested. 'Throw it out the window.'

'I wish I could.'

Though the pay was mediocre, especially when you considered the risk of getting turned into road pizza by a delivery truck or a sport utility vehicle, Hailey couldn't afford to lose her messenger job. Part-time teaching hardly paid anything, especially for an untenured junior faculty member, and her graduate stipend was only enough to keep her stocked with luxuries like coffee and tampons. The messenger job was flexible, it kept her in decent shape and she got to keep all her tips. Besides, Hailey loved being one of the guys, hanging out in the grimy rat-hole of a break room and comparing war wounds or playing poker. Truth was, she liked being in small, enclosed places with a horde of sweaty men. It kept a girl's hormones flowing.

But tonight she needed sleep, and the last thing she wanted to do was to call the Mercury dispatcher. One of the riders had probably called in sick, or shown up drunk, or had had to be hauled off to the emergency room.

'Where the hell is the phone?' she groaned, stumbling through the maze of empty beer and wine bottles that littered the floor. Her room-mates had already started celebrating the end of the semester. One of those room-mates, Jack, had passed out in the middle of the floor and was sleeping peacefully, using one of his bacteriology texts as a pillow. Hailey stepped over him, found the portable phone buried under someone's smelly T-shirt and dialled the messenger service's number.

'Okay, Ernie,' she said, when the dispatcher picked up. She had already kicked off her heels and was squirming out of her skintight pants. 'Let's make this quick and dirty. Where do you want me to go?'

Cade paced in front of the floor-to-ceiling window of his office, pausing every few seconds to brace his hands against the glass and peer down the hill. At this time of night – or was that a deadline dawn seeping across the sky? – there was nothing to see but the rain-slick street and a few delivery trucks making their 3 a.m. runs. Anyone who wasn't crazy, a criminal, or trying to meet the deadline on a software project was at home right now, snug in bed. He sat down in his ergonomic leather chair and spun around twelve times. Then he got up and looked out of the window. Still no messenger.

'So much for low-tech transportation,' Cade muttered. He had been using Mercury Couriers since he and Noah started Shiva Systems and, though their riders were usually efficient, they were prone to accidents and delays. Cade had always preferred to use the real pros, but Noah had a soft spot for the environmentally friendly messenger service, which employed university students to deliver packages all over the city.

Trust Noah to choose a trendy, politically correct, mom-and-pop company over an efficient nationwide corporation. It was a damn good thing that Cade was in charge of the business end of things, and Noah was the art director. If Noah's heart got any softer, he'd drop dead of circulatory failure.

At last, just when he was about to give up and go back to his office for a nap on the futon, Cade spotted a lone cyclist pushing up the hill. The rider was hunched over, bearing down hard on the pedals, helmet lowered, but as she (connoisseur of women that he was, Cade could tell it was a she) passed through the light of a streetlamp, Cade caught a glimpse of long, muscular thighs pumping up the incline. Through his fatigue and irritation, he felt a sexual spark. He'd never slept with a woman who had such athletic thighs and, before he knew it, Cade was lapsing into a fantasy that he was the one being pumped – all the way to the top.

Cade fought back a moan. Ever since Belinda started composing their wedding announcements, his sexual fantasies had taken on a fatalistic quality, and all of them were tainted by the word *never*. Now that he was going to marry Belinda, Cade would never have sex with a true redhead, a ballerina, a double-jointed contortionist, a stripper with breast implants, a neurosurgeon ... the list of possibilities that were being eliminated went on and on. Cade wasn't a traditional kind of guy. He would have been happy to have an open marriage and to let his wife have lots of extra-curricular adventures of her own, but Belinda was a born-again monogamist, and she took the phrase 'for-saking all others' as seriously as a heart attack.

Cade would never fuck the bike-messenger girl with the splendid thighs. He might as well accept it, and forge on. Downstairs, the outer door of the loft opened, and within moments Cade heard the rumble of the freight elevator. He walked out to the hallway and prepared to meet the messenger, his face set in a scowl. It was tough to be stern with these college girls; they tended to dissolve into tears at the slightest criticism. But his package containing Noah's artwork was over an hour late, and with the deadline at eight o'clock in the morning, the delay would put his programmers behind.

'Do you have any idea –' he started to say, as the biker's helmet appeared through the grating of the elevator, but the woman drowned out his words with a tirade of her own.

'Damn this city and every coffee-swilling, SUV-driving yuppie who lives in it!' she cursed, pushing her bike through the elevator door.

The rider was favouring her right leg, and Cade could see now that her left knee was scraped raw. Her face – what he could see of it through the mask of mud splatters – was twisted with rage. A pair of hazel-gold eyes, the colour of topaz, glared at him through the scrim of grime. From head to toe, she was smeared with mud and motor oil.

Cade was never going to fuck a girl with topaz eyes. The thought made him sigh in despair. An image hit him with the force of a falling boulder: those eyes flashing at him as he got ready to take the woman from behind, clutching her firm hips, climbing on board that taut ass. He would hold off at first, giving her the tip of his cock, nudging and teasing her lips. Snarling, she would turn her head to look at him with those eyes, and he would give her exactly what she wanted . . .

'You're hurt,' he said to the girl, sounding stupid even to himself.

'No shit, Sherlock. I got broadsided by a drunk who decided to open the door of his Ford Ranger so that he could do a little projectile vomiting in the street before he drove home. I got knocked off my bike and rolled halfway down the hill before I landed in a gutter. Then, as if he hadn't done enough, the jerk staggered over to me to see if he'd killed me. When he saw me lying in the street, he threw up the rest of his Bombay Martinis. I rolled into the gutter before he could splash me, but that's hard when you're already writhing in pain. So please excuse me for being late, but I'm sure you can appreciate why it took me a few minutes to pull myself together before I rode up the hill. The way this knee feels, I might as well have been riding up Mt Rainier. So I hope you appreciate this, dude.'

The woman reached into the pouch strapped to the back of her bike and produced a cardboard envelope, containing the CDs with the artwork that Noah had been waiting for.

'Why didn't you just send this stuff electronically?' the girl asked. 'It would have saved all of us a lot of grief.'

'We tried. It's a lot of huge, high-resolution art, and it crashed our server,' Cade explained. He stared at the girl's knee in order to avoid those angry yellow eyes. The abrasion was sticky and bloody, the torn skin studded with bits of gravel and asphalt. Cade felt queasy looking at it.

'Could I use your bathroom? I want to get this mess cleaned up before I head back home. My knee is starting to throb.' The girl was slowing down now, her rage softening into exhaustion.

'While you're in there, I'll get my friend. He can help,' Cade mumbled.

Noah would know what to do. He enjoyed rescuing hurt animals. Wounds made Cade feel sick. He pointed to the bathroom door and, as the girl headed towards it, Cade rushed into Noah's office.

The artist sat peering at his 24-inch computer monitor, oblivious to the uproar outside. He was gazing at a lush, electronically rendered version of a jungle, teeming with exquisite birds and beasts, a vision that the painter Rousseau might have designed, if he'd had access to a state-of-the-art computer. In the midst of the vibrant flora and fauna stood a glorious golden-haired maiden of inhuman proportions, the virgin warrior Yulana. As Cade watched, Noah reverted to a rendering screen, and with a few clicks of his mouse he enlarged Yulana's breasts from a D-cup to a double D.

'You are such a pervert,' Cade said. 'There's something twisted about having the hots for a woman you designed yourself. I'm sure it's a form of incest.'

'In case you haven't noticed, our customer base is composed of horny teenage males,' Noah reminded him. 'At the last focus group, the kids said they wanted Yulana to have bigger tits. Their words, not mine.'

'You just don't want to admit that you're in love with a pixelated blonde. This will take your mind off her for a few minutes – your artwork finally got here.'

Without turning away from the screen, Noah held out his hand for the package.

'But first you have a rescue mission waiting in the bathroom,' Cade went on. 'This is right up your alley. One of the couriers from Mercury got dinged by a car on her way up here; now she's cleaning herself up in our sink. If you can force yourself to stop looking at her luscious thighs, you'll see that she's got a big gash in her knee.'

'Are you serious? Someone's hurt?'

'She's hurt and she's a mess. Is there anything in the office that she could wear? She took a tumble on the street, and she's filthy.'

For the first time that night, Noah turned away from the monitor to face his friend. His dark eyes had already gone foggy with concern. Before Cade could explain any further, Noah had jumped up from his chair and was rushing to the bathroom. Having sent the saviour on his way, Cade rubbed his eyes and went off to grind some fresh coffee beans for the next caffeine infusion. On his way down the hall, he saw one of the junior programmers curled up under his desk. He had fallen asleep waiting for the artwork to arrive. Cade smiled. These kids they'd hired were hard-core, fully dedicated to the game.

The game. The words evoked memories, outrageous images that Cade had left buried for a long time. He wondered if Noah ever thought about the game that the two of them used to play, before Cade met Belinda, and Noah met his own fiancée, and both men retired from the sport of seducing and sharing women.

Cade's role was to identify the prey, then to hit her with the full force of his charm – the equivalent of a stun gun. After the woman had been snared, Noah would step into the competition, softening her up with his sensitive, sensual nature, and the game would be underway. The goal was to convince the woman that her ultimate sexual fantasy was to have sex with two men at the same time: Cade and Noah, of course. The two men worked as well together sexually as they did professionally. The game varied from one woman to the next, but no matter who the target was, Cade and Noah always tried to make her feel that she'd gotten the best of the situation.

The game didn't have a lot of rules; the men worked largely by intuition. Only one rule was set in stone: any method of seduction was permitted while they were reeling a woman in but, until they caught her, neither of the friends was allowed to fuck her unless the other one were present.

Nothing was more exciting to Cade than to join his best friend in bed with a beautiful woman. Cade's sexuality confused him sometimes. He was analytical by nature and liked to be able to categorise people, but he wasn't sure if he was ready to think of himself as bisexual. He wasn't attracted to men in general, or even to Noah under normal circumstances, but there was something about his best friend that drove Cade wild when they were naked together with a woman. He thought about that as he stood at the bathroom door, watching Noah pick gravel out of the bike messenger's knee with a pair of tweezers. Noah was wearing his glasses, and his profile was set in a frown. With one hand he extracted the tiny rocks; with the other he cupped the woman's shapely calf.

The woman's legs were works of art, toned and tight and longer than they ought to be, considering her height. She sat on top of the closed toilet lid, clutching the rim as she fought the pain. She had taken off her helmet, and her blonde hair stuck out around her head in sweaty tangles. Though Cade would never admit this to his fiancée, whose strawberry-blonde locks always hung in an impeccably sleek cap, he loved seeing a woman with her hair mussed, as if she'd just had a rousing tumble in bed.

When Noah dug too deep with his tweezers, the girl clenched her teeth and let out a low growl. That sound, combined with the look on her face and the fantasies firing his imagination, sent a flood of heat to Cade's groin. He folded his arms over his chest and shifted his legs so that she wouldn't be able to see the stone ridge in his khaki trousers. Not that she was all that interested in the state of Cade's penis at the moment, with the abrasion on her knee stinging and smarting.

'What's your name?' Cade asked. The question came out in a bark. Cade hated feeling like he wasn't in control.

The woman glared. 'Why do you need to know?'

Cade shrugged. 'A messenger gets hurt racing to my office in the middle of the night; I feel partly responsible. I'd like to know who you are.'

'Of course. You want to make sure that I don't hold you liable. You corporate drones are all alike.'

Her eyes scanned him, leaving a trail of disdain from his trendy haircut through his khakis to his Italian loafers. 'Don't worry, I don't have the time or the money to sue you, even if I had a reason to.'

Stung, Cade backed away from the door. She thought he was a corporate drone? He'd never thought of himself that way. Compared to his old prep-school buddies, who were all working as tax attorneys or podiatrists, Cade was a rebel. He'd bucked the system, starting his own software company, betting his trust fund on his gift for marketing and Noah's genius for game design.

It wasn't his fault that he'd been born with the markings of privilege. A person couldn't change his family background, any more than a tiger could help being born with stripes.

'Her name is Hailey.' Noah's voice, calm and soothing, cleared some of the tension from the air. 'And this is Cade, our CEO,' he said to Hailey. 'He's not a corporate robot; he just dresses like one. Hold on to your seat, now. This is going to sting.'

Hailey gritted her teeth when Noah applied the disinfectant. Cade couldn't help noticing that her nipples hardened under her cotton T-shirt as the astringent touched her skin. What would she do if he had her underneath him, naked and trapped between his legs, while he rubbed those nipples with a cotton ball soaked in something sharp and stinging? She would fight him, slash and claw at him, but he would pin her wrists above her head and hold her down while Noah stroked her, soothing her into submission. Noah's deft fingers would turn her into a butter girl, so warm and pliant that she would all but melt into the sheets. She would get the best of both worlds from her two lovers – one rough and one gentle, one forceful and one sensual. How could one man alone be everything that Cade and Noah were together?

Cade shoved his hands in his pockets and headed down the hall to wake up his programmers. No point in fantasising. The only action that he and Noah were going to see together in the future was a double wedding. The event had been in the works for over a year now and, if Belinda and Val had their way, it would be the social event of the century. Two successful men, two smart and stunning women, joined in blissful matrimony. Once those rings had been slipped onto

Cade and Noah's fingers, the friends would be bound to Belinda and Val for life.

That would be a good moment. No, it would a fantastic, earth-shaking moment.

But while they waited for that moment to come, couldn't Cade and Noah play the game one more time?

Hailey was glad when Cade left her alone with Noah, so she could sit back and enjoy the way his fingers were working over her leg. He was clearly a computer geek. A lot of the deliveries that she made at this time of night were for small software companies like this one, so she knew the type. But this geek knew how to touch something more than a keyboard and mouse. While he cleaned her up, his fingertips sank into the soft spot behind her knee, not just touching, but probing, as if he were wondering if she were sensitive there.

As it turned out, Hailey was very sensitive there. She had to chew her lower lip to keep from making any embarrassing sexual noises. Frowning as he worked, Noah didn't look like he was copping a feel but, when he put down the bottle of disinfectant and took hold of her thigh with both hands, Hailey sensed that he wanted to do something more than play doctor.

Primed by the scene at the Amazon Room, and the adrenaline rush from her accident, Hailey's nerves were on hyper-alert. A sticky melting between her thighs told her that she was more than a little aroused. Good thing her bike shorts were padded, so this considerate computer nerd couldn't see that she was creaming her pants. She must be as horny as a hyena if she was about to come from having her knee fondled. When he had patted that astringent on her wound, she'd thought she would jump out of her skin.

Hailey didn't usually go for men like Noah. She preferred the macho, meaty, sun-broiled types, men she could sink her teeth into. Noah was so lean that he was almost skinny, and the only light that ever shone on his pale skin was probably the glow of his computer monitor. On his knees in front of her, he looked like some throwback to the Middle Ages, a troubadour about to recite a love poem to his lady. With his ruffled black hair, deep bitter-chocolate eyes and refined features, he probably appealed to women who liked the tender, let's-commit-forever type, but Hailey wasn't into sensitivity, and she definitely wasn't into forever.

Noah's fingers climbed up her thigh, inching closer to the hem of her bike shorts. This time Hailey didn't even bother trying not to moan.

Maybe I shouldn't jump to conclusions, she thought.

'Your hamstrings feel like concrete,' he said disapprovingly as he kneaded the muscles. 'Don't you stretch before you ride?'

'Didn't have time tonight.'

'You're going to tear a muscle one of these days if you don't take time to stretch.'

'What, are you some kind of athlete?' she laughed.

'That's how the legend goes.'

Noah looked up at Hailey, and his grin was sheer sexual evil. She'd underestimated him. She didn't know what his game was, but he was a player. And when the bathroom light bounced shadows off his high cheekbones, he was diabolically cute.

'I want to hear the rest of that legend,' Hailey said.

'Maybe I'll tell you someday.'

Hailey leaned forwards. 'Why not now?'

Noah's fine features wrinkled as he caught the smell of motor oil on her clothes. 'What we need to do right now is get you out of that greasy shirt.'

'You're right,' Hailey admitted, looking down. 'I'm a dirty girl.'

'Are you?' Noah asked softly. He handed her a Shiva Systems T-shirt that didn't look all that much cleaner than the one she'd been wearing. 'This thing was lying around the office. I can't remember when I washed it, but it's better than what you've got on. I can't do much about the shorts . . .'

Noah gazed wistfully at Hailey's thighs, as if he'd like nothing better than to get her out of those shorts, too.

'I'll take whatever I can get,' Hailey said.

She stood up and was starting to pull up her shirt, when Noah surprised her by getting to his feet and doing it himself. Acting passive and obedient for once, she raised her arms to help him. He took his time, brushing her silken inner arms as if by accident. Her nipples sprung to life. After the shirt came off her head, Hailey saw that Noah had noticed how the twin points protruded through her sports bra. In fact, he seemed to be having trouble looking anywhere else. He held the T-shirt in one hand, but he wasn't in any hurry to cover her up with it.

Hailey stood still and let him get an eyeful. If Noah were the kind of man she usually went for, she'd be all over him by now, but she sensed that she shouldn't push. Besides, she couldn't remember the last time a man had admired her this way. His pupils were so wide that his eyes looked like wells, and that hungry stare was as thrilling as a touch. When he actually did touch her, she wasn't ready for it – the contact made her gasp.

'You've got a bad bruise here,' he said, running the knife-edge of his hand down the length of her torso. His thumb traced the central seam of her lean abdomen, coming to rest in the shallow pit of her pierced navel. She quivered when he toyed with the gold ring. 'Did you break any ribs?'

'I don't know,' Hailey said. 'I didn't bother to have it checked out.'

'You should have had an X-ray.'

'Bones can heal without X-rays.'

Noah frowned. 'You really should take better care of yourself.'

'I would, if I had the time.'

'Then find someone else to do it. That shouldn't be hard, for a woman like you.'

Noah's hand found the curve of her hip and stayed there. His own hips were centimetres from hers, and Hailey could feel how much he wanted to pull her close to him. The warm rush of his breath tickled her cheek. She could smell the perspiration on his neck, fresh and salty, and the scent of baby shampoo from his hair. If she took a half-step forwards, she'd be close enough to bite his earlobe. But before she could do it, he was easing her down onto the toilet seat again, turning his attention back to her injured leg.

Strange guy. Definitely worth pursuing, but she'd have to bide her time.

'Why don't we get together later?' Hailey asked. 'I was planning to meet some friends at the Waterfront Brewery for happy hour around 5.30. The place is a meat market, but you might enjoy the conversation. All we talk about is sex.'

'Hey!' Cade burst into the room, putting an end to the promising moment. 'What are you doing, Noah? Open-heart surgery? We've got a product to deliver in three hours. Last time I checked, you were still the design director around here.'

Cade's voice was scratchy, as if he spent a lot of time

shouting orders at people. His staff probably hated him, but Hailey would bet money that he was good at his job. Nice package, too, she noted. Not even his preppy khakis could hide the impressive bulk between his legs. Cade's physique was the opposite of Noah's; he looked like he spent most of his free time at the gym, and his skin had the flush of outdoor exercise. Or maybe that was the flush of one too many Bushmills; he could be the type who spent a lot of time schmoozing over cocktails at the country club.

As Cade stood staring down at her, a weird thought crept into Hailey's mind. Had the CEO been standing outside the door for the past few minutes, watching Noah touch her? No wonder he was growing before her eyes. The swelling in his crotch must be making him uncomfortable, but he insisted on standing there, maintaining his dominance.

Hailey didn't mind at all. The small room buzzed with tension, and Hailey could smell testosterone wafting off both of the men. She couldn't figure out the dynamics between the aggressive CEO and the sensitive designer. There was a competitive energy between the men, but no murderous jealousy or potential for combat. At the heart of that tension sat Hailey, dirty and knocked about and having the time of her life.

'Well?' Cade pressed. 'Are you going to get to work on that art, or do I have to light a stick of dynamite under your ass?'

Noah heaved a sigh of resignation and let Hailey go. From the awkward way he adjusted his Levi's, Hailey guessed that he had enjoyed touching her as much as she'd enjoyed being touched. Sparks were whizzing all around the room. Hailey only hoped she'd be around when one of them ignited. Noah tried to help her stand up, but Cade dismissed him.

'I'll take it from here,' Cade said. 'You can go back to your office.'

'Whatever you say, your majesty,' Noah said, executing a mock bow.

Once Noah was gone, Cade held out his hand and lifted Hailey to her feet. His hand had a powerful grip, and the palms were harder and warmer than Hailey would have expected. Standing eye to eye, she and Cade sized each other up. She had spent enough time around cats to win any human staring contest, but Cade gave her a run for her money, holding her gaze without blinking. She let him win, a sure sign that she was attracted to him, in spite of his rudeness. His clear, true-blue eyes would have been nice to look at, if they weren't so bloodshot.

'You look like you need a cup of coffee,' Hailey said.

'There's enough caffeine in my blood right now to animate a zombie, but what the hell. I'll make another pot. Care to join me?'

Hailey checked her watch. 3.45. Dawn was so close now that sleeping was beside the point. 'Why not?'

Cade paused. 'Better yet, why don't I buy you breakfast? There's an all-night diner down the block.'

Though it wasn't exactly the offer of the century, Hailey took a moment to consider it. Cade's face was sincere enough – with that straw-coloured hair and clear skin he could be a former choir boy from Kansas – but rapid calculations were going on behind his baby blues. Hailey could see herself being moved around in his brain like a chess piece. The thought of being manipulated by a man like Cade wasn't unappealing. In fact, Hailey could already feel the anticipatory buzz of a rousing sexual competition and, when she scanned Cade's sturdy, muscular build, she knew that he'd make a worthy opponent. But before she jumped into whatever game he was plotting, she wanted to make sure she could win.

'You're being very friendly, all of a sudden,' she said. 'Ten minutes ago, I thought you were going to throw me out of your office. Now you want to feed me. What's the catch?'

'Catch?' Cade was all innocence. 'I'm offering you a five-dollar breakfast at a greasy spoon, which serves some of the worst coffee you've ever had in your life. I'm not asking for your first-born. I just want some company.'

'What about your deadline? That's why I ended up in this mess, after all.'

'Noah and the programmers can take it from here. They don't have far to go, and they'll work faster if I'm not breathing down their necks.'

'All right. On my budget, I'd be a fool to turn down a free meal.'

Hailey followed Cade out of the office and into the freight elevator, wheeling her battered steed. If Cade made a move before she was ready, she could always block him with her bicycle.

A free meal – or the chance for some fantastic sex, she thought. She liked sparring with the CEO; he was different from the ivory-tower academics she met at the university and the scam artists she knew from the clubs. He looked like a trust-fund baby, but he had a canny edge about him that told her he was tougher – and wilder – than he seemed.

And what was going on between him and Noah? Taken separately, each man was intriguing, but as a pair, they were doubly hot. From the steam that rose between them when they were standing together in the bathroom, Hailey got the feeling that they liked to operate in tandem, in more ways than one.

If she played her cards right, she might get the chance to work under both of them.

2 The Perils of Pair-Bondage

Except for a waitress and a couple of off-duty cops eating breakfast at the bar, the diner was empty. The waitress, an overblown brunette who looked like the heroine of a corny country ballad, fluffed her tower of hair and licked her teeth when she saw Cade, then glared at Hailey through narrowed eyes as she sat the couple at a booth. Noting the other woman's dagger-like fingernails, Hailey decided that if the waitress wanted Cade, she could have him.

'Coffee, hon?' the waitress asked.

She addressed the question to Cade, turning her nose up at Hailey. The badge pinned to her ample right breast informed them that her name was Dusty. Of course, Cade already knew that. When the waitress thrust her hip at him, he let his hand glide down the curve of Dusty's rump. As he touched the waitress, he gave Hailey a long, mocking stare that sent a bolt of lust through her body. From the gleam in his eye, Cade looked like might be a touch insane. That was fine with Hailey. Smart and successful, crazy and perverted. What more could a woman want?

'That's a definite yes on the coffee. And keep it coming, darling,' he told the waitress.

'You frequent some upscale places,' Hailey remarked, as she pried open the sticky menu. 'Dusty sure has a thing for you.'

'Dusty's a good woman,' Cade said, his voice soft with nostalgia.

Hailey leaned across the table. 'You slept with her, didn't you?' she whispered.

Cade smiled, then leaned back and stretched his arms along the cracked orange vinyl booth. 'Are you always this curious about the sex lives of strangers?'

'As a matter of fact, I am. Sex is my livelihood.'

Dusty delivered the coffee, and Cade poured. He was right: Hailey had never tasted such a vile brew. She wondered if the waitress had laced her cup with poison. At least the oily black liquid packed a wallop of caffeine.

'OK, I'll take the bait,' Cade said. 'I'm assuming you do something else for a living besides delivering packages. Unless you offer some other service that I'm not aware of. If that's the case, I want to be a customer.'

Cade slid forwards in the booth. As if by accident, his inner thigh brushed Hailey's sore knee, but it wasn't the pain that made her shudder.

'I'm a graduate student in biology,' Hailey said, doing her best to keep her hands steady on her coffee cup. 'Evolutionary biology, with an emphasis on conservation genetics. I'm doing a study of sexual selection and mating strategies in felids.'

'Felids? That's got to be the most interesting word for pussy that I've heard in a long time.'

'I'm just telling you what's in my thesis proposal.'

'So what's your thesis?'

'In the short term, I'm working on a study of conservation genetics in wild cats, to prove that larger breeding pools make for healthier species. In other words, females need more options to choose from. Otherwise you get too much inbreeding, and the species suffers.'

'And in the long term?'

'I want to change the way people think about female

monogamy. I want to prove that the idea that females have to be monogamous in order to maintain a stable social structure and conserve the species is bullshit.'

Cade sputtered into his coffee. For the first time in their conversation, he didn't have a smart retort.

'What's wrong?' Hailey asked. 'Do you have a different opinion?'

Cade gave an awkward laugh. 'Well . . . yes and no.'

Dusty broke in to take their order. Cade asked for the house special. Hailey ordered the same thing, though she had no idea what the 'special' was. She just wanted Dusty to propel her pelvis away from their table so that she could find out what had caused Cade to lose his cool all of a sudden.

'What do you mean, "yes and no"?' Hailey pressed.

'I'm not exactly monogamous myself. That's probably not a shocker, is it? What I mean is, I like to explore. I crave variety. I love all kinds of women; there doesn't seem to be any type that I'm not attracted to.'

'So what's the problem?'

'The problem is, my fiancée's the exact opposite. She wants to mate for life. Longer, if that were possible. You'll probably kill me for saying this, but I think deep down, most women are like Belinda, and most men are like me.'

With his cheeks flushed red, Cade looked like a kid who'd been caught in the bathroom with his father's issue of *Playboy*. It didn't surprise Hailey that Cade was a womaniser, or that he was engaged to be married. Men who loved erotic variety always seemed to have a self-destructive need to make commitments they couldn't keep. She thought of her friend Marco, who had sworn he would be with his trapeze-artist girlfriend forever. Two weeks from now, Hailey would go back to the Amazon Room and find him with a new 'pet'. Pair-bonding – pair-bondage, as Hailey called it – was a romantic illusion, as far as she was concerned.

Now she could see why Cade had been rude to her back at the office, and why he had then done an about-face and invited her out to breakfast. He couldn't help himself. The chase was scripted in his DNA. He would never stop pursuing women that he found attractive. Hailey only hoped that his future wife had her eyes wide open.

'Fair enough. But what makes you so sure that your fiancée is monogamous by nature?' Hailey went on. 'Maybe she's just trying to meet social expectations. Or maybe she hasn't had enough experience to know what she wants.'

'Belinda never needed much experience. She's got an amazing sexual imagination; I think she was born with a copy of the Kama Sutra imprinted on her brain. When I first met her at the country club, I thought she was a typical princess. She was prancing around in her microscopic tennis skirt, looking like the kind of girl who runs off to take a scalding hot shower after she gives her boyfriend a handjob. When she challenged me to a game of squash, I figured it would be a fun way to spend the afternoon. I'd let her win, just in case her daddy was some billionaire high-tech mogul.'

'Major sacrifice on your part,' Hailey said sarcastically.

'OK, I'm not above using politics to get ahead in my career. When I'm passionate about something, I'll do anything to make it work. That's why I fought so hard to get Belinda. She wasn't an easy catch, believe me.'

'Did you let her win?'

'I didn't get a chance. She slaughtered me within the first ten minutes. She shot all over the court like a greased thunderbolt; I could barely keep track of the ball. By the time she'd beaten me – which didn't take long – I was pouring sweat, and she was "lightly perspiring", as the Southern belles like to say. I think one strand of her hair had slipped out of her hairband. I slunk off to take a shower, feeling thoroughly humiliated.'

The waitress broke in to deliver their breakfast specials: giant burritos smothered with salsa and cheese. Ravenous, Hailey dove in. The soft, steaming tortilla was stuffed with scrambled eggs and cheese, potatoes and spicy sausage. Cade didn't touch his food. He was gazing at the dark-blue sky outside the diner window with a muzzy look on his face, as if he couldn't remember how he'd ended up in a greasy spoon at four o'clock in the morning. Hailey recognised that dazed, stupefied look. She'd seen it on male friends who were madly in love and engaged to be married, but couldn't reconcile those two states.

'You're probably not used to being humiliated by women,' Hailey teased, trying to snap him out of his trance. 'Did it turn you on?'

Cade grinned. His eyes returned to Hailey. 'Not as much as what happened next.'

'What happened?'

'It was pretty intense. Are you sure you want all the gory details?'

Hailey set her fork down and wiped her mouth with her napkin. She'd quickly polished off most of the enormous burrito, and she couldn't take another bite. 'Listen, I'm getting most of my sex vicariously these days. Tell me everything.'

Cade leaned across the table. At this range, Hailey could see all of his imperfections: the cowlicks in his hair, a crooked tooth, a thin white scar that creased the corner of his lower lip. His white Oxford shirt was wrinkled and sweat-stained; he'd probably been wearing it for at least 48 hours. He wasn't the stand-offish golden boy that she'd seen when she first walked into his office. He was a very flawed, very sexy man. Very warm, too – she could feel the heat radiating from his skin. A man like Cade had to have a high metabolic rate, a necessity when you had to move fast and stay on top.

'I'll tell you everything,' he said, 'if I can touch you while I talk.'

Hailey raised an eyebrow. 'That's a sketchy proposition, coming from a man who's about to tie the knot.'

'Look, Hailey. I love Belinda more than my own life –'

'But you'll never be able to keep your hands off other women. Face it.'

'As soon as we get married, my hands will be tied forever.'

'No they won't, and you know it. You are always going to want more than one sex partner. Why not accept it now, before you make any vows that you can't fulfill?'

Cade groaned. 'It's too early in the morning for premarital counselling. Can't I touch you without feeling like I'm heading straight for hell?'

Hailey looked around the diner. The cops had finished their breakfast and departed. Dusty the waitress was standing back at the grill, gossiping with the cook.

'Under the table, or over?' she asked.

'That's my decision. If you agree, you have to let me do what I want.'

'You're used to getting what you want, aren't you?'

'Every time. Well, 99 per cent of the time.'

'All right, then.' Hailey pushed their plates out of the way and leaned over so that she and Cade were almost nose to nose. 'Let's play touch and tell.' She was as aroused by her own curiosity as she was by the lust in Cade's eyes as he began to tell his story.

'After Belinda beat me at squash, I slunk off to the men's locker room to take a shower,' Cade began. 'The locker-room was empty for once; it was the middle of the afternoon, in between the lunch-hour and the after-work rush. I stripped down and threw my clothes on the floor, then headed for the showers.'

Hailey closed her eyes. She tantalised herself with the image of Cade naked, his athletic torso gleaming with sweat. He wouldn't have much chest hair, maybe a smooth golden fuzz covering his pecs, thinning across his abdomen and forming a soft ridge trailing down to his pelvis. The fur would darken and thicken at his groin. She imagined him casually toying with his balls as he got ready to shower, enjoying himself the way men did when they were alone; she saw his penis curving into a lazy half-hard-on as he fondled it with one hand. He would be thinking about the woman who had just beaten him on the court, and in his imagination he would be winning the game. Hailey saw Cade's hand on the faucet, then clouds of steam swallowed her vision.

Cade took Hailey's right hand and turned it over. He dabbed his fingertips in his glass of iced water, then made figure-8s in the cup of her palm. Hailey gasped at the chilly sensation. He knew what he was doing; the simple motion played an exquisite tune on Hailey's nerves.

'I love it when I get to take a hot shower alone at the club after a hard work-out,' he continued. 'I've never been into the locker-room male-bonding routine.

I like to take my time, soap down thoroughly, not have to worry about whether the guy next to me is comparing his goods to mine.'

'Sounds intimidating,' Hailey agreed, though she was thinking that Cade probably didn't have anything to worry about. Based on what she'd seen of him with his trousers on, he had plenty of mass to work with. A steaming shower with a naked man sounded like paradise right now. Scalding hot water pulsing against her mud-splattered skin and washing the sweat from her hair ... Cade on his knees in front of her, sliding a bar of soap back and forth between her pussy lips, then replacing the soap with his bare hand, and finally standing up to replace his hand with his cock ...

'So I figured I'd be able to relax under the hot water and nurse my pride for a half-hour or so before anyone else came in. I had the water turned on so high that I didn't hear footsteps behind me on the tiles. All of a sudden, someone threw a towel over my face. Crazy scenes ran through my mind. I thought it was another guy, and that he was about to take me from behind.'

'Did that bother you?'

Cade paused and studied Hailey's face, as if he were trying to decide how she would judge him if he told her the truth.

'No. Not really. It kind of aroused me. I even thought about a couple of men at the club who I wouldn't mind getting together with, if I were into men.'

Cade was running his hands up and down Hailey's forearms. The friction made the tiny hairs on her skin sizzle with static. As Cade's hands reached her elbows, his thumbs brushed her nipples. She couldn't tell if he'd done it on purpose, but the brief contact turned the knots of flesh into two little stones.

'It wasn't a man, was it?' Hailey asked.

Cade shook his head. 'I knew it was a woman as soon as she grabbed my goods. The grip was firm, but I could tell it was feminine. A woman will never grip as hard as a man wants her to. Not even a woman like Belinda.'

Now it was Cade's turn to close his eyes, as he reminisced.

'Hey! You can't stop now,' Hailey protested. 'How did you know it was Belinda?'

'It was sheer body memory; I remembered the way she had made me feel when I watched her flying around the court. Then all of a sudden, here she was, pressing the length of her tall, strong body against my back, and I knew that this was what she had wanted to do all along. She didn't say a word, just started to move. She kind of flowed, kind of danced against me, like a snake, and the whole time she was holding this towel over my eyes, and stroking my hard-on. Back and forth, taking her sweet time. She'd been a ball of lightning when she had a racket in her hand, but nothing was going to rush her now – not even me, begging her to stroke me harder. '

There was no doubt that Cade meant to stimulate Hailey's nipples. The balls of his thumbs circled them, making the tight points at the centre painfully hard. She squeezed her thighs together and prayed that he wouldn't stop.

'Then she started whispering into my ear, telling me all the things she wanted to do to me. She wanted to get me onto all fours and ride me. She wanted to push me against the shower wall and spank me. She wanted to plunge her fingers into my hole and fuck me until I came. Her hot talk was driving me wild, but her fantasies were all about *her* being in control.'

'You don't like to have a woman in control?'

'I don't mind, when I'm in the mood for it. But I'm not going to be some rich girl's sex slave. I had to turn the tables on her, before she got the wrong idea. At this point, I didn't care whose daughter she was. She had dominated me on the court, but I had to teach her that she wasn't going to dominate me anywhere else.'

'How did you manage that?'

'As much as I hated to pull her hand off my cock, I had to do it. I grabbed her wrist, turned fast and took the other arm. Then I twisted her around so that she was facing the wall, and I pressed her up against the tile. Not very hard – I didn't want to hurt her. I just wanted her to know that she couldn't have everything she wanted. Instead, she was going to get what *I* wanted.'

Cade was unconsciously re-enacting the scene with Hailey, seizing her forearm and rotating it. She could feel the force behind his grip. What really excited her wasn't his strength, but the way he restrained it. She felt a rush of envy for Belinda. The spoiled, ultra-competitive rich girl must have been taken totally by surprise.

'It wasn't easy to hold her down,' Cade went on. 'Belinda's almost as tall as I am, and she's a natural athlete. I had one of her arms behind her back, and the other pinned above her head. I locked one of her legs with mine, then I rubbed my erection against her hip so she could feel how turned on I was. I was pure concrete – never been so hard in my life. She knew I wasn't going to let her go, not in that state. She whimpered that her elbow hurt. I told her that I'd move her arm if she promised to behave. I told her that we were playing a new game, and I was making the rules. I asked her if she understood what I was telling her. She bent her head and nodded. I couldn't see her face, but I knew that she was starting to feel humble. I also knew that she was getting excited.'

'How so?' Hailey's throat felt raw. She was surprised that she'd managed to talk at all. One of Cade's hands had slipped under the table and was weaving arabesques down the length of her outer thigh. The other was cupping her jaw, trancing the parabola under her jawbone with his thumb. His face was so close to hers that she could see a reflection of herself in his dilated pupils. He could have kissed her, if he'd wanted to.

'When I let go of the arm that I'd pinned behind her back, she put her hand up on the wall, beside the other one. She could have walked away, if she'd wanted to. I would have let her go; I'm not into forcing women to do anything against their will. But when she arched her back and offered me her ass, I knew that she wasn't going anywhere. That's when I almost caved – when I saw her long, beautiful body stretched out for me. Those incredible muscles in her back ... her lean waist ... her full hips. I wanted to get down on my knees and worship her. But I knew that I had to maintain the power position, so I braced myself for the ride of my life.'

'Wow,' was all Hailey could say.

'Wow is right. I wanted to be inside her like crazy, but I didn't have a condom and I wasn't going to take her without one. I reached down between her legs and lubed my hand with her juices. Touching her cunt was like sinking my fingers into a bowl of warm butterscotch pudding; she was so warm and wet down there I couldn't believe it. I rubbed her wetness all along the cleft between her cheeks, making a nice slippery channel for my cock. She cried out when I took my hand away from her pussy, but I wasn't going to give her an easy orgasm. I told her that I was going to come first, and that if she wanted to do the same, she was going to have to work for it. She wasn't happy about that, but I was too far gone to care. I came in close, locked my legs around her, and started gliding up and down that long, wet groove. Her ass cheeks were so firm and tight that it was almost as good as fucking her. She was moaning with frustration, but I wasn't going to go in. I drew it out as long as I could. I wanted to make her feel every ridge and vein in my cock; I wanted to imprint her with my flesh, if that makes any sense.'

'It makes sense,' Hailey whispered.

'I couldn't hold out as long as I wanted to; after only a few minutes, I could see a red mist over my eyes, and my balls started to tighten. I was holding her so tight I knew I was going to leave bruises on her arms, but I couldn't stop. When she started grinding her bottom into my groin, I came like a psychopath. I never thought the spasms would end. They say men can't have multiple orgasms, but I swear I did. Every new sensation brought on another rush: feeling her ass cheeks tremble against my cock, seeing my come splash against her skin, hearing her cry out.'

'So she *did* come, even though you told her not to?'

'Oh, no. She was close, but she wasn't there yet.'

Cade was stroking both of Hailey's thighs, a no-holds-barred caress. The contact reawakened the pain in her injured knee, but she didn't care. She'd never been touched this way before. He was fondling her greedily, like a man who was about to give up one of his greatest pleasures. His fingers were kneading the soft, damp swellings of her deep inner thighs, the only part of her legs that refused to turn taut and toned, no matter how much she worked the muscles. She wondered if he planned to make her come. She wasn't going to push for it, though she felt like a little more nudging could drive her over the edge. Hailey was going to be passive in this situation. Though she didn't believe in marriage, she was wary about treading on Belinda's territory. Cade's fiancée sounded like someone who could and would murder a female opponent, given the opportunity.

'Did you let her come?'

'I thought about telling her she couldn't,' Cade continued. 'I really wanted to punish her. But at the same time, I wanted to watch her fall apart with pleasure. I didn't know what would happen between us, if I'd ever see her again, so I thought I'd better seize the opportunity. After I came down, I let her go and pretended that I was going to wash up and leave. She gave me this incredulous look, and made a noise like a wounded animal. She was so hot she couldn't even speak, and she thought I was going to leave her like that.'

Hailey didn't have to make contact with Cade to know how excited he was, recounting this part of the story. The beat of his pulse was as powerful as an electric current; the table was practically shaking with it.

'Go on,' Hailey urged, in a choked voice. 'What did you do?'

'I told her that I'd let her come, but she'd have to do it herself.'

'Masturbate? In front of you?'

'That's right.'

'I bet she wasn't too happy about that.'

'Hah! She was embarrassed beyond belief. To this day, it still amazes me that a woman could be so assertive one moment, then turn into a shy little girl the next, all because I asked her to pleasure herself. I'm not kidding – she looked like a schoolgirl, with her hair hanging down, her face bright red. She stood there in the running water, biting one of her fingernails and thinking about whether she could do it.'

'But she did, didn't she?'

'Oh, yes. Did she ever.' Cade took a long, shuddering breath. 'She was awkward at first; you'd think she'd never touched herself down there before. But once she decided to let go, she gave it all she had. She fingered her pussy like a madwoman, and while she was doing that, she pulled on her nipples. God, I loved watching her do that, tugging them so hard that I was sure she was hurting herself. I'd never been that rough with a woman's breasts before, never would have dared. Soon she was swaying back and forth; she had to lean against the wall to keep from falling down. She was so far gone, I don't think she remembered I was there. She had her head thrown back, her eyes closed, and she was making this low keening sound that was getting me hard all over again. She was seconds away from exploding, but I wasn't done with her yet.'

'Not yet?'

'No way. I was going to make this girl pay for beating me on the court.'

'You're a bastard.'

'Don't I know it! I told Belinda to step away from the wall, that I wanted to see her use the water on herself. I told her to stand under the water and open herself up for me, so I could watch her inside while she came.'

'You said that?'

'Oh, yeah. You should have seen the look on her face. Daddy's princess was totally offended, but she followed my orders. She had to go into a half-squat to open herself up as wide as I wanted her to. It was amazing, watching the water stream down along her open slit, and the steam float up around her. Just before she came, an amazing blush spread all over her body, starting with her belly and moving all the way up. Her climax was outrageous. She was bucking back and forth, and her hair was whipping around her face, splashing water everywhere. I went numb watching her. Couldn't feel a thing above the waist, but below, I was on fire.'

Hailey couldn't help it; Cade's hands and his voice were going to bring her to her own orgasm. Cade wasn't even aware of what he was doing any more. His fingers were clutching her thighs, and his thumbs were working their way into the crescents of flesh just below her pussy. If she hadn't had her bike shorts on, he could have split her wide open.

'Stop it,' Hailey begged. 'Stop!'

Startled, Cade yanked his hands away. Too late. There was nothing he could do to reverse the building momentum inside her. Out of the corner of her eye she saw a young couple coming into the diner – two lovers who'd been out partying all night, stopping off for something to eat before going home to bed. Her eyes met theirs just before the starshower went off between her legs. She saw the curiosity on their faces, and the smug satisfaction on Cade's, as she bit down on her lower lip and let the orgasm rock her.

'Amazing,' Cade said. 'That was almost like living through it all over again.'

'Glad I could help you out,' Hailey said. It took her a few seconds to catch her breath. 'What did you do to me? I thought all you were going to do was touch.'

'Did I do anything else?' Cade asked, all boy-next-door innocence.

'You know what you did.' Hailey drank in deep breaths of air in a futile attempt to compose herself.

'Think there's anything you could use in your research?'

'You reinforced my belief that pair-bonding runs counter to the nature of human sexuality.' Hailey glanced up at the old Coca Cola clock above the grill. 'Speaking of sexuality, I've got to get home and shower. I actually have to stand up in front of a classroom of college freshmen this morning and act like a respectable woman.'

'Will I see you again?'

'I don't know. Depends on my delivery route.'

'Let's not make it so random.' Cade held on to Hailey's hand. He gave her a longing look that sparked a fire in the pit of her belly; she'd never known that cool blue eyes could hold so much heat. 'I like you. You stimulate my brain.'

Hailey pulled her hand away, though she hated to break the contact. She liked Cade, too, but getting tangled in someone else's pair-bond was always risky.

'I've got to run,' she said. 'We'll see what happens.'

The waitress was strolling over with their bill as Hailey clambered out of the booth. From the dirty look she gave Hailey, Hailey guessed that Dusty had watched the scene unfold. Counting the waitress, Cade and the couple who had just walked in, four people had watched her performance. The worst part was, she'd had two orgasms in one night, and both of them had been second-hand.

Way to go, Hailey said to herself in sarcastic self-congratulation. Girl, you have *got* to get a sex life of your own.

Cade took his time getting back to the office. He set off on a brisk walk around the block, thinking about what had happened at the diner. Hailey pushed new buttons in his erotic imagination. He'd never had a woman with her mix of qualities – sexy and smart, brash and outspoken, and totally resistant to the idea of living happily ever after with a romantic hero. When was the last time he'd had a challenge like that?

Then there were those luminous topaz eyes of hers. And her long, sculpted legs, with those velvet pockets right below her pussy. She had felt like a furnace down there; it was all he could do to keep his hands off the source of that heat. He had loved the way she fought off her orgasm, and the way she finally gave in to it, lifting her hips off the booth and arching her back as her fingers clawed the table-top. With her golden eyes fully dilated, she had shot Cade a look of pure fury. Cade loved nothing more than making a woman come in public and, with a wildcat like Hailey, his satisfaction doubled.

When Cade walked through the door of Shiva Systems, the office was as quiet as a theatre after a long, crazed performance. He didn't have to consult with Noah to know that the product was finished, but he went in to see him anyway.

'Did you send the kids home?' Cade asked.

Noah nodded. 'All's well. We'll ship the beta version of Yulana this morning.'

Noah always referred to Shiva's latest game by the name of his favourite character, not by its actual title, *Mutant Quest*. Cade had to admit that the stacked blonde warrior was going to sell more copies than the mutants she chased, but he was starting to get worried about Noah's infatuation with Yulana. It might be normal for an artist to fall in love with his creation, but should he really be spending every spare moment sitting in front of a computer screen, drooling over her?

'Okay, buddy, time to call it a night,' Cade said.

'Deadline's over; you can go home. Val's probably keeping the bed warm for you. You might be able to nab her for a quickie before she goes to work.'

'Hmmm.'

Noah used his mouse to rotate Yulana in a full circle, so that he could admire her statuesque curves. By Yulana's side stood her loyal familiar, the majestic blue panther Azuro. Sometimes Cade thought Noah was as infatuated with that feline mutant as he was with his warrior virgin. Noah was a cat fanatic.

Hailey was a cat fanatic.

This plan that Cade was brewing just might work, as long as he didn't push his friend too hard.

'Hey, dude.' Cade took hold of the back of Noah's chair and turned him away from the computer monitor, so that his friend was forced to face him. 'What's going on? Everything all right at home?'

'Everything's fine,' Noah said. He took off his glasses and rubbed the bridge of his nose. 'Val's right on track with the wedding plans for September. I'm helping by staying out of the way.'

'Staying out of the way doesn't mean you have to live at the office.'

'I'll head home soon. Give me some time to unwind. Are you hungry?'

'Not any more. I took Hailey to breakfast.'

Noah looked up, his wiped-out face lighting up. 'Hailey? Did she come back with you?'

Cade laughed at his friend's eager-puppy reaction. 'Hailey had to get on with her life. She's got better things to do than hang out with game freaks all day.'

'Too bad,' Noah said with regret. 'I liked her.'

Cade eyed his buddy. It occurred to him that he hadn't seen Noah looking so animated in weeks. If he played this right, it might be easier than he thought to convince Noah to resurrect their game.

'I liked her, too.' Cade moved behind Noah and casually began to knead his friend's shoulders. Working out the knots in Noah's muscles, Cade launched into his master manipulator mode. 'I got to know a lot about Hailey at breakfast,' Cade said. 'And I think there's a way we – more specifically, *you* – could help her.'

'Help her? How?' Noah's tense shoulders were softening under Cade's skilful fingers.

'As it turns out, you and Hailey share a passion. She's a biology student, and she's writing a thesis about cats. Big cats.'

'Are you serious?'

'Dead serious. Can you imagine how wet she'd get if she knew about your zoo?'

Noah frowned. 'It's not just a zoo, Cade. It's a wildlife rescue park. We don't keep animals exclusively for display; we're dedicated to rehabilitating exotic cats who've been abandoned by people who are under the misguided impression that they'd make good house pets.'

'OK, OK. Spare me the public-relations speech. The point is, Hailey's studying the mating habits of felids. And she's working at a dangerous, low-paying part-time job to help support herself while she's in school. Don't you think she'd jump at the chance to work for you this summer?'

'It's not my park. I couldn't make the decision to hire her,' Noah said. Though his words were cautious, his voice had quickened with enthusiasm. The screensaver had popped up on the computer monitor, hiding Yulana. For once, Noah didn't notice that his warrior maiden had left his field of vision.

'Noah, for all practical purposes, it *is* your park. You're the one who scrapes up the money to run that place. If you want Hailey to work for you, you've got her. Besides, it's not like she wouldn't be qualified. She loves cats.'

And she loves sex, Cade thought, but Noah would find that out soon enough. From the gleam in his best friend's eyes, he suspected that Noah was already thinking along those lines – or he would be, if he weren't so tied up in his fiancée's agenda. It wouldn't take much more effort to draw him into another round of the game. Judging by the listless way Noah been acting lately, it might even be good for him to have some distraction from Val.

Though Cade never would have said this to Noah, he didn't trust the woman that Noah was going to marry. Noah was a gentle-natured, introspective artist; Val was a redheaded steamroller. The short, curvaceous attorney had barged into Noah's life and left her mark on everything he did, said and owned. Or used to own. Val had been controlling Noah's property months before he had asked her to marry him.

Was it Noah who popped the question? Cade wondered. Or had Val come to bed one night holding a pair of fur-lined leather cuffs in one hand and a prenuptial contract in the other? Together, Belinda and Val were a deadly duo. The two women had planned the double wedding, they had planned the honeymoon and they had mapped out their futures as married women for the next five or six decades.

Not that Cade was nervous or anything. Cade was the master and commander of his own life . . . as far as he knew.

'Noah, I've got a great idea,' Cade urged. 'Why don't

we both go up to the lodge after the final version of the product ships? We deserve a vacation. We could spend a few weeks hiking and fishing, get out of the girls' hair. You could spend time at the cat park, help Hailey get settled in for the summer. We could both help her get settled in, if you know what I mean.'

Still massaging Noah's shoulders, Cade gave his friend's deltoids a meaningful squeeze. Noah rolled his head to one side, then the other. Then he froze as he registered what Cade had said. He turned to look up at Cade, and in his eyes was a look of excitement mixed with pure terror.

'Are you talking about what I think you're talking about?' Noah asked.

Cade nodded. 'Exactly.'

'No. No way.' Noah tried to stand up, but Cade held him down.

'Why not?'

'Damn it, you know why not!' Noah cried. 'We're getting married. We're settling down. We're not chasing other women any more – we're going to be tied down to Belinda and Val for the rest of our lives. That's what this whole three-ring circus is about!'

'Relax, buddy. Take a deep breath.' Cade eased Noah down into his chair. 'Listen to what you're saying. "Tied down." "Three-ring circus." Is this a typical case of cold feet, or are you having serious doubts?'

'I don't know. I really don't.' Noah's glasses slipped onto his lap as he buried his face in his hands. He didn't even notice that they'd fallen off. He ran his fingers over his scalp, rubbing so hard that his hair crackled with static.

'Settle down. Breathe deeply, and close your eyes. Let's take a walk down memory lane,' Cade said, in a mesmerising tone. 'We're going back five years, ten years, all the way to our sophomore year in college. We're going back to have a three-way reunion with the woman who taught us what sex is all about. Tell me, Noah, do you remember Lady Janessa?'

3 Mating Games

Janessa Klein, aka Lady Janessa, was the object of Cade and Noah's daydreams, wet dreams and bathroom masturbation sessions from the moment she moved her double-wide feather mattress into their college dormitory. She was a pocket-size Aphrodite, a Comparative Lit major with hazy violet eyes and a cloud of fine, frizzy black curls that looked like nothing less than a hip-length pubic muff. Noah adored her for her Romantic beauty and her poetic spirit; Cade went wild over her beestung lips and the way her braless breasts jiggled under her Venetian lace blouses. For such a small girl, she had an incredibly deep, smoky voice that made the two room-mates hard whenever she spoke to them.

Unfortunately, Janessa hardly ever spoke to Cade and Noah, except to turn down their repeated requests for dates. Once in a while, she would let one of them light her Gauloise cigarettes or carry her books across campus, but she made it clear that she was so far out of their league that she might as well be living on another planet. While Cade and Noah endured the ache of stifled lust, or dated other girls who were more willing but less desirable, the Lady Janessa reserved her favours for the chairman of the Romance Languages department, a married Frenchman who was twice her age. He used to drop her off in front of the dormitory in his black Karman Ghia, saying goodbye with a slithering ten-minute tongue kiss that left Cade and Noah grinding their teeth with envy.

If the professor hadn't been so smelly, condescending and flat-out unappealing, the two best friends might have given up on Janessa. But their pride couldn't handle being rejected in favour of a spindle-legged Marxist who smelled of stale tobacco and cheese and wore the same black turtleneck for weeks at a time. The world wasn't supposed to work that way. Noah and Cade were young, fit and brimming with lust and, by all rights, Janessa should have belonged to one of them.

To *one* of them? Maybe that was the problem. For months they'd been competing, in a comradely way, for Janessa's attention. They'd been operating under the assumption that only one of them would be the winner, and end up with the fair lady. But what if one man wasn't enough for her? What if what she really wanted wasn't the fairy tale of a committed relationship with a nice college boy, but the wild kingdom of a threesome with two young studs?

Late one night, as Cade sat by the window of his dorm room, staring down at the driveway and watching Professor Camembert paw Janessa like a madman, he had an idea. Not just any idea, but a lightbulb-over-the-head epiphany that would change his sex life for the next ten years.

'Hey, Noah! Wake up,' Cade hissed, shaking his room-mate into consciousness. 'I've got it. I know how we're going to get Janessa.'

'Huh? Wassa matter?' Noah sat up on one elbow and blinked at Cade. Though Noah slept like the dead, he had come to life at the sound of Janessa's name.

'Janessa. She's not like other girls. We can't treat her that way.'

'We don't treat her like other girls,' Noah grumbled.

'More like a goddess. Doesn't do any good.' He flopped back down in bed.

'You're dead on – the way we've been treating her hasn't gotten us anywhere at all. Lighting her cigarettes, carrying her books, leaving flowers and wine outside her door. She thinks we're pussies. Look at her down there, french-kissing a married man. The girl's a rebel.'

'So what do you think she wants?' Noah peered up at his friend, new interest in his near-sighted eyes.

'I know she doesn't want the boy next door,' Cade said. 'But I think there's an excellent chance that she might be interested in the *boys* next door.'

'Huh? What are you talking about?'

'You and me, dude. We've been going head to head for this girl. From now on, you and me are going to work together. Instead of competing, we're going to be playing on the same team. We'll be combining our strengths to get Janessa.'

'Sexual symbiosis,' said Noah, catching on at last.

'Whatever you want to call it. The point is, we've had no luck on our own, but together we can get the woman we want.'

Speaking his fantasy aloud, Cade realised that it was what he'd wanted all along. His cock hardened as he thought about how Janessa would react when she found herself tumbling into the trap that Cade and Noah would set for her. As he and Noah plotted, Cade struggled to keep himself under control. It wasn't just Janessa he was thinking about, but Noah. When he watched his friend do his nightly push-ups, or slip off his jeans before bed, Cade felt his pulse quicken to a new beat. He'd never given much thought to having sex with another man, but Noah was different. There was an intense, quiet heat about him that made people take notice, even when he wasn't doing anything to call attention to himself. His body was slim but hard, and when Cade caught a glimpse of his friend's dozing cock, long and pink, nestled in a hood of sleek black pubic hair, his throat went as dry as a bone.

On Friday afternoon, the game began. After a lot of coaxing, and some outright begging, Cade convinced Janessa to come to his room the following day to proof-read a paper he was writing on Shelley and Keats. Cade, a business major, didn't read anything more literary than the *Wall Street Journal*. But that didn't matter, as long as he got Janessa into his lair, with the door locked securely behind her.

'I guess I don't mind taking a look at your paper,' Janessa said, her husky voice dripping with disdain, 'as long as it doesn't interfere with my plans for the weekend.'

'Oh, it won't,' Cade lied. 'Your plans won't be affected at all.'

For the next 24 hours, Cade caught himself lapsing into fantasies about Janessa and Noah. He drove himself into a frenzy wondering what colour Janessa's cunt-lips would be. He thought about Noah's penis, about what it would be like to feel that sleepy snake waken in his mouth, about tonguing and nibbling the shaft until his friend groaned for release. He thought about Janessa watching him and Noah make love, and diddling herself with her dainty fingers while she enjoyed the show. He thought about watching Lady Janessa go down on Noah while Cade mounted her from behind and gave her something that her French professor couldn't: nine inches of stone-hard, grade A, prime young cock. By the time Saturday night came, he had all but worn himself out with his fantasies, and he wondered whether reality could possibly measure up.

As it turned out, reality *didn't* measure up – at least not in the way Cade expected. Saturday afternoon came and went, with no sign of Janessa. Noah reported that he never heard her door open or close, which suggested that she hadn't been home since Friday night. Getting more dejected by the minute, Cade and Noah hung out in their room and tried to study while they waited for Janessa to show up. At ten o'clock, when she still hadn't appeared, they decided to give up and go out for a hamburger and a pitcher of beer.

'Better luck next time,' Noah reassured his friend.

Noah obviously hadn't been obsessing over this plan the way Cade had; he had almost sounded relieved. As they put on their coats and walked out the door, Cade wished he could knock some sense into his room-mate. He was mad at Noah for trying to soothe his frustrated sex drive with a silly platitude, and he was mad at himself for thinking this scheme would work on a bitch like Janessa. But most of all, he was mad at Janessa herself, who happened to be walking up the stairs to her room that very second.

The woman of their dreams giggled to herself as she carefully placed one foot, then another, on the treads. With her hair frizzing into a flyaway thundercloud, and mascara smudges under her eyes, she looked like she'd been ridden hard and put away wet. She was wearing a thick woollen coat, which she clutched around herself, and a pair of black pumps. One of her heels had broken off, and she was wobbling as she climbed.

'Hey, boys,' she said, in that molasses-rich voice. 'You didn't start the party without me, did you?'

Cade and Noah stood frozen. They'd never seen the Lady Janessa drunk before, or even tipsy; she was always cool and serene and self-possessed. But if they were shocked by her intoxication, they were blown away by what she did next.

'Why is it always so fucking hot in this building?' she complained.

Then, without warning, Lady Janessa threw open her coat and let it fall into a heap of wool at her feet. She wasn't wearing a stitch underneath, except for the damaged shoes. Her naked body was everything Cade and Noah had ever dreamed of, a scaled-down Venus with round, high breasts tipped with pale nipples the size and shade of cultured pearls, and a neatly trimmed bush that spread like a dark, scalloped fan along the lower slope of her belly. Her plump thighs pooched out at the top, and her hips flared into a pear shape; unlike most of the girls in their co-ed dormitory, Janessa wasn't purging, fanatically exercising or even dieting. She was the lushest, most scrumptious woman that Cade had ever laid eyes on.

And she was too drunk to fuck.

If he hadn't been too proud, Cade would have bawled in despair. There was no way that he was going to take advantage of a woman who was intoxicated enough to let two geeks see her naked, but god, she looked even better than he'd imagined. While he stood there, dumb as a rock, Noah took over, rushing down to scoop up Janessa's coat. Cade was too stunned to do anything but squeak in protest as Noah covered up that glorious body. Capably lifting Janessa off her feet, he carried her up to the landing. Janessa laid her head on Noah's shoulder, closed her luminous eyes and started to snore.

'What are we going to do?' Cade asked.

'What do you think? We'll put her to bed and let her sleep it off. Go ahead. Unlock the door for me.'

'You mean you're going to put her to bed in *our* room?'

'Well, I don't have the key to hers.' Noah shrugged. 'And apparently she doesn't either. She's not carrying a purse, and I don't feel anything in her coat pockets.'

'Why did this have to happen?' Cade moaned. 'My balls hurt so bad, I wish they'd explode and put me out of my misery.'

Noah glared at him over the snoring bundle of Janessa's body. 'Could you think about something besides sex for five seconds?'

'No. Why should I?' Cade retorted. 'As long as I'm not getting any, I'm going to keep thinking about it. She's not sleeping on *my* bed, by the way.'

'Don't worry. I'll let her use mine. I'll sleep on the floor tonight.'

'Of course you will. Always the freaking Good Samaritan.'

Sulking, Cade threw himself down on his bed. Before he knew it, the long days of lust and longing caught up with him, and he fell into an exhausted sleep.

Hours later, he woke in a darkened room. At first he couldn't remember where he was; he only knew that he was lying in a bed, and that he was fully dressed. Gradually his gritty eyes made sense of the shapes around him, but something was different in the room he shared with Noah. First he smelled a pungent, musky odour, familiar yet out of place. Then, in the light that filtered through the blinds over his windows, he saw the shifting forms of two pale, nude bodies on the floor.

Janessa.

Noah.

Janessa lay on top of Noah, her head between his thighs, her lips making juicy sounds as she sucked him.

Her long hair covered her face, but from the noises she was making, Cade could tell that she was relishing the taste of Noah's sex. As she gobbled, her fingers crawled up Noah's abdomen, stopping at his nipples. She coaxed the two disks into hard pebbles, then pinched them with her fingertips. Noah made a strangled sound, half pleasure, half agony.

Cade swallowed. A sour taste filled his throat. He didn't know whether he had a right to feel betrayed, but he knew that he was the loser in this scenario. He lay motionless, trying not to make any sound that would catch the lovers' attention. There was a certain masochistic thrill in watching from the sidelines, while two people you'd been lusting after made love. Without his glasses on, Noah looked angelic in the moonlight, while Janessa roved over him like a greedy witch, kissing and nibbling and licking.

Janessa tossed her hair out of the way so that her lips could reach the base of Noah's shaft. In that motion, she caught Cade's eye. For a second she faltered, self-conscious. Then Cade saw a sly smile form on her lips, and he knew that she had read his mind.

'Looks like we have an audience,' she said, shaking Noah out of his trance. 'Should we invite him to join us, or should we torture him by making him watch?'

'Get down here, Cade,' Noah said. His voice was harsh, guttural. Cade had never heard him sound like that before, his voice so thick with desire that he could barely get the words out. Cade fumbled as he tried to squirm out of his jeans and sweatshirt. He was so close to having his fantasy come true that his hands were shaking, and his heart was pounding hard enough to wake the whole campus. His cock arched away from his body in a trembling parabola, a bead of arousal pooling from the slit. His balls rode high against his body, already set to release their load. He only hoped he could last long enough to spare his dignity.

Somehow he managed to roll onto the floor, landing on his side with a thud that knocked some of the fire out of him. At first he didn't know what to do, where to begin. It was awkward, trying to find a place for himself in between two people who had been getting along just fine without him. Should he touch Janessa first, or Noah? Use his mouth, his hands or his cock?

Janessa solved Cade's dilemmas by pushing him onto his back, so that he and Noah lay side by side. Planting a hand on each man's chest, she sat upright, rising above them like a goddess straddling two horses.

'I've been waiting for this,' she said. 'I know you two have had your eyes on me for a long time. To tell you the truth, you didn't interest me all that much, until tonight. When I saw you together, as fucked up as I was, I knew that I had to have both of you – at the same time.'

He'd been right, Cade thought jubilantly. Though his plan hadn't worked as expected, the basic idea had been sound. This time, he would let Janessa play the game her way. Next time, Cade and Noah would set the course and make all the rules.

Janessa turned out to be a gifted tutor, showing Cade and Noah how to find their way in this new situation. She could have taken centre stage, claiming all the fun for herself; instead, she licked Cade's palm and guided his hand to Noah's cock.

'I want to watch you finish him off,' she said to Cade. 'Go ahead. I'll be right here.'

She clasped Cade's hand with her fingers as he stroked Noah's erection. As much as he'd wanted to fuck Noah, Cade felt strange when he was gripping his friend's penis. Janessa's reassuring touch kept him going, and Noah's moans let him know that he was moving at the right pace. Cade knew Noah so well that it wasn't hard for him to guess what his friend wanted next. Never letting go of the root of Noah's cock, he moistened his index finger with saliva, then probed the cleft between Noah's buttocks until he found the snug sphincter.

Noah had once confessed to Cade, over a third or fourth pitcher of beer, that he liked to touch his anus while he jerked off. Cade did him one better, inserting the length of his finger into his friend's rectum and wiggling it back and forth as he tugged Noah's cock with his other hand. A low sound, like the rumble of thunder, came from deep in Noah's chest, building into a howl as it made its way to his throat. Cade stroked faster, moving his hand up the shaft to concentrate the pressure on the swollen crown. With the ball of his thumb, he dug into the groove at the base of the glans. If the crest of Noah's cock was as sensitive as Cade's, this should send Noah skyrocketing into space.

Noah's body stiffened from head to toe. For a few moments he was silent, then he shouted as his hips thrust back and forth, his cock pulsing in Cade's fist. Janessa's hand was still clinging to Cade's. She was panting, and the locks of curly hair that fell across Cade's forearm were soaked with sweat.

'Let me in. Let me in!' she demanded. Cade moved out of the way, and Janessa swooped down to lap up the milk that bubbled from Noah's twitching cock.

No time to waste – at his level of arousal, Cade wasn't going to last much longer than Noah. With Janessa in a prone position, Cade seized the opportunity to climb on top of her and grab her from behind. She struggled, but only because she'd lost her precious control. Within seconds, after Cade's shaft was planted firmly inside her, she was bucking against him, throwing the weight of her small body into his groin. Her cunt was a honey trap – sweet and tight. He had a short taste of bliss, rocking back and forth inside her, before his instincts forced him to cut loose and give her everything he had.

The climax took him with the force of a tornado. Cade almost passed out from the sheer strength of it. He lost all awareness of who or where he was; the world held nothing but the spasms that were seizing his body. In the back of his brain, he was conscious of a warm, radiant glow that he'd never had before during sex. He couldn't think of what to call it, until after he'd come down from the skies.

I'm happy, he thought, turning to look at Noah's dozing silhouette. Though he'd been hit by a thousand sensations during sex, Cade had never felt the clear, simple pleasure of making love with a good friend.

Before he could dwell on his happiness, Lady Janessa had planted herself on Cade's face and was demanding cunnilingus. He took hold of her thighs and lost himself in her sap-covered bush. Her flesh tasted dark and primal and dangerous; Cade recognised the taste of his own fluids mingled with hers. She was so raw from the reaming he'd given her that she couldn't stand much more than a butterfly flicker against her clit, but that was all it took to bring her to a climax. She rode his mouth like a fury, twisting and grinding for an unbelievable length of time. When he realised that he was giving Janessa multiple orgasms, Cade increased the pace and pressure of his lapping, and finished by pulling her straight down on top of him, with his tongue buried deep in her juicy crevice.

The flutter of her velvet muscles against his mouth was a sweet victory. Cade had wanted Janessa for so long that drawing these orgasms out of her was like hitting a jackpot. After she came to rest, then dismounted, Cade felt himself stiffening again.

'Time for round two,' he announced.

Spent, Janessa and Noah grunted faintly in reply.

Cade shook Noah by the shoulders. His friend was staring into space as if he'd been slapped on the side of the head with a bag of wet cement. Janessa Klein did that to men, even in memory.

'Come on, buddy. Don't go to sleep on me,' Cade said.

'We made a good team, didn't we?' Noah asked.

Janessa Klein had been the beginning. Over the years, Cade and Noah had perfected their approach, honed their strategies, until they were able to get just about any woman they desired. After college they'd expanded their shared interests and started to tinker around with computer games. Their early efforts blossomed into a full-scale business, which soon devoured all of their spare time. Then Belinda and Val came along, and before they knew it, Cade and Noah had shelved the one game that they most enjoyed.

'We *still* make a good team, Noah. Nothing's changed.'

'Oh yes, it has. Everything's changed,' Noah said.

Cade squatted down on his heels and peered up into Noah's face. For weeks Noah had been looking pale and worn-out; he had lost weight, and in the early morning light he almost seemed gaunt. Cade had assumed that the changes in Noah's appearance came from the stress of launching a new product, but he was starting to suspect that Noah's relationship with Val was breaking him down.

'We're still a good team,' Cade assured Noah. 'We've

just gotten rusty. Don't you think we should play one more round, before we retire?'

Noah set his jaw. He didn't say anything for several long moments, and for a while Cade was sure that he was going to deliver another sermon about the importance of fidelity.

'Fuck it,' Noah finally said, pounding the arms of his chair with his fists. 'Let's play.'

Cade jumped to his feet, hooting with glee. 'Dude, you won't regret this!' he shouted.

Though he didn't say it, Cade was convinced that the game was going to save Noah from making a huge mistake.

Five-thirty on a Friday afternoon: the bowels of rush-hour hell. Hailey wove through the traffic on her bike, dodging the commuters who couldn't wait to shove their way under each other's bumpers as they merged onto the bridge.

She slowed down when she spotted an open Jeep with a driver wearing nothing but jogging shorts, a pair of sunglasses and a smile. He turned to check Hailey out as she pulled up beside him. That grin had a gleam of competitive psychosis, but Hailey didn't mind insanity in a good-looking male. She wished she could toss her bike into the back of the Jeep, jump into the passenger seat and head off wherever he was going. The weekend was supposed to be glorious – sunbursts dancing across the Pacific, blue skies spreading wide behind the blue mountains, which were still capped with spring snows.

She let the Jeep driver go on his way as she headed down towards the wharf district. Another Friday 'seminar' at the brewery, this time with the added festivity of an end-of-semester celebration. Hailey locked up her bike outside and wiped the sweat off her face with her forearm. She clasped her hands, lifted her arms over her head and stretched as high as she could, closing her eyes as she luxuriated in the feeling of extending every muscle and tendon. Mercury Couriers had gotten their money's worth out of her this afternoon. Considering that she hadn't slept the night before, Hailey hadn't done badly at all.

She stepped gratefully into the cool interior, and breathed in the smell of hops as she looked around for her cohorts. There they were, at a table near the back, already halfway into a pitcher and fighting like hyenas. The stage was set for a Friday-night fight and, except for Hailey, the players were all assembled.

First there was Parker, a thirty-something doctoral candidate in cultural anthropology, and her lover Alicia, who wasn't enrolled in the seminar but always came for moral support. Across from Parker sat Hailey's room-mate Jack, and Stacy, a senior biochemistry major who had all but moved into Jack's room. Then there was Etienne Grimaud, an associate professor of biology, and a couple of his disciples, who thought he was hot because he'd published a book on homosexuality and evolution. That book had gotten Etienne more dates than an unpublished lecturer like Hailey could ever dream of.

'Hey, honey, wanna buy me a beer?' asked one of the men at the bar, ogling Hailey's hips in their skin-tight bike shorts. These men didn't realise that every time they opened their mouths, they provided alarming evidence that the human race was devolving.

'I'll buy you a whole pitcher,' Hailey shot back, 'as soon as hell freezes over.'

The drunk didn't even hear Hailey's retort; he was already in hot pursuit of an unlucky barmaid who happened to be walking through his range of vision. Hailey bolted away from the gauntlet of horny beer-guzzlers and made a beeline for her friends' table. By the time she got there, she'd been fondled twice, goosed once, and was primed for an argument.

'It's not hard to see why we're evolving in reverse,' Parker was saying to Jack's sweet young girlfriend, Stacy. It wasn't even six o'clock, and steam was already coming out of Parker's ears. She looked like she was about to chomp poor Stacy's head off. 'Take a look around one of these days, if you can pull your head out of the latest issue of *Baby Bride*. Every mall has a bridal shop, full of archaic costumes that mean absolutely nothing. You've got these behemoth multi-passenger vehicles rolling through the streets, and all these shop windows crammed with more trendy household products than any single household could ever use. People have gotten so far from their origins that soon they wouldn't be able to find their own genitals with both hands. Half a million years from now, if we haven't bombed ourselves into oblivion, people are going to be reproducing like fungi. We'll be throwing spores out to the four winds and praying that they landed in a fertile location.'

'Nothing wrong with that,' Jack said, resting his arm protectively on Stacy's shoulders. 'The reproductive habits of fungi are highly efficient. As a species, we could do a lot worse than follow their example. Better yet, we should reproduce like bacteria. If we could just exchange chromosomes without having to get naked and do the nasty, our lives would be so much easier. Sexual reproduction started with bacteria. You should remember that, Hailey, when you're studying your mammals.'

'If I ever forget, I'm sure you'll remind me,' Hailey said.

'You mustn't tease Hailey about her cats,' Etienne scolded Jack. 'One of these days she'll make a marvellous lion-tamer. Perhaps we'll all watch her perform in Las Vegas.'

For once, Hailey didn't have an instant retort. She was used to her friends making digs about her field of study, but tonight the jokes sounded stale.

'Hailey, thank god you're here. You've got to help me,' Parker pleaded. 'Jack's gone and decided to hang himself. You've got to help me convince him that he's making the biggest mistake of his life.'

'What are you talking about?'

Hailey pulled up a chair. She would have loved to pour herself a beer, but the pitcher was empty and, with the brewery so packed, she didn't have a prayer of getting her own drink anytime soon. She made do with Jack's half-full mug. He didn't seem to mind. In fact, he looked suspiciously placid and content this evening.

Stacy's face crumpled and reddened like a squashed tomato. She burst into tears, tore away from Jack and pushed through the crowd to the ladies' room. Etienne gave Parker a brittle smile. Jack buried his face in his hands.

'Am I missing something?' Hailey asked.

Jack lifted his head. 'I asked Stacy to marry me. She said yes. I told her not to tell these monsters that we were engaged, but she's young and naïve, and she thought they'd be happy for us.'

Parker rolled her eyes. 'Just goes to show you how perceptive she is. She's been hanging out with us for months now, and she still doesn't have a clue what I'm about.'

'Stacy thinks you're a closet romantic,' Jack

explained to Parker. 'She thought your frozen heart would melt when you heard the news.'

'I agree with Stacy,' said Etienne. 'Every neo-Darwinist is a romantic. Social Darwinism as we interpret it is a tribute to the notion of the romantic hero, the one who goes through trials and tribulations to single himself out from the rest, so that he can win the object of his love.'

Parker slammed down a fist on the table. 'Goddamn it, how many times do I have to tell you I'm not a Darwinist? I don't believe in the almighty power of random genetic mutations!'

'But your speech is full of the language of natural selection,' Etienne persisted. 'When you speak of mating, you talk about the struggle for survival, about reproductive fitness. You say that you're a firm believer in symbiotic evolution, but your words are all about competition.'

'Look, frog boy, if you want to analyse the vocabulary in my academic papers, that's fine, but don't go deconstructing everything I say in a bar,' Parker fumed.

'I give all language equal weight,' Etienne replied smoothly. Nothing could ruffle his composure, not even the wrath of a militant anthropologist. 'Why should I assume that the things you say in print are more sincere than the things you say here? Unless you're a hypocrite, of course.'

Hailey's head was pounding. Ordinarily she would have jumped into the fray by now, defending Parker against Etienne. Tonight she just wished she could transport herself to an exotic locale, where she could think about absolutely nothing while mute, muscular slave boys brought her piña coladas and rubbed almond oil into her overworked muscles. She was getting tired of these academic arguments, which never changed from week to week. If Jack wanted to get married – to 'hang himself', as Parker put it – why should anyone try to stop him? At least he was pairing off with another human for once in his life, instead of fantasising about swapping chromosomes with bacteria.

Looking around the table at her friends, Hailey suddenly realised how much she needed a change of scene. There was Parker, who was always battling the world from the top of her soapbox; Jack, who spent so much time with microbes that he couldn't see the macroscopic issues that were staring him in the face; and Etienne, who was so satisfied with himself and his cult of elitists that it was a wonder he bothered to hang out with mere mortals at all.

And let's not forget about me, Hailey thought. She wasn't any better than the rest of them. She had gone into biological studies because she loved the idea of spending time outdoors, travelling to isolated locations, studying exotic animals and working on ways to conserve endangered species. Sure, she had done her share of fieldwork, both at home and abroad. She had observed feline behaviour in captivity, and had traveled to Costa Rica to work on a study of population genetics in jaguars at a biological station in the rainforest. But nowadays she spent most of her time observing her students as they struggled to stay awake in class, and the only wilderness she'd visited recently was the Amazon Room. How had she let her dreams get so far off track?

'Hailey, help me out here,' Parker said, shaking Hailey by the elbow. 'These guys are killing me tonight. Hailey? Earth to Hailey!'

As Hailey squirmed in her chair, trying free her arm

from Parker's insistent claws, she caught a whiff of Noah's body on the T-shirt she was wearing. She'd been wearing the shirt all day, even to class. Whenever she moved the right way, she could smell Noah's scent, and it reminded her of how close they'd been early that morning. When they'd stood next to each other, she'd felt each fibre in his body vibrating, like the wires on a fine baby grand piano.

Then there was Cade – all driving heat, the perfect foil to Noah's calm, soothing sensitivity. Cade had known exactly what he was doing when he told her about the scene with Belinda in the shower. He was a champion manipulator, and he had an agenda for Hailey. She only wondered how long it would be before she found out what that agenda was.

'Leave me alone, Parker. I need a drink,' Hailey said.

There was an edge in her voice that shut her friends up at once. They watched her, their mouths hanging open, as she stood up and left the table. She could feel their startled eyes following her as she cut a path through the crowd, bypassing the bar and stalking out of the brewery. Later she could apologise for ditching her buddies; for now, she was fed up with the same weary arguments and the same old routines.

'Hailey? Hailey – wait.'

Someone called out to her as she unlocked her bike in the parking lot. Figuring it was one of her gang, Hailey ignored the voice, but she couldn't ignore the firm masculine hand that took hold of her wrist.

It took Hailey a few seconds to recognise Noah. He wasn't wearing his glasses, and his brown eyes squinted in the slanted light of the evening sun. He looked different outdoors, stronger and healthier, nothing like the pale, withdrawn computer geek she'd met that morning.

'I thought I'd take you up on your offer,' he said. 'Sorry I'm late. I'd been up for four days in a row, and I had to get some sleep.'

'My offer?' Hailey was having trouble thinking; her cognitive abilities had been overwhelmed by memories of Noah's hands touching her knee, her ribs, her thighs. Now that he had her attention, he could have let go of her wrist, but he held on, rubbing the base of her palm with his thumb, dandling her hand back and forth.

'Happy hour. Remember?'

'Oh, damn.'

Hailey had completely forgotten that she'd invited him to meet her at the brewery. What had she been thinking? Noah didn't belong in a meat market like that. Noah was the kind of man you would take to a secluded, out-of-the-way spot for an intimate conversation, followed by hours of passionate sex, with plenty of soulful eye contact. Noah might want to recite poetry afterwards, or sketch a portrait of his lover sleeping, but, when she was in post-orgasmic bliss, Hailey could be flexible.

'Looks like you're already leaving.'

'Yes. No. I mean, I don't know where I'm going right now.' Hailey laughed and ran her fingers through her hair, hoping she didn't look too awful. If she'd remembered that Noah might be here tonight, she would have at least used a comb before she left the house. 'Noah, it's so good to see you. Listen, why don't we go somewhere else?'

'Where?'

'Anywhere but the waterfront. I'm up for an adventure.'

'Funny you should say that,' Noah said with a grin. 'That's exactly what I wanted to talk to you about tonight.'

An ocean breeze ruffled his black hair, and the light exposed a sprinkling of freckles on his nose. He looked like he could be about fifteen years old right now – young and full of energy and ready for anything, like the boys Hailey used to run around with when she was a muddy-faced tomboy.

'Are you going to ask me to run away with you?' Hailey teased.

'Something like that. Hailey, I'm about to make you the deal of a lifetime.' Noah's voice deepened. He sounded like the announcer of a game show, offering a free washer-dryer to an overexcited housewife. 'I'm offering you the chance to spend this summer in a fabulous location. Not one, but two dashing men will be your hosts, catering to your every whim, while you spend your time doing something you love, all expenses paid.'

Hailey planted her hands on her hips. 'What's the catch?'

'You're the catch,' Noah said lightly.

'Come on. Be serious. What are you offering me?'

'A job. A vacation. A research opportunity. Whatever you want to call it. Are you interested?'

'That depends on what's involved.' Hailey's hopes were soaring, but her mouth was dry. Was Noah playing a joke on her? Dangling a carrot just to see if she'd be fool enough to follow?

Noah pulled Hailey's bike off the rack, jumped on and set off down the sidewalk, pedalling slowly enough for her to keep up with him at a jog.

'Noah! Slow down!' she shouted.

He turned his head and stuck his tongue out at her. 'No way! You speed up!' he shouted back.

Noah lowered his head and started pumping for real. Even in the heat of frustration, Hailey couldn't help admiring the way Noah's glutes shifted rhythmically under his shorts, or the way his solid hamstrings tightened every time he stepped down on one of the pedals. He was in better shape than she'd thought, and before long he was in serious danger of outracing her.

Hailey wasn't about to let herself be beaten by a computer geek. Heart and lungs on fire, she tore after him down the sidewalk.

After a few blocks Noah let Hailey catch up with him, then he hopped off her bike and wheeled it along for her. Walking side by side with Noah, Hailey felt like a schoolgirl letting a boy carry her books. But when Hailey was a kid, boys had known better than to offer to carry things for her, and she'd always left her textbooks to gather dust in her locker.

'You're a nice guy, Noah,' she said. 'A rare gentleman.'

'Ouch.' Noah flinched. 'I guess that destroys any possibility that you could find me attractive.'

'What are you talking about? I like men who know how to act considerate once in a while.'

'You're different from most women, then. Most women prefer sexy jerks.'

'Bad boys do have a lot of sex appeal,' Hailey agreed. She wasn't about to tell Noah how many of those bad boys she'd chased in her lifetime, or how many she'd caught.

'Why do you think that is?'

'Bad boys generate a sense of danger, of risk, and that sets off women's hormones. They're aggressive, so they probably have higher levels of testosterone than the average male. And mothers don't like them, so that automatically makes them attractive. No girl wants to date a man that her mother would approve of.'

'That explains why I had such a bizarre sex life as a teenager,' Noah said. 'I'd start out having a crush on a girl, but I'd end up in bed with her mother.'

'You're joking,' Hailey laughed. 'Did that really happen?'

'Almost . . . once. Well, I know for sure that one of the girls' mothers was attracted to me. Or maybe I just imagined it. I've always had an overactive imagination.'

'You need an overactive imagination in your line of work.'

'That's true,' Noah agreed. 'When you spend eighteen hours a day in front of a computer, it's hard to find your ideal woman. Sometimes you have to invent her.'

'Invent her? What are you doing up in that office of yours, cloning women like some kind of mad scientist?'

'Not quite. I'll show you, if you come upstairs with me.'

Hailey hadn't noticed where Noah was leading them. They had been walking and talking for longer than she realised, and had just climbed the hill to the old warehouse that housed Shiva Systems. Before he opened the door, Noah stopped, took Hailey by the shoulders and turned her around to face him. Coming from Noah, the dominant gesture surprised and aroused her.

'Before we go up there, I have to make sure you understand something,' he said. 'Thousands of people have seen my art in the games we design, but only one person knows what Yulana means to me.'

'I suppose that person is Cade,' Hailey said.

Noah nodded solemnly. 'If I introduce you to Yulana, you have to promise me that you won't laugh, call me a pervert or make jokes about geeks who spend all their time fantasising about computer-rendered women. I already get enough of that shit from Cade.'

'I understand. No jokes,' Hailey promised. 'Do you

want to make a blood pact? Or how about we swap spit and shake hands?'

'Your word's good enough for me,' Noah said.

He opened the door for Hailey, and they took the freight elevator upstairs. Now that the product had shipped, the offices of Shiva Systems were all but empty, except for a couple of junior programmers who were banging away at a pinball machine in the darkened break room.

'Kirk and Tuan are engaged in a fight to the death,' Noah explained. 'That game's been going on since eleven o'clock last night.'

'I see,' Hailey said, although she didn't really understand this dim, murky world of indoor recreation. Some of these game fanatics seemed to live in a world of perpetual night-time, always sitting in front of one machine or another with the blinds shut against the sun.

Noah's desk was a disaster area. The surface was littered with papers, loose CDs, Power Bar wrappers and a jumble of action figures and three-dimensional puzzles. The only pristine spot in the room was Noah's enormous monitor, which was surrounded by several inches of clean space. Unlike some of the other monitors in the office, this flat-panel beauty wasn't plastered with Post-It notes and superhero stickers.

Noah pulled up a chair for Hailey, then sat down and switched on the computer.

'Welcome to my world,' he said.

He clicked on a desktop icon, and the monitor displayed a forest from a dream. Trees with fantastical shapes arched over a narrow pathway, which led to a distant blur of multicoloured light. From the glittering blue-green depths of the foliage, hidden animals watched, blinking their golden eyes. Suddenly the masses of leaves took on life, forming a series of swirling letters that spelled out the words *Mutant Quest*.

'*Mutant Quest!*' Hailey laughed in delight. 'Hey, we're in the same line of work. I'm always on the lookout for random mutations.'

Noah grinned. 'You'll see plenty of 'em. Watch this.'

He clicked an icon, and a panel of characters popped up on the screen.

'You can play as an animal, or as a male or female human,' he explained, guiding his cursor over the panel. 'Yulana is my favourite character to play. She's a virgin warrior, a princess whose father was killed by a rogue mutant bear. The object of the game is to find the evil scientist who's responsible for all these monsters.'

'An evil genetics engineer – I love it. Let me guess – once you find him, you shoot up his lab with automatic weapons.'

'No, it's not that easy. First you have to convince him to tell you where all his mutants are hiding. You can bribe him, threaten him or seduce him, depending on your characters' powers. As you find your way to his laboratory, you can buy or steal weapons or gifts to help you get what you need.'

'How does Yulana defeat him?'

'Yulana has it all,' Noah said blissfully. 'Strength, intelligence, cunning and, of course, loads of sex appeal. In fact, she's a lot like you.'

He clicked Yulana's icon, and a magnificent blonde dressed in armour appeared before Hailey's eyes. Hailey did a double-take.

'A lot like *me*?' she said. 'I'm flattered but, the last time I checked, I didn't look anything like that.'

Yulana's wavy hair rippled to her waist, and her

jewelled breastplate didn't hide the fact that she had huge breasts. Her mighty thighs looked like they could snap a man's neck, if any man were fortunate enough to get that close. From the forbidding glare on Yulana's haughty face, Hailey guessed that the warrior princess spent a lot of time defending her virginity. By her side stood an astonishing animal, a muscular panther whose fur was a brilliant shade of blue.

'Yulana's looks are all for show. That's what the kids want to see. I was thinking of other traits, qualities that aren't pasted all over the screen. Her bravery. Her brains. The way she comes off as sexy, but she's got plenty of armour.'

'Wow, Doctor Freud. How much do I owe you for that thirty-second psychoanalysis?'

'It's on the house. What do you think of Yulana?' Noah asked, with an artist's shy pride.

'She's awesome. But tell me something – is Yulana a woman you want to fuck, or is she a woman you want to *be*?'

Even in the half-light of the monitor, Hailey could see that Noah's face had gone red.

'A little of both,' he said. 'She'd be my ideal mate, but she's also who I would be if I could choose to be anyone I wanted. Not very realistic, is it?'

'The best dreams aren't realistic at all,' Hailey said. 'There's nothing wrong with dreaming big, as long as you're able to make some compromises along the way.'

'Oh, I've made plenty of those,' Noah said.

His cool, distant tone made it clear that he wouldn't welcome any questions on the subject. He rotated the figures of Yulana and the blue feline, letting Hailey see the two splendid creatures from all sides. Both were rendered in loving detail; Noah must have devoted months to these creations.

'I love the panther,' Hailey remarked.

'That's Azuro. He's Yulana's animal guide, and he's also a mutant.'

'That's what I figured, from the blue coat.'

'Can you really tell he's a panther?' Noah asked. 'Only one kid in the focus group was able to identify what species he is, and only three seemed to notice the genetic mutation. Most of those guys care more about Yulana's boobs than Azuro's chromosomes.'

'I can definitely tell he's a panther. You've done your homework on feline anatomy.'

'Cats are another passion of mine. I've got five of the little monsters at home, but my favourites are the large exotics.'

'Mine too!' Hailey cried. 'That's my thesis topic – sexual selection in felines.'

Noah turned away from his alternative reality to smile at her. 'I know. Cade told me.'

'You and Cade share a lot, don't you?'

'We share just about everything.'

'Even women?'

'A gentleman wouldn't tell.'

'If you won't tell me, I'll have to ask Cade. He doesn't seem to have a problem sharing information,' Hailey said.

Heat spread through her loins as she thought about the incident at the diner that morning. Cade and Noah were like night and day; it was a miracle that they were such close friends. While Cade had no hesitations about discussing his erotic exploits in public – and giving Hailey an orgasm in the process – Noah wouldn't even talk about his sex life behind closed doors.

'Cade must have told you about my feline rescue project, then.'

'Um ... no. That's not exactly what we talked about.'

'I'm one of the founders of a rehabilitation park for wild cats. It's a small place up in the mountains, out of the way of everything. We do tours in the summer, and we run a little gift shop to bring in money, but we're mostly funded through private donations. Well, mostly *my* private donations.' A shadow crossed Noah's face. 'My fiancée thinks it's a complete waste of money, in spite of the tax write-off.'

'Your fiancée? Cade didn't tell me you were engaged.'

Hailey was stunned at how disappointed she felt. If Noah were engaged, she wouldn't have a chance with him. Hailey could feel how strongly he was attracted to her – she could feel it deep in the pit of her belly, where it counted – but unlike Cade, Noah would be a one-woman man.

'Sometimes I forget I'm engaged myself,' Noah said. He sounded like he was only half kidding. 'Can we not talk about personal things right now? I want to make you an offer.'

'All right,' said Hailey, more than willing to drop the topic. 'Tell me your offer.'

'The park always needs volunteers, especially people who know about animals. We're busy in the summer months, so we especially need help then. Cade has a lodge up there, with plenty of room. We couldn't afford to pay you, but we could offer you free room and board at the lodge while you work at the park for the summer. Who knows – you might even be able to use the cats for your research. We've been trying to breed the white tiger, though we haven't been successful so far. Does it sound like something you'd want to do?'

'Sounds fantastic, but I've got so many commitments ...'

'Such as?'

Hailey's voice tapered off as she thought about the summer. She was supposed to teach a summer-school class, and she had planned to meet with her thesis advisor every other week. She couldn't abandon her courier job, or some young punk would snatch it from her. And she couldn't leave her room-mates to cover her share of the rent while she wandered off to the mountains to play with exotic cats.

Noah was leaning forwards in his chair, his elbows propped on his knees. His dark eyes studied her intensely. He was not even remotely her type. On top of that, he was engaged to another woman. But Noah and Hailey had so much in common that they could still be great friends ... friends who were wildly attracted to each other.

'What else have you got going on?' Noah pressed.

'Nothing,' Hailey said. 'Nothing that can't be rearranged. I'd love to come.'

'Good,' Noah said. 'Cade and I will make sure that you do.'

Hailey wasn't sure, but she could swear she detected a double entendre in Noah's words, and in his secretive smile.

4 Welcome to the Jungle

It didn't take much effort on Noah's part to convince Hailey to spend the summer at the 'cat ranch', as Cade liked to call it. In fact, making the decision to go was a lot easier than finding the lodge in Sasquanatee County. Hailey got lost several times along the two-lane road that wound through the mountains, but she didn't mind. All she had to do, when she started to worry, was to close her eyes and breathe in the super-oxygenated air of the Pacific Northwestern rainforest. Fresh, sweet and delicious, that air left her feeling like she'd had a few sips of fine champagne.

Sitting on the hood of her car by the side of an overgrown logging trail, Hailey let herself get drunk. Suddenly it didn't matter that she didn't know where she was. Life had slowed down to the calm pace of her breathing. A map lay open beside her, but she had gotten tired of studying the lines and squiggles that represented the roads up here. Somehow, at some point in time, she'd find her way to the lodge. For now, she was having a great time doing absolutely nothing in the silent forest.

One by one, she released the worries that had been buzzing around in her brain. Her room-mates could find someone to cover her rent for the summer. Her technophobic thesis advisor could learn how to use e-mail, so that Hailey could send him the draft she'd be working on. Though she wouldn't be earning extra income teaching summer school, she'd make up for it with the money she'd save on rent. Life in the city would sort itself out. Meanwhile, she was feeling more relaxed and sensually open than she'd felt since her trip to Costa Rica.

Costa Rica. That was where she'd fallen seriously in love with evolutionary biology – and where she'd fallen seriously in lust with Alessandro.

The country was Hailey's vision of paradise, an evolutionist's playground. There were so many species of birds, amphibians and mammals that it would have taken a lifetime to record a fraction of the variations. Everyone Hailey met seemed to be a biologist; the country was such a fertile research ground that it drew scientists from all over the world to explore its riches. Hailey had been part of a team of grad students who were collecting data on jaguars and their mating patterns. When she wasn't hunting for scat samples, or squatting under a cover of leaves trying to record her rare sightings of the elusive cats, Hailey was honing her own mating skills with an Italian ornithologist who had a lot more than birds on the brain.

While Hailey was studying the sexual habits of cats, Alessandro was equally enthralled with the mating patterns of birds. Hailey did a lot of her research at twilight or after dark; Alessandro did much of his work just before dawn. He looked a bit like a bird himself, a sleek and seductive bird of prey, with piercing eyes that singled Hailey out one night in a packed cantina where she was partying with her friends.

She saw him cutting sideways through the cantina, his slim body parting the crowd like a cool knife slicing a fresh chocolate cake. Through the haze of tequila, Hailey recognised him as a fellow academic. She had heard him present a paper at a conference the year before, and she knew that she should probably treat with professional decorum. But on that humid night, all she cared about was the sheen of his tanned skin against his white shirt, and the predatory flash in his eyes. There was too much racket for polite introductions or superficial chat; Alessandro simply took Hailey's arm, pulled her off her bar stool and led her to the dancefloor.

The tiny space was crammed with young, half-naked, perspiring people, all of them moving and gyrating like a single organism. Alessandro let the crowd help him with his seduction. Standing behind Hailey, he held her lightly by the waist and rotated her hips to the beat of the loud Latino pop. He and Hailey rode the waves of the other dancers, moving in one direction, then another, depending on where the sea of bodies drifted. In the midst of so many gyrating people, their skin-to-skin friction was unavoidable, and it almost seemed like an accident that Hailey's hips kept meeting the hollow of Alessandro's pelvis.

Before long, her bottom was rotating against him like a ball in a socket, and she could feel his hardness with every move. His fingers kept inching up her waist, which was bare under the cut-off jersey top she wore. Soon the edges of his palms were tucked in the sweaty crevice under her breasts, and Hailey was leaning back against the warm plank of his chest.

At that moment, one of the drunks on the dancefloor decided that Hailey's breasts would look even better if they were bathed in tequila. When she felt the first stinging splash against her chest, she almost hauled off and punched the guy. But as the liquor started to work its way into her skin, puckering the sensitive flesh around her nipples and leaving a fiery trail down the central groove of her abdomen, Hailey's anger changed to full-blown lust. She wiped some of the booze off her skin with her index finger, then turned around and popped her finger into Alessandro's mouth.

When the Italian began to suck on her fingertip, Hailey knew she'd struck gold. He put more effort and skill into that simple activity than a lot of men put into a whole night of lovemaking. His lips and tongue crafted a world of sensations, all of them focusing on that one small part of her digit. Just when she thought her pleasure couldn't get more intense, Alessandro did something that she never would have expected from a high-ranking ornithologist: he lifted up her top and began to lick the rest of the tequila off her body.

The other revellers must have noticed what he was doing, but most of the women were near-naked by now, and Hailey was beyond caring what anyone thought. She closed her eyes, leaned her head back and watched the whirling disco ball above her head as Alessandro's tongue painted her throat, her collarbone and the top of her breasts. When he pushed down her bra to suck her nipple, she closed her eyes and gave in to the feeling. A throbbing pulse between her pussy lips echoed the rhythmic suction. He kept his mouth fixed to that stiff button as he eased her body back, holding her steady with his arms.

The music changed to a catchy pop tune with a mambo beat, one of those obnoxious top-ten hits that worms its way into the brain like a tropical parasite. Hailey would hear that song again and again for the rest of that year, and every time she heard it she would think of what Alessandro did to her next. He brought her back to an upright position, then lifted his knee and began to grind the round ball of his kneecap against her pussy.

After the stimulation he'd already given her, it didn't take long for him to make Hailey come. He held her face in his hand, so that she was forced to meet his keen, dark stare as she climaxed. Those hot black eyes pulled more spasms out of her than she had thought possible. When the last of them had finally ebbed, she reached for his cock, hoping to reward him. But Alessandro backed away, smiling and pointing at his watch, and disappeared into the crowd.

He came back for his reward a few hours later.

It was the time of day that Hailey called 'the ugly hour', too close to dawn to be out partying, but still too dark for normal human beings to be walking around. After closing down the cantina with her friends, Hailey had found her way back to her room at a local hostel and had passed out on her bed. She woke to the sound of sharp, insistent knocking.

'Who the hell?' she grumbled into the pit of her pillow, then immediately passed out again. When she woke up, she was being dragged into her clothes by someone far more alert and efficient than she was. She must have forgotten to lock the door the night before; now she was being forcibly dressed by a stranger. How often did that happen?

Hailey opened her bleary eyes to see that the man in her room wasn't a stranger – it was her bird-watching friend, the man who had made her come so hard the night before.

'What are you doing, lying around in bed so late?' Alessandro scolded. 'You've already wasted half the morning.'

'Morning's not till noon,' Hailey said. 'Go away and come back later.'

'No way. I have incredible things to show you.'

'Like what?' Hailey perked up. She loved sex first thing in the morning, though the fact that Alessandro was getting her *into* her clothes didn't look promising.

'You'll find out soon enough.'

Alessandro dragged her off the bed, down the stairs and out to the street, where his muddy Jeep was waiting. He strapped Hailey into the vehicle and, before she knew it, they were rushing through the cool, deep-blue morning and heading for the mountains.

'Are you going to tell me why you kidnapped me?' Hailey asked, when Alessandro stopped the jeep on the side of a road in the foothills.

'I needed an assistant this morning,' he explained.

'You're joking, right?'

'No. Not at all. Your colleagues speak very highly of you.'

'Are you so desperate for help that you have to pick up assistants in bars?' Hailey asked.

Alessandro pulled a heavy backpack out of his Jeep. She assumed that he was going to strap it onto his back; instead he handed it to Hailey, along with a pair of binoculars.

'I'm hard to work with,' he said, giving her a look that brought back every ripple, quiver and shudder that she'd felt last night. 'Very hard. Now, are you ready to work, or not?'

'I'm ready,' she said meekly.

Hailey thought she was getting the worst of it with the ten-ton backpack, but Alessandro ended up carrying most of the gear. He led them up a steep, muddy trail that twisted through the trees. It took them forever to climb the trail to the cloud forest. Every few feet he would stop, put his finger to his lips to warn Hailey to keep quiet and point up to the canopy of trees. Training the binoculars on the place where he was pointing, Hailey would see a flicker or flash of some exotic species: a macaw or a toucan. As the sun rose, she could see the colours of their feathers more clearly, and she started to recognise them by their hues and calls.

'You'll see a wider variety of species here than almost anywhere else on earth,' Alessandro told her when they finally stopped in a level clearing to set up their gear. He'd brought everything with him: a laptop computer, recording equipment, cameras, a rucksack full of cooking utensils and food, and even a tent. 'That's why I never want to leave this place. I can't stand a restriction of variety.'

Supposedly he was making a professional comment about the birds, but Hailey knew male double-speak when she heard it.

'What you're telling me,' she said, 'is that we should enjoy each other while we can, but that I shouldn't expect anything permanent.'

He smiled. 'Does that bother you?'

'The only thing that bothers me is your assumption that I want to marry you and have ten kids with you, just because we shared a hot mambo and a few slurps of tequila last night.'

'You know, there are some species of birds that supposedly pair-bond for life,' Alessandro said. He was already starting to set up the tent, before the rest of the gear was unpacked. 'But in other species, the bond isn't solid at all, and it's not always the male who seeks variety. When the male leaves the nest in search of food, the female fools around with other males. It increases her odds of having viable offspring if she mates with more than one.'

'What's your point?' Hailey planted her fists on her hips.

'My point is, I never make assumptions when it comes to female sexuality.'

'You're making a big assumption by setting up that tent so early in the morning,' Hailey shot back.

Alessandro laughed. 'Believe me, I wouldn't make assumptions about you. You can't blame me for being an optimist. I like to make love before I start working. It releases tension, puts me in a good mood. I thought there was a good chance that you might want me to fuck you, and that if you did, a little privacy would be nice.'

'Privacy? Are you kidding? You didn't seem all that concerned about privacy last night on the dancefloor. The whole cantina was watching while you practically ate me alive.'

'In the cantina, there were only people watching,' Alessandro said dismissively. 'Here there are birds and animals and insects going about their daily business. I don't want to disturb them any more than I have to.'

This attitude wasn't surprising to Hailey. A lot of the biologists she knew didn't hold a very high opinion of their own species. Humans weren't as metabolically resourceful, sexually diverse or physiologically resilient as some of the other creatures on the planet. Unfortunately, not even the most dedicated scientist could curl up with a protozoan on a cold winter's night, or get a hot-oil massage from an arthropod.

The tent was ready and waiting. Alessandro stood in front of it, holding the flap open.

'Now, Signorina,' he said with mock gallantry, 'shall we finish what we started last night?'

The morning was perfect. The air felt gloriously sensual: soft and silken and veiled with mist. The temperature was on the cool side, but once her skin was pressed against Alessandro's, Hailey knew that she wouldn't feel the chill. She could already sense a loosening in the core of her body, along with a warm, sliding rush between her thighs and a tingling in her extremities. Alessandro's eyes were level with her nipple line, and her arousal was as obvious as a pair of headlights in a fog.

They had to take their clothes off before crawling into the low, narrow tent. Hailey was so eager that she fumbled with her buttons and got her ankles tangled in her jeans. Alessandro wasn't doing much better; he almost tripped over himself as he hurried to peel off his T-shirt and shorts. His gleaming nut-brown skin was smooth all over, except for a soft layer of black fur between his pecs, which thinned to a single black line along his abdomen then fanned out into a thick pubic pelt. His cock was semi-erect in the cool air. Hailey had to smile to herself; true to his word, Alessandro was optimistic, but he wasn't making any assumptions.

Hailey got into the tent first. Alessandro followed. The tent's yellow nylon walls filtered the sunlight, giving Alessandro's skin a burnished golden glow. The tent was strictly for sleeping; there wasn't even enough room for Alessandro to move around on all fours.

'My tent's not very romantic,' he admitted, lying down beside Hailey.

'I love it,' Hailey said.

They were so close together, in that yellow cocoon, that they could have counted each other's pulse without lifting a finger. There was something intensely intimate, Hailey thought, about lying stark naked against a man she hardly knew, who was just as naked as she was. Their tangled awkwardness felt sweet and familiar, almost like being married, but the fact that they were almost strangers made it new and exciting. Alessandro must have felt the same way, because there was nothing half-hard about him now. The full length of his penis pressed against Hailey's lower belly.

She reached down to touch his erection. He was uncut, and the sleeve of his foreskin moved smoothly against her hand, as if it were made for her palm. Under that velvet layer, the shaft was warm and resilient, ridged with a light network of veins. He had a condom with him but, before he put it on, Hailey got to know his cock with her fingers. Then she wiggled down and got to know it with her lips. His crisp black pubic curls had a musky, peppery scent. The crown of his cock was slim and bullet-shaped, about the same circumference as the shaft, and he slid like a firm eel into her mouth, his cock long, but not too long to fit comfortably into her throat. While she sucked him, Alessandro cupped her head in one hand and moved his hips, gently at first, then with more urgency.

'Turn around,' he said.

She lifted her head and looked up at him. 'How?'

'I want you on top of me, with your cunt on my mouth. Hurry.'

Rocking the tent's frame, Hailey managed to clamber into the position he wanted. They had told her she'd need to be in good shape for this trip, but no one had warned her about the perils – or the pleasures – of doing 69 in a one-man tent. It took her a few minutes to work out the rhythm of licking while being licked, sucking while being sucked; she had to divide her mind in order to do justice to Alessandro's cock while enjoying the way his tongue was exploring her pussy.

A rain cloud passed overhead, and a brief morning shower sprinkled the tent. The sound of the falling water mingled with the sounds of mouth and tongue on cock and pussy and, before she knew it, Hailey forgot that there was any trick to doing 69 at all. She dropped any trace of self-consciousness and moved to the hypnotic rhythm of the rain, rotating her hips against Alessandro's mouth and letting his tongue wend its way through the whorls of her sex. He gripped her ass cheeks, pushing her firmly onto his face, using the hard shelf of his chin to create pressure on her mound while his lips tugged at her clit.

She did her best to give his sleek cock and firm round balls their due, but soon it was hard to concentrate on anything but the welling warmth between her legs. His tongue flickered in and out of her lower lips like a fish caught in a net, prodding and provoking the tiny knot buried in the folds. Before long, his erection slid out of her mouth, as Hailey lost herself to a body-wracking orgasm. After the storm had worked its way through her, she collapsed face-down in the crevice between Alessandro's thighs. Maybe it was the richness of the rainforest air, or the challenge of a new lover, but Hailey couldn't remember ever having felt so exhilarated during sex.

Alessandro gave her ass a light slap, reminding her that he was still there.

'Ride me,' he ordered.

Hailey managed to turn herself around so that she and her new lover were face to face again. His cock glided effortlessly into her well-lubed channel, but under the low flaps of the tent it was hard to sit up and mount him with her whole weight. Hailey started out fucking him slowly and carefully, respecting the limits of the nylon cocoon, but when he clutched her hips and drove himself into her, she threw caution to the winds and rode him wildly. The tent was a wreck, anyway. From the birds' perspective, the nylon structure must have looked like a giant yellow caterpillar, humping and writhing in the middle of the jungle.

Alessandro's climax was as powerful as Hailey's had been. She knew he was close to coming when he started issuing guttural commands in Italian then lost the ability to speak altogether. She gave the last few minutes everything she had, milking him with her inner muscles as she posted up and down, and when he exploded, he shouted something in his native tongue that didn't exactly sound like a novena. His last thrusts gave her a second orgasm, more forceful than the first. As she was coming she heard a frenzied shriek somewhere in the jungle, and for a moment she didn't know if the sound came from some wild animal or her own mouth.

Alessandro was as good as his word. He didn't want anything permanent, just a few weeks of hot sex in every possible place and position that Hailey could think of. Since Hailey was high on imagination, low on inhibitions and passionate about biology, she held his interest longer than most women. When they weren't making love, they were talking about their work; he taught Hailey to respect birds almost as much as she respected cats, and she managed to convince him that felines were more genetically similar to humans than he'd realised. There didn't seem to be any reason, Hailey thought, why such a free, uncommitted relationship had to end.

Then one night a stunning Norwegian ecologist caught Alessandro's eye at a bar. He walked away to buy the other woman a drink, and Hailey never saw him again.

That was the way mating was supposed to be, Hailey thought. Lots of intensity, lots of heat and as much variety as possible. But after Alessandro, she found herself being self-protective around men. She loved sex as much as ever – the sight, the sounds, the smells of it – but when it came to landing another partner for herself, she kept finding an excuse to hold back.

In fact, she realised with a jolt, Alessandro was the last real lover she'd had in ages. Instead of finding a new mate, Hailey had been surviving on memories of him for far too long. She could still remember their early-morning activities in the tent, with the racket of exotic birds drowning out her moans and the moist air stroking her bare back like another pair of hands. She remembered the way Alessandro had laved her pussy with his tongue, and the way the ribbons of moisture had tingled in the morning coolness when he stopped licking. She remembered how his elegant English had turned monosyllabic when she took the dominant role and pushed him onto his back, then climbed aboard his cock and rode him like a crazed witch. She would never forget how hard she'd climaxed when she heard a monkey scream in the trees, and it really came home to her that she was a beast like all the rest of them.

The forests of the Pacific Northwest weren't much like Costa Rica, but the sensations of being outdoors were just as arousing. Leaning back against the windshield of her car, Hailey spread her legs wide and loosened a few buttons on her blouse. The moist, cool air passed the hems of her cut-off denim shorts, caressing her inner thighs, tickling her pussy. It flowed down the collar of her shirt and covered her breasts with its freshness. She felt like she was getting a free luxury spa treatment. She arched her spine, threw her head back and stretched for all she was worth. Sometimes a good stretch felt better than sex.

Unless you happened to be doing it with someone like the guy who was watching her.

The tall, long-haired stranger didn't appear very friendly, but he was definitely easy on the eye. The guy looked like he could be part of the native fauna, like some large, gorgeous species that dwelled in the trees. His dark-red hair was about the same colour as the redwood bark, and he was motionless enough to be part of the scenery.

'Hey,' she said, reluctantly bringing her knees together. 'Can I help you with something?'

A silly question, considering how much help Hailey needed herself, but it was the only thing that came to mind. In her mellow mood, Hailey hadn't noticed that she had an audience. As audiences went, he wasn't a very flattering one. Glowering from the shadows of the redwood trees, he didn't look like he appreciated finding a scantily clad woman in the middle of the woods. He could be one of those back-to-nature environmentalist fanatics who hated any kind of intrusion on the wilderness. Hailey had met more than her share of those in the biological-sciences department. She hoped this one wasn't armed or anything.

'Are you lost?' asked the forest fanatic.

'Well ... yes,' Hailey admitted. 'You could say I'm lost.'

She rounded her shoulders to cover her breasts. She would have liked to button her blouse, but figured she'd call more attention to herself if she did that. She couldn't read this guy's stare. Maybe he wanted to rape her. More likely, he wanted to give her some anti-logging pamphlets and send her back to the city.

'Where were you heading?'

'There's an exotic-cat rehabilitation park somewhere

in this area. I've got a job there for the summer. I'm trying to find a lodge that's part of the park. Two friends of mine are staying there.'

The man made a snorting noise that might have been laughter, derision or both. 'That figures,' he said.

'What's that supposed to mean?' Hailey bristled.

He shoved his hands in his pockets and scuffed his boot along the loamy ground. Hailey could swear that he was trying to hide a smirk.

'Did I miss something? What's so funny?'

He straightened, all business again. 'You're not too far from where you're trying to go. If you don't mind giving me a ride, I can take you up there.'

By now, Hailey *did* mind. 'No thanks. Just tell me where to go, and I'll find my way.'

'Stay on this trail for about a half-mile,' said the fanatic, unperturbed. 'Keep your eyes peeled for a tree with a slash of white paint on the trunk. It's not easy to see, and it's the only way the road is marked. If you'd come from the west, the lodge would be a lot easier to find.'

'Like I said, I got lost,' Hailey said. This man was exasperating beyond belief. She hoped he wasn't a fixture around here. 'How do you know so much about the park, anyway?'

'I'm the cat handler,' he said. 'And the park's curator, and business manager. You name it, I do it around here.'

Oh great, Hailey thought. So much for not being a fixture. Not only was he permanent – he would have total control over Hailey's work. If he decided that he didn't trust her, he'd never let her near the cats.

'Look, you might as well ride up there with me,' she sighed, sliding off the hood. 'Since we're going to be working together, we should get to know each other. I'm Hailey.'

'My name's Rick.'

As the cat handler approached the car, Hailey watched his smooth, rhythmic walk. Definitely a feline type, he carried himself with a smooth, unselfconscious pride. Hailey would bet anything that Rick didn't have to work very hard to find his mates; females always enjoyed a challenge.

Hailey was no exception. As she guided her car along the trail, she had to fight the urge to flirt. In the narrow confines of her old Honda, Rick's closeness triggered all her senses. She could smell the piny scent of the soap he used, hear the sound of his breathing, feel the dense masculine hardness of his body. She sensed a loosening in his muscles; he was warming up to her. When he looped a strand of his long auburn hair behind his ear, she noticed that he wore a small silver earring, and had a Chinese character tattooed on his neck. Maybe Mr Back-to-Nature wasn't all that pure or natural, Hailey mused.

'That tattoo must have caused you some pain,' Hailey said. 'What does the character say?'

'It means "tiger",' Rick said. 'I got it to celebrate Seka's birthday.'

'Who's Seka?'

'The love of my life. She's a gorgeous white tiger that we rescued from a ranch in Arizona. We didn't think she'd make it past her second year; that's why I got the tattoo.'

'Did she give you that scar on your hand?' Hailey asked, pointing to a jagged seam that ran diagonally from the base of his index finger to his wrist.

'Nope. That was Mingus. He's a bobcat.'

'Your job sounds dangerous.'

'I'd rather handle cats than corporate clients,' Rick replied. 'Eight years ago I was wearing three-piece suits instead of tattoos. I'd rather have a chunk gouged out of me any day than go back to that.'

'Don't blame you a bit. What did you do?'

For the first time since they'd met, Rick looked like he'd been caught off guard. He cleared his throat and mumbled something.

'I didn't hear you,' Hailey said. 'What did you say you did?'

'Look, there's the tree up ahead,' he said, sounding glad to change the subject. 'This is where you turn.'

Rick's hand came to rest on Hailey's leg. He guided her thigh to the right, as if her lower limb were a gear shift. She turned the car in that direction, and he let go. The contact lasted only a second or two, but those seconds were loaded and ready to fire. Rick was hardly a touchy-feely guy; he was more like an I-need-to-be-in-control kind of guy, and the touch was his way of showing her who was boss.

'You really do spend a lot of time around cats,' Hailey said. She tried to sound cool, but her voice had an embarrassing tremor.

'What makes you say that?' Rick asked.

'You're territorial. I'm surprised you haven't marked me with your glands by now.'

'Kind of hard, when you're driving.'

She couldn't look at him, because she was trying to guide the car down the fern-edged logging trail, but she knew that Rick was taking a subtle inventory of the lines and curves of her body. She could still feel the imprint of his palm on her thigh. How would it feel to have the cat handler controlling, manipulating, handling *her*?

Not so fast, Hailey warned herself. She'd better scope out this situation before she dove head-first into a casual fling. She stepped on the brakes.

'Why are we stopping?' Rick asked. 'The park's another mile up the road.'

'I know that. Now that you've shown me the turn, I think I can find my way by myself.'

'Are you sure about that?'

'I'm sure,' she said, giving him a meaningful glare. 'There are some things that I do much better on my own. One of them is driving.'

She expected Rick to be put out, but he only looked amused. He opened the car door and slid out gracefully, without protest.

'Stop by my cabin later. Anyone can tell you where it is. I'll show you the park,' he said, leaning down to peer through the passenger window. 'Unless you'd rather give yourself the tour.'

'I'd rather think things over before I let you give me anything,' she said, and started the engine.

She tried to resist glancing in the rear-view mirror as she drove on, but she caught herself taking a peek. She immediately wished she hadn't. Rick was strolling down the middle of the road. His hands were buried in his pockets, and he wore the most aggravating, patronising smile she'd ever seen.

Too bad that smirk didn't make him any less of a hunk.

After the encounter with Rick, it was a relief to reach the sanctuary of the lodge. She recognised the sprawling old Craftsman-style house by the sexy man who sat on the front porch. Cade was relaxing with a beer in his hand, his bare feet propped up on a wooden footstool. Wearing faded jeans and a clean white

T-shirt, he looked delicious – like one of the older high-school boys Hailey used to lust after when she was fourteen.

'This place is perfect!' Hailey cried, climbing out of the car.

The lodge looked like a natural outgrowth of the woods: its broad porch was all but buried in lacy green ferns, and the roof was furred with moss. On one side of the front steps stood a painted totem pole, and on the other rose a mountain lion, carved out of burl wood, that was at least as tall as Hailey. Behind the house rose the forest, skeined with fog. The huge, mist-covered trees could have been creepy but, in Hailey's frame of mind, the evergreens' dark depths held thousands of sensual possibilities. A person could really let go in a place like this, far from the stresses and petty rules of civilisation. Up here, no one could see or hear you, and if they did, there was no one around to tell.

'Glad you like it,' Cade said. 'It belonged to my grandfather. He used to come up here to fish, relax, have orgies with loose women.'

'I don't doubt it. Promiscuity's in your genes.'

Cade lowered his head. 'I bow to your insight, Miss Evolutionist. Care for a beer?'

'I'd love one.'

Hailey threw her old duffel bag on the porch and sat down next to Cade in one of the redwood gliders. She accepted the frosty green bottle of beer that Cade handed her, and took a deep, grateful swig.

'So do you think that promiscuous behaviour makes the species stronger?' Cade asked.

Hailey took another sip. She wasn't in the mood for a debate, but a casual chat with an attractive man on a summer afternoon was another thing altogether.

'I hate to say it, but I do. And I think that goes for both men and women. A woman has a better chance of having viable offspring if she has more sex partners.'

'If that's true, then why do girls get so rabidly jealous when they think their man's cheating on them? Hell, why do we even use a word like "cheating" when it comes to sex, if your theory is right?'

'I think a large part of jealousy is projection. Women get jealous of their men because deep down, they want to be playing around too. Only it's not OK for a woman to be promiscuous, so she has to go in the opposite direction and be a rigid monogamist instead. As far as "cheating" goes, I think it's a strange choice of words. We use the word "cheating" when we talk about games, or tests, but we wouldn't think of a monogamous relationship as a game, would we?'

'Not as a game, but it's definitely a test,' Cade said. 'A test of will.'

'What about your fiancée? Don't you think it's a test for her, too?'

'No; I think it comes naturally to her. We had this discussion early in our relationship. She told me flat out that she didn't want me "cheating" on her, and that I could trust her not to "cheat" either.'

'All right, then. Knowing yourself as well as you do, why did you agree to that?' Hailey asked. 'It kills me to hear men talk like this – about how they caved in to monogamy, when what they really want to do is play the field. Why not just avoid marriage from the beginning?'

'Because men do this insane thing called falling in love,' Cade said. 'We can separate love and sex. Women can't. We can't get the women we love unless we agree to give up having sex with other girls.'

'Listen to yourself. The person you love is a

"woman"; the one you have mindless sex with is a "girl". Do you automatically associate monogamy with maturity, and vice versa?'

Cade picked at the label on his beer bottle. 'I guess I do. I mean, marriage is what you do when you get older, right? You make a choice, you take a vow, you settle down.'

'And you bring loose women to your lodge when you want a little nookie on the side. Is that how it goes?' Hailey taunted him. 'Wouldn't it be better to be honest about what you want? If monogamy were a natural condition of maturity, then it should be easy for you to settle into it. You don't have a burning desire to play cops 'n' robbers any more, do you?'

'No.'

'Then maybe you should consider the possibility that your desire to have multiple sex partners is a natural part of who you are, and that it's not going to go away just because you slide a ring on your finger, or hit your third or fourth decade.' Hailey stretched and yawned. 'I'd love to hear what Belinda has to say about this.'

Cade silently continued to peel at the label. His forehead was wrinkled up like corrugated iron.

'Cade, is something wrong?' Hailey asked.

'You'll get a chance to ask her yourself,' Cade said. 'She's driving up tonight. She'll be here by dinner-time.'

'So? What's wrong with that?'

'To tell you the truth, I didn't expect her to come so soon. I thought we'd have some more time to show you around, get you settled in.'

'But it's great that she's coming! I can't wait to meet the Monogamy Princess. Maybe I can convince her of the error of her ways. Then you two will go on to have a long and happy marriage, but you'll be able to enjoy other people to your hearts' content.'

'Nice fantasy, but it'll never happen.'

'Maybe it's you who can't handle the thought of sharing your mate,' Hailey suggested.

'Just wait till you meet her. Then you can decide,' Cade said glumly.

'Don't sound so depressed. I'm sure she's the catch of the century, or you wouldn't be with her.' Hailey slapped Cade's knee. 'What do you need me to do? Chop veggies? Set the table?'

'Not a chance. You're the guest of honour tonight. I want you to lie back, have another beer or two or three, and wait until the meal is served. Noah's in there slaving away over the stove. He's making his famous maple salmon. It's guaranteed to make you climax on the first bite.'

'Noah's cooking? God, I love a man who can cook,' Hailey said, sighing with pleasure.

'His cooking is nothing compared to his artwork. The guy's a genius,' Cade said. 'Wait till you play *Mutant Quest*.'

'I can't wait.'

Hailey saw an odd expression flit across Cade's face, but the look was gone before she could analyse it. Something was cooking here at the lodge, and it wasn't just Noah's special salmon. She could feel goose bumps puckering on her skin – a sure sign that her body was responding to the challenge. Cade's fiancée would add even more spice to the meal.

Then there was Rick.

'By the way,' Hailey asked idly, 'what's up with your cat handler? Is Rick always such a charmer, or does he just turn on the sex appeal for lost female motorists?'

Rick's name seemed to catch Cade off guard. His eyes narrowed, and his grip tightened on his beer bottle.

'When did you meet Rick?'

'In the woods. I had a heck of a time finding this place, and he gave me directions. Funny how he showed up. He seemed to come out of nowhere.'

'Rick's hard to avoid,' Cade said. 'You'll have to get used to his attitude. It's best if you can find a way to steer clear of him.'

'Not possible, if I'm going to be working with the cats. In fact, I was planning to meet up with him this evening. He offered to show me the park, and I figured he'd be the best one to do it.'

'Why don't you hold off on the tour? Noah can show you around after dinner.'

'But Rick –'

'We'll see about him,' Cade said, in a vaguely ominous tone. He stood up. 'Look, I'm going to help Noah with the fish. Help yourself from the cooler when you're ready for another beer.'

'I'd be glad to.' Hailey swung her legs around and rested her feet on the footstool that Cade had abandoned. Funny how the mention of Rick had driven Cade away. Maybe he was running off to polish his shotgun.

Men were so predictable, Hailey thought, sipping her brew in contentment. A man would whine and whimper when he had to curtail his sexual activities, but at the first sign that a competitor was interested in one of 'his' women, he launched into attack mode.

Hailey polished off her beer, then slipped into a half-doze in the comfortable old gliding chair. The sound of a car motor woke her, and she opened her eyes to see a champagne Lexus convertible pulling up to the lodge. The sleek automobile stopped next to Hailey's Honda, making the green hatchback look like a junker in comparison.

Hailey knew right away who the driver was. Even if she hadn't seen the telltale strawberry blonde bob, or the flawless, upper-crust features, she would have known that the car belonged to Cade's fiancée: the vanity plates read BELSBABY. Did Belinda mark all her property that way, or was it only her car? Hailey had a sudden vision of the word BELSBOY tattooed on one of Cade's buttocks, and she laughed out loud.

Belinda didn't look too happy to find a strange woman laughing at her on the porch. Her forehead creased behind her designer sunglasses, and her lips puckered into a pink knot. Hailey couldn't blame her. It was always disturbing to find a new female on your home turf.

Hailey pulled herself off the chair and held out her hand to Belinda.

'I'm Hailey,' she said. 'I'm going to be working at the cat park this summer. You must be Belinda. Cade's told me about you.'

Boy, has he ever, Hailey added to herself. Looking Belinda up and down, she remembered the story about the shower. Cade hadn't exaggerated when he said that Belinda had a body to die for. Three or four inches taller than Hailey, she managed to be athletic and voluptuous at the same time. Her fair skin had just enough of a tan to convey health, without making her look like a skin-cancer risk. And as if all that weren't enough, she was wearing an off-white linen blouse and skirt that had survived a long car trip with only one or two creases.

Belinda waited for a beat before shaking Hailey's hand. She didn't have much of a handshake, more like one of those charm-school finger-squeezes.

'He didn't tell me anything about you,' she said. 'But there are always new people around in the summer.'

New *people*. A strategic choice of words: Belinda managed to neutralise her rival by ignoring her femininity. Having gotten Hailey neatly categorised and out of the way, Belinda was already gazing over her head and into her fabulous future.

'I'd better go see what Cade's up to,' Belinda said. 'Nice to meet you, Hilary.'

'Nice to meet you, too.'

Hailey didn't bother to correct Belinda. She had a feeling that Cade's fiancée had mangled her name on purpose. Watching Belinda's long, straight back as she stepped through the screen door, Hailey took note of an interesting detail. Perfect Belinda, whose hair didn't get mussed in a convertible and whose linen didn't wrinkle, had a blemish in her appearance. The backstrap of her bra was twisted, as if she'd fastened it too fast . . . or as if someone with clumsy, masculine fingers had fastened it for her. What could that mean? Hailey chalked it up as evidence to explore later, and went back to the glider to drink another beer.

Dinner was weird. The meal was delicious. Noah's maple salmon melted on Hailey's tongue, and the crisp, fruity wine that Noah served with it gave her a delicious buzz. Yet in spite of the food, no one seemed to be in the mood for conversation, except Belinda. She rattled on and on about her job (she was a sales agent at a trendy art gallery), her efforts to find a new condo for herself and Cade to start their married life ('Daddy' was going to cover the down payment) and, of course, the double wedding.

'So Val and I were thinking, why don't we go back to ecru for the bridesmaids' dresses, and ditch the mauve? Ecru works better for September, and mauve is so senior prom. And then we could do those miniature

Japanese mums, the way we planned in the beginning. God, I don't know where Val came up with mauve in the first place. Her sisters and cousins are all pale redheads. Redheads look like cadavers in mauve.'

Belinda threw her hands in the air in exasperation. The solitaire on her ring finger flashed like a lightsabre. Hailey drank more wine, listened to Belinda and watched the two men. Cade was forking food into his mouth, while gazing at his fiancée as if he'd rather be forking her instead. No matter what Cade's views on monogamy might be, it was obvious that Belinda held his heart in one hand and his balls in the other.

As she listened half-heartedly to Belinda's chatter, Hailey had to remind herself that this was the same woman who had driven Cade into a frenzy in a public locker-room. Apparently Cade had brought out a side of Belinda that most people couldn't imagine. Too bad Belinda couldn't be a hot, wet wildcat all the time. She'd be a lot more fun.

Wouldn't it be interesting, Hailey mused, if Belinda's naughty side could come out on a more permanent basis? Maybe her sexuality was like a suppressed gene that wouldn't express itself without a certain amount of tinkering.

Noah didn't seem to notice Belinda one way or the other. His eyes were fixed on a snarling badger's head that hung above the flagstone fireplace. Cade's grandfather had been an amateur taxidermist, and the results of his work decorated the walls and shelves of the dining-room. Hailey thought they made the room look like a road-kill hall of fame, but Cade had seemed so proud of his grandfather's hobby that she hadn't said a word.

It was hard to describe the lodge's décor. 'Backwoods kitsch' would be a polite way to put it, but 'American psychotica' could also fit the bill. The place was packed to the rafters with enough World War II memorabilia, hand-carved Native American totems and dusty knick-nacks to fill a museum or a junk shop, depending on how you looked at it. On top of the mantel stood a forest of shot glasses, souvenirs from truck stops, gift shops and gas stations in 47 states. An array of beer steins from Germany and Switzerland decorated a wall high above the table. In every room of the house, some kind of collection was displayed, from swords to salt-and-pepper shakers.

'Belinda keeps threatening to throw everything out,' Cade had told Hailey during a tour of the lodge. 'But I won't let her touch this stuff. All this junk has been here ever since I was a kid.'

Then there was the house itself, a rambling assortment of rooms that made sense at first, but gradually lost all logic. The original core of the lodge was still sound, but Cade's grandfather had added on so many bedrooms, bathrooms and closets over the years that the place had turned into a maze. One of the hallways even dead-ended in a blank wall.

'My grandfather was ... eccentric,' Cade said apologetically. 'It got worse as he got older. We tried to stop him, but he just kept building.'

The dining-room held as much clutter as the rest of the house, but the room was so vast that it seemed to swallow everything but the dead animals' heads and the massive oak table. The dining-room was the heart of the lodge, the room where the old man had held family powwows, holiday dinners and meetings with his old war buddies. The four people who sat at the table now – Cade and Belinda, Noah and Hailey – didn't even take up half of it. Fat beeswax candles shed an unsteady light on the few plates and dishes they had set out. If it hadn't been for Belinda's endless talking, the huge, shadowy room might have been spooky.

As soon as Belinda stopped to take a breath, Hailey stretched and yawned. 'Man, I'm tired,' she said. 'I'd hoped to see the cats tonight, but it's getting too dark to see much of anything. After all this food and wine, I'm more in the mood for some indoor activities. Noah, why don't you show me your new game? I'd love to have a crack at it before it's released to the general public.'

Silence fell. Hailey looked around the table. Everyone was frozen in place, like characters in an old *Twilight Zone* episode.

'Was it something I said?' she asked. 'Hello?'

Belinda sighed and rolled her eyes. 'The lodge is a game-free zone. We don't talk about characters, stories, weapons or 3-D tits around here.'

'She had to set some ground rules,' Cade added, 'or Noah and I would drive her crazy.'

'It's bad enough that the boys eat, sleep and breathe games in the city,' Belinda complained. 'When they come up here, they need some relief from all that.'

The 'boys' might say the same thing about your bridal monologue, Hailey thought, but she smiled sweetly and said she understood.

'We let Noah bring a laptop with him, but he can only use it in his bedroom, and only after dark,' said Belinda.

'The hard drive's loaded up with porn,' Noah said dryly.

'It is not! You wouldn't do that to Val,' Belinda cried.

'Val wouldn't care if Noah downloaded a little smut now and then,' said Cade, but he didn't sound convinced.

Belinda was glaring at Cade, Noah looked miserable,

and Hailey didn't want the warm glow of the wine to be blasted away by another debate. She stood up and cleared her throat loudly.

'OK, forget I mentioned you-know-what. I'm going to do the dishes.'

'I'll help,' Noah offered.

Cade and Belinda didn't mind leaving all the work to the other two. As Hailey and Noah cleared the dishes off the oak table, the pair made their escape, arms wrapped around each other's waists. Cade already had one of his hands wedged between Belinda's firm ass cheeks. That hand was going to leave one hell of a wrinkle in her linen.

'They make a good couple,' Hailey said to Noah, following him into the kitchen. 'You know, he comes off as a player, but when they're in a room together, he never takes his eyes off Belinda. I think he's crazy about her.'

'He is. No doubt about it.'

'You must feel the same way about your own fiancée. What did you say her name was?'

'Val.'

Noah piled dishes in the rust-speckled sink, then turned on the water full blast. Hailey got the distinct impression that he wanted to change the subject, but she was too curious to let it go. She hopped up to sit on the counter beside the sink and crossed her legs, carefully resting the wounded one on top.

'Well? Tell me what she's like,' Hailey said. 'No, let me guess. She's a creative type, like you, but she works in a different field. Maybe she's a journalist, or a musician, or a dancer. She's one of those delicate, pre-Raphaelite redheads. Am I getting warm?'

'You're stone-cold. Val's an attorney, and she's about

as delicate as a freight train. You're right about the redhead part, though.'

'How did you meet her?'

'Through Belinda. Val does contracts for her. Belinda set us up on a double date a couple of years ago, and the rest is history.'

'Your history, or hers?'

'Both. What do you think?' Noah said irritably.

The steam from the water had fogged up his glasses, hiding his eyes. Hailey got the feeling that she wouldn't have seen much expression there anyway.

'I think she doesn't sound like your type,' Hailey said.

'How do you know what my type is? The fact that you've had a lot of experience analysing biological specimens and studying the mating habits of animals doesn't automatically make you an expert on any one human male.' He said it gently, but firmly enough that Hailey knew she couldn't go any further.

Not for the time being.

Best to slow things down, anyway. On the journey up here, Hailey had decided that her mission for this summer was to act as an enzyme. She would be a chemical catalyst for some sort of change in Noah and Cade, but she wouldn't become part of the resulting compound, and she wouldn't be altered or diminished in the process.

But it was hard to think like an enzyme when all of her molecules were hopping around, begging for the chance to bang up against Noah's. The more she got to know him, the more he attracted her. She liked the way his shaggy black hair always looked like it needed a trim, and she liked the way he bit the corner of his lower lip when he was thinking. She especially loved the way he walked about with a distracted look on his face, which turned into an intense, full-on concentration when he spoke to Hailey.

Watching him with his brown, corded arms buried in soap-suds, she remembered the way he'd touched her when he was patching up her knee – he'd been skilful and considerate and hungry all at once. He'd be that way in bed, too, but to the hundredth power.

Noah was a simmerer. He had a lot of hardcore desires brewing in the primitive part of his brain; he just hadn't let them come to the surface. Cade, on the other hand, was at a full boil. He knew exactly what his impulses were, but he couldn't decide what he should do about them.

Hailey was going to help both men figure out what they should do. She was developing an hypothesis about Noah and Cade and their brides-to-be, based on the evidence she'd been gathering. Felines were her first love, but it could be fun to take a detour into the realm of human mating strategies, especially if she were pulling a few of the strings. If her theory proved accurate, everyone was going to get exactly what he or she needed by the time this summer was over.

Of course, Hailey wasn't going to wait that long to get *her* needs met, but Noah and Cade didn't have to know that.

'Start rocking. Now!'

Cade clapped his hands. The smack of one hard palm against the other sounded like a shotgun firing. Good thing the attic was well insulated, because once he got going, it was going to sound like a rifle-range in here.

Belinda shook her head until her blonde hair was a blur around her face. It was the only way she could refuse, with the gag filling her mouth. Cade was almost ashamed of how much he enjoyed gagging his fiancée. Lucky for him she enjoyed it, too, or he might have felt like an archaic jerk. When she wasn't talking, her eyes became ten times more expressive. At the moment, they were saying, I hate your guts, you asshole. How could you invite another woman up here without telling me?

'I know why you're pissed off, Belinda,' Cade said soothingly. 'But it doesn't matter, because you're going to come for me anyway.'

God, she looked incredible, sitting stark-naked on the painted antique rocking-horse, her hands tied behind her back. The angle of her arms made her breasts jut forwards, and the slight sway in her back caused her lower abdomen to pooch out. She was always trying to diet that pooch away, but Cade thought it was one of the sexiest things about her. That soft swelling of flesh was the polar opposite of her taut, toned behind. Belinda hated the fact that she couldn't do anything about her belly. Cade loved the fact that there was part of her that she couldn't control.

Actually, her belly wasn't the only thing Belinda couldn't control about herself; it just happened to be the most visible.

'You know you want to come for me,' Cade said. 'You're just holding back out of spite. Well, I have ways of handling spiteful little girls. If you don't start rocking by the time I count to three, I'm going to show you some of those ways. Do you understand?'

Belinda screwed her eyes shut – the ocular equivalent of sticking out her tongue.

'One,' Cade said. 'I hope you know what you're in for.'

Belinda turned her head towards the opposite wall. She really must be furious. Cade could hardly blame her. She'd cancelled a dinner appointment with one of the West Coast's hottest sculptors so that she could drive up here and help her fiancé celebrate the end of his product cycle, and the first thing she'd seen when she got out of her car was a gorgeous female stranger sitting on her porch.

'Two,' said Cade in a menacing tone. 'You're pushing it tonight, Belinda. Just keep in mind, this rebellion is going to cost you.'

Belinda continued to pretend he didn't exist.

The funny thing was, now that Belinda was here, Cade wasn't thinking about Hailey quite as much. In fact, he would have been hard-pressed to recall what Hailey looked like, if someone had asked him to describe her at this very moment. But that didn't make her any less of a threat, as far as Belinda was concerned. Belinda had put on a good show at dinner, talking up a storm so that no one would know she felt insecure. But Cade knew that her competitive juices had been flowing like crazy.

In fact, Cade could have sworn that he could hear those juices squeaking against the English saddle when Belinda shifted her weight on the horse.

He was probably the first man who had ever bought an expensive English saddle for a rocking-horse, but he couldn't resist. Cade had found the battered rocking-horse at a flea market in the city a few months ago. He'd had the giant toy repainted in antique shades of cream, blue and gold, then he'd brought the restored treasure up to the lodge, planning to give it to Belinda as a wedding gift.

The second he saw the horse, he'd had a vision of Belinda that brought his blood to a boil. In his years designing software, Cade had gotten good at predicting glitches. The last thing he wanted was for his bride to end up with a crotchful of splinters. That's how he managed to pay a small fortune for the best English saddle he could find – all for an old wooden toy. And after that awkward dinner with Hailey, he'd decided that he'd better introduce the horse tonight, instead of waiting till after the wedding.

'Three,' Cade said. He was looming over Belinda now, ready to show her how serious he was. She was headstrong, a daddy's girl whose path in life had been paved with golden asphalt. He was going to have to devote a lot of time and effort – and a lot of discipline – to maintaining his dominance in their relationship.

He wouldn't have had it any other way.

'All right, that's it. Now you're in for it, Belinda.'

Belinda sat like a stone, her blue eyes staring straight at the wall. Cade took her by the elbows and helped her stand up and dismount. She was furious, but compliant, and by the speed of her pulse and the moist heat of her skin, Cade could tell that she was looking forward to what he had in store for her.

'You could have had it the easy way,' Cade said, 'but you're so stubborn that you'd rather suffer than do what I tell you to. I've been managing my own company for a long time, and I've never had anyone on my staff who was as hard to manage as you. The good thing is, I don't have to take the kind of crap from my fiancée that I take from my spoiled-brat junior programmers.'

Cade led Belinda over to an old steamer trunk that stood in a dusty corner of the attic. As soon as he guided her in that direction, her body started to shake. She'd paid a few visits to that trunk before.

'You know what's coming, don't you?' Cade taunted

her. 'You probably wish you could go back to the rocking-horse, but it's too late now. Get down on your knees.'

He tried to help Belinda lower herself to the floor, but she managed it gracefully on her own. Before she leaned her torso across the broad, rounded lid of the trunk, she gave him an insolent look.

'Oh, so you don't need my help?' Cade laughed. 'Trust me, getting up is going to be a lot harder than getting down.'

Cade had never spanked a woman before he met Belinda. Though he liked to play rough once in a while, he had always thought that spanking another adult would be silly at best, and at worst barbaric. The first time Belinda goaded him into smacking her bottom, he couldn't believe he had done it. The second time, he started to get into the master-and-punisher role, and he gave her a few more swats than she wanted. By now, Cade and Belinda had perfected these disciplinary rituals so that they each got exactly what they needed. Now, as she waited for her punishment, Belinda's bottom was already twitching with anticipation.

'Not so fast,' Cade said. 'First you need a warm-up.'

He reached down into the crevice between her cheeks to finger her plush triangle. She wiggled impatiently; Belinda got annoyed with sensual stroking when she was in the mood for pain. But Cade could never resist the temptation of handling her pussy when she was on her knees like this. There was something so primal about seeing her in that submissive posture, with her pussy lips exposed. He ached to fuck her, but that might put a premature end to the evening's activities.

'This isn't what you want, is it?' he whispered, moving his index finger slowly in and out of her channel. 'Some women would love to get this treatment all night long, but this isn't good enough for daddy's little princess, is it?'

Belinda grunted in contempt.

'What about this, then?'

Cade's light, fast swat landed right in the middle of her bottom. He balanced his weight on one arm, his palm on the steamer trunk, while he used his free hand on Belinda's backside. At first her squeals of pleasure shook the rafters. Then Cade picked up the pace and pressure of the spanking, and before long the squeals had been replaced with pleading shrieks. He'd gotten to be an expert at translating the sounds that Belinda made when she was gagged, and right now she was begging him to ease off.

He did ease off, but only after another half-dozen sharp smacks. He couldn't get enough of the way her toned flesh quivered after every blow, like the aftershock of a small earthquake, or the way his palm painted her skin with marks that looked like primitive cave paintings.

'Had enough, princess?' he asked when he was done.

Belinda nodded. She lay across the trunk, her ribcage puffing in and out as she regained her breath. Sweat gleamed on her skin. Cade thought he saw a funny set of marks on her upper arm, a line of faint bruises that might have been fingerprints. But when she lifted herself off the trunk, he couldn't see the marks any more. If someone had manhandled her, maybe one of those strung-out artists that she worked with, Cade had no doubt that the guy was in far worse shape than Belinda.

'You're going to play nice for me now,' Cade went on. 'I spent a boatload of money on that old piece of junk. You're going to sit down on that horse, you're going to rock on it, and you're going to come on it. Understand?'

He lifted Belinda to her feet, then gave her a push in the direction of the rocking-horse. She shuffled across the floor like a contrite child, then raised a leg and lowered herself onto the horse again. She held herself stiffly, trying not to rest her whole weight on the saddle, and Cade smiled, satisfied with his work.

'Go ahead,' he said. 'Let's pick up where we left off, before I had to spank you.'

Belinda started to rock. She moved reluctantly at first, her muscles weighted with resentment. She hung her head low, letting her hair swing back and forth across her sullen profile, so that Cade could see just enough of her face to know how pissed off she was.

'That's good, baby,' Cade encouraged. 'Keep going. Rock it out of your system.'

Belinda's jaws worked as she ground her teeth against the gag, but she was finally obeying. Using nothing but hip action, she made the horse move, faster and faster, until the rockers creaked and Cade thought the wood might split. Her breath came in huffing pants through the wad of cloth, and her cheeks were fire-engine red under her flying hair. Her full breasts were a blur of flesh, bouncing like something out of Cade's overblown teenage fantasies. Each time the horse came to rest, Belinda's bound hands slapped her buttocks, and her bottom landed on the saddle with a juicy thud. The rocking-horse, staring at Cade with one glass eye, looked alarmed.

Cade was feeling worried himself. Most of the blood in his body had rushed to his groin, leaving him light-headed. If he didn't get Belinda off that horse and do something to relieve the pressure that was building in his groin, he would pass out.

'You can stop, baby,' he said. 'Belinda? Stop. That's enough. Time to give me some attention now.'

His fiancée was in a private erotic frenzy, undulating on the horse as if it were the world's largest sex toy. Her powerful thighs clamped it so hard that her muscles quivered, and rivulets of sweat trickled down the groove between her jostling breasts. Then, all of a sudden, Belinda stiffened. A muffled squeal rose from her mouth as she arched her back, thrust her hips forwards and came.

Cade wished he could have captured her orgasm on film, so that he could play it for himself in slow-motion over and over again. The first spasm almost doubled her over, then she whipped back, like a cowgirl riding a bucking bronco. At the pinnacle of her climax, her beautiful body rose straight off the horse, and she seemed to hover in midair, suspended, until her orgasm ended, and she landed back on the saddle with a thud.

Belinda stared at Cade with dazed blue eyes. He walked over to her and, with unsteady hands, removed the gag, then untied her wrists.

'Water,' she demanded hoarsely.

'Not yet.' He stood in front of her, letting her see the ridge of his erection so that she'd know exactly what he needed her to do.

Still sitting on her mount, Belinda unbuttoned his jeans and pushed them down around his knees. Before pulling down his boxers, she teased his prick through the cotton, rubbing both palms against the shaft and creating a promising friction between the cloth and his skin. When she pulled down his shorts, his rigid penis sprang away from his body. He knew that her mouth was dry from the gag, but his pre-come fluids gave her some moisture to work with.

First she lubed her tongue on the creamy liquid beading at the tip of his cock, coating the crown of it in the process. Then she lifted the shaft so that she could lick the sensitive underside of his glans. When her tongue strummed at the strand of skin dividing the base, his knees buckled and he almost collapsed. All of his nerves seemed to converge on that one tiny point. He gripped Belinda's head in his hands and pushed her forwards.

Feeling his urgency, she swallowed more of him. She was voracious, just the way he liked her. Cade wished that Belinda's country-club friends could see her now, sitting naked on a rocking-horse and sucking cock like a hooker delivering a ten-dollar blowjob. She moaned as she reached the last possible gulp; she hadn't quite swallowed him all the way, but she was close enough.

Cade closed his eyes, sank his fingers into Belinda's tresses and let himself go. He guided her head back and forth at the pace that suited him best, and she didn't resist at all, even when he pushed her further than she'd thought she could go. The last thing he heard, before he lost himself to his orgasm, was Belinda's whimper of surprise when she swallowed him down to the root.

Always the overachiever, Belinda gave Cade's balls a gentle tug and twist while he was coming, setting off fireworks at the base of his brain. They said men weren't capable of multiple orgasms, but anyone who'd experienced one of Belinda's blowjobs would have grounds to argue.

Cade wished he weren't attacked by nagging suspicions every time his fiancée completed one of those blowjobs, or rode his cock like a jockey racing for the finish line, or showed him some dazzling new sexual trick that put all of his former girlfriends to shame. He wished he could believe Belinda when she told him that he was only the third lover she'd ever had. He just didn't see how she could be so good in bed without lots of practice ... more practice than a lifetime total of three men could have given her.

Hailey would howl at his double standards, but Cade didn't care. He didn't want to marry a woman whose tally of lovers was higher than his own.

'Honey?' Belinda was looking up at him, a satisfied smile on her face. 'Are you OK?'

'Much better than OK. You're an expert.'

'I know,' she said, turning her engagement ring so that she could get a better view of the whopping diamond. 'I love my new toy.'

'Are you talking about the rocking-horse, or about that ring?'

'Both,' Belinda laughed. 'You're the most wonderful fiancé in the world. Now can I have that drink of water? Or better yet, bring me a glass of water and the rest of that bottle of wine.'

Cade pushed his suspicions to the back of his mind and went downstairs to get a drink for his bride-to-be.

5 Sexual Competition

Early the next morning, Cade and Noah met at a trailhead near the lodge for their daily run. Noah was already waiting for Cade. He wore a Shiva Systems T-shirt and shorts, trainers with mismatched socks, and a strange scowl. Cade had never seen his friend look so determined, or so grim. They usually jogged along in companionable silence, but today Noah had something on his mind.

'Cade, we need to talk about Hailey,' Noah said, as they set off through the trees. 'I have to know where the game's going, before this whole thing slips out of our hands.'

'Nothing's slipped out of our hands yet,' Cade reassured him. 'We've got Hailey right where we want her. She's on our turf now.'

But Cade had to admit that Belinda's unexpected arrival had been a setback. As soon as his fiancée had showed up, Hailey had backed off, deferring to the other woman. And the rocking-horse episode last night had broken Cade's focus on making a new conquest.

'You don't understand. This is *important* to me,' Noah panted.

Noah was in good shape; he could only be huffing and puffing because he was upset. His shoes were pounding the dirt trail so hard that his heels sprayed flecks of loam. Cade glanced at his friend curiously.

'What's wrong, buddy? Things got off course last night, but it's no big deal. We're still in control. The summer's just beginning. Belinda's going back to the city tomorrow, and we'll get to work on Hailey again.'

'We can't screw this up,' Noah repeated.

'We won't. Have a little faith.'

Noah's attitude was way out of character. He had always been the laid-back one in the friendship; in fact, he was mellow to the point of being a doormat, as far as Cade was concerned. When Val had come into his life, she had marched right over him. Up until recently, Noah had seemed to like being controlled by the curvy, dominant redhead. Could he be gearing up for a rebellion?

'Hey, Noah,' Cade asked, 'how do you feel about Hailey, compared to other women we've been with?'

Noah's puffing escalated. 'I like her better than most of them.'

Enough to dump Val for her? Cade wanted to ask, but he avoided the temptation.

Cade had selfish reasons for wanting Val out of the picture. He and Noah were so close that, for all practical purposes, the woman Noah married would be an in-law, a constant presence at holidays, parties and family vacations. Val was a bad influence on Belinda. When the two women got together, Cade felt like he was on trial for being a man. They watched him like a couple of jealous hawks, as if they were *both* engaged to him, and if he so much as crossed his eyes in the direction of a good-looking woman, they accused him of lechery. The fact that the accusations were true didn't make them any easier to live with.

'I think Hailey's terrific,' Cade said. 'In fact, if you wanted to chase her by yourself –'

'What? No way.' Noah stopped in his tracks. 'This game only has one rule, remember?'

'I remember. We can chase the woman separately,

we can touch her, and we can even make her come, but when we do the final deed, we've got to be together.'

'That's right. You set this up, Cade – you have to go through with it.'

The men stood face to face, breathing heavily. Noah's face was flushed. His lips were open, and his nostrils flared. A light coating of sweat had made his T-shirt cling to his skin, and Cade could see that his nipples were erect. Cade knew, probably better than anyone else, how sensitive his friend's nipples were. They turned into hard, sharp points whenever Noah's emotions ran high and, when he was sexually aroused, pinching them could bring him to a climax. Women loved watching Cade do that trick, if they hadn't figured it out for themselves first.

I'm such a pervert, Cade thought, not without satisfaction. My best friend's going through an emotional crisis, and all I can think about is what it takes to make him come.

'Don't worry. We'll go through with it,' Cade promised. 'Nothing can stop us.'

'Nothing,' Noah repeated, with a curt nod. He lifted his hand, and the men exchanged a high-five.

The rumble of an engine tore into the morning quiet. An ancient Ford pick-up truck appeared on the trail ahead of them, lumbering along like a dinosaur. And just like those prehistoric monsters, the truck was faster than it seemed. Noah and Cade had to leap to either side of the logging trail to avoid being run over. As the vehicle roared by, Cade caught a glimpse of a strongly cut male profile, and a streamer of long reddish hair.

Cade and Noah stared at each other in the wake of the truck.

'Shit,' Noah said. His shoulders sagged. 'I forgot about Rick.'

'I didn't. That horny bastard's not going to get in our way,' Cade blustered.

He didn't sound very convincing, even to himself.

It wasn't hard to find the cat handler at six o'clock in the morning – all you had to do was follow the aroma of freshly baked, mind-altering muffins to April May's house. April May ran her own underground bakery out of her ramshackle cottage, selling marijuana-laced muffins in the morning and brownies in the afternoon. In the early hours of the day, while Cade was out slogging along on his morning run, Rick could often be found fucking April May, a lifelong hippie who had never lost her taste for free love.

Cade found Rick's truck parked at the side of the drainage ditch that ran along April May's property. True to her nature, April May had left her front door wide open, so that anyone passing by could hear the melodic hums and howls she made during sex. Cade hadn't intended to stand around gawking, but he couldn't help getting an eyeful when he walked up to the cottage.

In today's performance, Rick had April May pinned to her divan. Feet planted on the floor, he leaned against the back of the couch, his hands braced against the frame, while his pelvis pistoned back and forth. All Cade could see, behind Rick's back, were April May's shapely legs, which were spread at an angle that she could only have achieved through a lifetime of yoga practice. Her fingers clutched at the crocheted afghan that covered the divan, as its wooden back creaked dangerously under Rick's thrusting.

That's one way to split lumber without using an

axe, Cade thought. He propped himself against the door frame, folded his arms across his chest and settled back to enjoy the show. The two of them should really charge admission to these morning events. Everyone who lived in the surrounding woods – men, women and frustrated adolescents – had seen or heard Rick and April May. As a testimony to the endurance of human interest in sex, people came back time after time to get their vicarious thrills.

April May wasn't Rick's only lover: far from it. Most of the women in the county had sported his bite marks on their bodies at least once, and most of the men wanted to kill him. He'd already survived a couple of murder attempts. Like all tomcats, Rick had at least nine lives. Still, with the number of enemies he had in the area, it was a miracle he had any lives left. Men hated Rick, and Cade was no exception.

Watching the undulating expanse of Rick's back, the smooth contractions of his buttocks and the swing of his heavy, pendulous balls, Cade was assaulted by memories of his high-school years. Cade had been a scrawny nerd who vanished into the walls whenever a jock or a stoner bass guitarist appeared; Rick was one of those alpha males, fifteen years older now but still drawing women like lemmings to the ocean.

As envious as he was, Cade had to pay silent tribute to Rick's technique. The cat handler used every muscle in his long, toned body to orchestrate his lovemaking, shifting his weight from one side to another in time to his lover's moans. Even if Rick and April May had been total strangers to Cade, he would have known right away that they had been lovers for a long time. They moved together effortlessly, finding their pleasure in well-known angles, trusted rhythms. When April May raised one of her legs in a graceful arabesque, Rick reached up to stroke the lovely limb from ankle to inner thigh, as if it were a piece of sculpture that he knew by heart, but didn't value any less for its familiarity. When she lifted her bottom off the couch, he scooped up her cheeks and pressed her firmly against his groin, so that he was lodged inside her from stem to stern.

After a few forceful thrusts, Rick paused in the dance to pull out and slide to the floor between April May's thighs. For a second Cade was treated to the sight of the glistening pink conch between her thighs, spread wide for the world to see, then Rick lowered his head so he could attend to her with his tongue. He shook his head back and forth like an animal shaking the hell out of its prey, driving April May into a frenzy. She massaged her breasts while he licked her, her slim fingers forming a web across the flesh. Cade thought she would come when she began to tug at her nipples, but Rick put a stop to that. He got off his knees, resumed his old position, and sank deep into her again.

The volume of April May's moans was reaching a crescendo. With her fingers digging into Rick's shoulders, she pumped her hips like a madwoman, until a shattering cry marked her climax. Rick's ass cheeks, working furiously to keep up, clenched one last time, and his back shuddered as he followed his lover to the finish line. When he came, he threw back his head and gave a throaty groan.

Cade felt like breaking into sarcastic applause, but Rick would probably take him seriously, and he didn't want to give the other man any additional ego reinforcement. Instead, he stepped back out of sight and waited a few minutes for the couple to get decent.

Rick wasn't one to linger in the afterglow of love. In less than thirty seconds he was dressed and heading out the door. April May followed him, beaming under her tent of fuzzy brown curls. Those curls had a lot of grey in them, but April May's body was as slim and limber as any 25-year-old's. Even if you didn't attend her morning performances, you could see most of her best features under the see-through calico dresses she wore. She never bothered with the conventional props of middle-class life, like panties or a bra.

'Hey, Cade. I haven't seen you in ages.'

April May hugged him. She was stoned, either on sex or pot, or both.

'It's been a while since I came to the lodge.'

'Still doing that thing with the computers?'

'Sure am,' Cade said.

April May scratched her head. 'One of these days I'm going to get a computer. Join the modern world. Or maybe not. I kind of like my world the way it is. Don't you?'

Rick had pushed through the door without acknowledging Cade's presence. He was already halfway to his truck, keys jingling in his hand.

'Sorry to rush, April May, but I have to catch up with Rick,' Cade said. He tried to disengage himself from April May's arms, but she was clinging to him like a Virginia creeper. Her skin was still warm from her morning exercise, and her hair smelled of sex and patchouli.

'Come back and see me sometime? We could ... you know.' She pantomimed the motions of smoking a joint.

'Definitely,' Cade said. Rick was starting up the truck. 'Now I've got to run.'

He broke away and ran for the truck. Rick saw him coming, but didn't bother to switch off the noisy engine.

'Rick! I need to talk to you,' Cade shouted over the din. 'Turn that off!'

Cade leaned against the side of Rick's truck, so that the other man couldn't ignore him. Rick finally acknowledged his existence with a narrow-eyed frown. He switched off the engine.

'What do you want?' the cat handler asked.

'Keep your hands off Hailey,' Cade said, 'or I'll ruin the sweet little set-up you've got going here.'

There was no use mincing words with Rick. He was a competitor, and he needed to be warded off. Not that Cade's words were going to have any effect on Rick. The cat handler ate other men's threats for breakfast. Still, Cade felt obliged to give him fair warning.

Rick yawned and ran a hand over his thick auburn hair, a preening gesture that made Cade want to punch him. 'Who's Hailey?'

'Kind of hard to miss her. Athletic blonde, smart-ass attitude, drives a junker Honda. Ring any bells?'

'What can I say?' Rick shrugged. 'She doesn't stand out in my memory.'

'Bullshit. You know who I'm talking about. She gave you a ride yesterday.'

'OK. Now I remember. Mostly I remember the attitude.'

'Good. Don't touch her. You've got your choice of women around here; leave this one alone.'

Rick sighed. 'Look, Cade, I've got hungry animals to feed. Is this conversation going anywhere, or did you just have an urgent need to get in my face this morning?'

'Hailey's going to be working for you for the next couple of months. I want you to keep the relationship professional. She's a serious student, and she wants to do research on the cats. Don't distract her.'

Rick grinned, shook his head and fired up his engine again. 'I'd like to help you out, Cade, but you're under a serious misconception.'

'What's that?'

'You think I'm like you. You think I spend all my time chasing women. Did it ever occur to you that I'm hardly ever the one who does the chasing?'

Rick lifted his foot off the brake, and the truck heaved out of the mud. For the second time that morning, Cade had to jump out of its way.

'I'll keep things professional with Hailey,' Rick said, 'but if she gets unprofessional with me, all bets are off. That's the best I can do.'

The truck rumbled away, leaving Cade standing in the middle of the road. He could feel his shoulders sagging, the way Noah's had earlier. Back in the city, Cade was the top male, but Rick was the king of the jungle around here. Maybe Hailey would be smart enough to avoid becoming a notch on the king's bedpost.

But if history repeated itself, she wouldn't.

Hailey was up early, but not as early as Belinda. As Hailey was stepping out of the shower in the guest bathroom, she could hear the other woman's voice in the room next door. From the way the conversation was going, Hailey assumed that Belinda was talking to her fiancé.

'I don't mind a few bruises now and then,' Belinda was saying in a reproachful tone, 'but you got too rough last time. I'm not going to spend the summer wearing long-sleeved blouses just because you can't keep your sadistic impulses under control.'

Hailey, who'd been rubbing her hair dry with a towel, froze. Belinda liked rough sex play – now *that* was a lot more interesting than new condominiums and bridesmaids' dresses. Hailey waited for Cade's reply.

It never came.

'Listen,' Belinda went on, her voice rising, 'I've got fingerprints all over the back of my arm and inside my thigh. If we're going to keep seeing each other, you're going to have to tone it down. Why don't you channel your aggression into your work? Then maybe I could sell a few of your paintings once in a while.'

Hailey had to clamp her hand over her mouth to hold back a shriek of surprise. Belinda wasn't talking to her husband-to-be; she was talking to one of her artist clients, probably some foul-mouthed bohemian who'd never set foot in a country club.

'I've got to go. Think about what I said. I don't want to have to cut you off till after the honeymoon,' Belinda warned.

Wrapped in a skimpy towel, Hailey opened the bathroom door. Belinda was standing in the hallway, lowering her travel bag to the floor with one hand while she folded up her cellphone with the other. She looked up and caught Hailey's eye. For a few tense moments, the two women stared at each other across the corridor. Guilt, embarrassment and fear flashed across Belinda's patrician face, but she quickly regained her composure.

'My clients are such a pain in the ass,' Belinda said. She tossed her power bob and stuffed her cellphone into her purse. 'They won't leave me alone for a second.'

'I see what you mean,' Hailey said. 'About the pain part, anyway. Some men can't help leaving marks; it's part of their need to dominate.'

She gave Belinda a conspiratorial wink, then darted

into her bedroom. But before she could close the door, Belinda shoved her way in, then slammed the door and locked it. Hailey didn't even have time to exclaim before Belinda had one of her arms locked behind her back and a leg wrapped around her ankle. In her black Donna Karan ensemble, Belinda looked like a blonde urban ninja.

'How much did you hear?' Belinda demanded.

'I heard enough,' Hailey said.

Belinda's face was a flaming mask of rage. She shoved Hailey back onto the bed, then climbed on top of her and pinned her down by the wrists. Hailey's own adrenaline was rushing at full force. She could have lunged up at her attacker and bitten her on the neck, but since Belinda was bigger and stronger, flight seemed like a better response than fight. Hailey kicked at the air with her legs and twisted her upper body with all her strength, but Belinda held her down.

Finally Hailey decided that her best option was to play dead. She went limp all over, and Belinda's grip relaxed. By now, Hailey's towel was a distant memory. She was totally naked, with a big blonde ninja holding her down. Someone should really be filming this, Hailey thought. They could make a fortune selling the footage on the internet.

The energy in the room was so intense the air crackled. Belinda's cheeks glowed pink from the exertion of their struggle. She smelled of sweat and honeysuckle body spray. Hailey suddenly knew exactly what it would be like to feel Belinda's feminine weight lowering down on her, to feel the contrast of the cool fringe of the blonde's hair with the heat of her skin. But it was hard to think of Belinda as a potential lover when her eyes were narrowed to murderous slits.

'Don't think for a second,' Belinda hissed, 'that I

won't murder you if Cade finds out about this.' She wrapped her fingers around Hailey's throat, pressed her thumbs against windpipe and squeezed.

'I believe you,' Hailey said.

'Do you?' Belinda squeezed harder.

'Won't tell. Promise!' Hailey squeaked.

Belinda released her death grip on Hailey's throat, but she didn't let her captive go. She lowered her hips and thighs onto Hailey's body and arched over her, supporting her weight on her arms. She bore down onto Hailey's mound with her pubic bone, until the pressure was so intense that Hailey didn't know whether to moan in pleasure or screech in pain. When Belinda began to rotate her hips, Hailey chose the moaning option.

'I could kill you right now,' Belinda said. 'Do you realise that? Or I could make you come. I could do anything I wanted.'

Hailey flashed back to a dark night in Costa Rica. She'd been out doing research in the jungle, using an infra-red nightscope, when she had come face to face with a jaguar on the prowl. She'd caught the reflective sheen of the cat's eyes, then she'd felt every hair on her body rise as the animal lowered itself into a crouch. But Hailey's partner had tripped over some equipment at that exact moment, falling into the undergrowth and making a racket that sent the jaguar running.

Hailey was lucky she'd come out of that confrontation in one piece. Would she be as lucky this time? A territorial upper-class professional woman could be more deadly than a jungle cat. Belinda's blue irises were almost edged out by her enormous pupils, and her nostrils were flared. The predatory curiosity in her eyes was making Hailey very nervous, and more than a little aroused. Belinda placed an exploratory hand on

Hailey's breast, then tweaked Hailey's nipple with her fingernails, crooning to herself when the areola stiffened into a rosy pink cap. The fact that those nails had an expensive French manicure didn't make them look any less like claws.

Belinda shifted her weight, moving aside to get better access to Hailey's nakedness. Hailey could have used the opportunity to escape, but she felt frozen in place like a small animal, paralysed by excitement rather than fear. Belinda's hands left Hailey's breasts and her nails raked a path down Hailey's taut abdomen, seeking signs of moisture in the furry notch between her thighs. Her eyes lit up in triumph when she discovered that Hailey was wet.

'So you *do* like women,' Belinda mused. 'I wondered about that, when I first met you. You looked like such a tomboy. Cade's very attracted to athletic girls. I bet he wishes he could be right where I am now, feeling how turned on you are.'

Belinda moved down the bed, her mouth following the trail that her claws had left on Hailey's belly. Her full lips left moist impressions of themselves on Hailey's skin.

'I love taking the women Cade wants,' the blonde murmured. 'You smell like fresh apples. You're making me hungry.'

Thank god for Green Apple Bodywash, Hailey thought, or else Belinda might be murdering her now instead of having her for breakfast. Hailey was melting under Belinda's mouth, her thighs parting, her hips moving. As Belinda kissed Hailey's inner thighs, her bobbed hair, still slightly damp from the morning's shampoo, slid across Hailey's skin like silk curtains.

Belinda slid off the bed and knelt between Hailey's

legs. She opened Hailey's pussy with her fingers, never letting Hailey forget how sharp the nails were, and bent down to devour her. She didn't just lick; she pulled Hailey's delicate inner lips into her mouth and sucked for all she was worth, as if Hailey's sex were a ripe orange, and she was savouring every last drop of juice. The measured sucking made Hailey feel like she was made of cotton, light and fluffy, ready to float off the bed at the slightest puff of wind.

That puff of wind was Belinda, pulling back to blow on Hailey's open pouch. The soft friction of the air on Hailey's overstimulated flesh made her shiver violently. She couldn't take that exquisitely delicate feeling, not when she was so close to coming. Hailey forgot that she was supposed to be the passive one. She reached down and took hold of Belinda's head, pressing her face back down.

'Lick me,' she begged. 'I have to come.'

Belinda's tongue dove straight for Hailey's clit. Hailey used swatches of Belinda's silky hair to guide that tongue in circles, in figure-8s, and finally in a direct, up-and-down motion that brought Her to a shattering peak.

When she came to her senses, Hailey realised that Belinda was climaxing too. The blonde had been fingering herself as she made love to Hailey, and Hailey's orgasm pushed her to the brink. After Belinda's moans had died into murmurs of satisfaction, she did something that none of Hailey's lovers had ever done before. With her rough, slightly dry tongue, she licked Hailey's pussy clean, taking her time, like a cat washing one of its kittens. The gentle, almost maternal gesture filled Hailey with contentment. For a competitive, self-centred bitch, Belinda made a wonderful lover.

'You've forgotten everything you heard me say on the phone, haven't you?' Belinda asked when she'd finished, looking up at Hailey from the foot of the bed.

Hailey nodded.

'Good.'

Belinda rose to her feet. She caught a glimpse of her reflection in a spotted antique mirror and stopped to check her hair and make-up. Then she sank into a chair and tried to catch her breath. Hailey lay flat on her back and did the same thing.

'You're great in bed, but you fight dirty,' Hailey said, palpating her sore neck. It didn't feel like Belinda had dislocated any vertebrae.

'Sorry about that,' Belinda said. 'I didn't mean to hurt you. I can't lose Cade; we've got our whole lives planned together. But I can't seem to give up the others, either.'

'Others? You mean there's more than one?'

'Of course.' Belinda lifted her chin aggressively. 'It's better that way, isn't it? If I had one other lover, he'd be more of a threat. Cade's the only man in my life that I'd ever want as a husband. But I have to have the rest of them, too. They all meet different needs.'

'I know what you mean, Belinda,' Hailey said. 'You don't have to explain yourself to me.'

Suddenly Belinda dropped her defences and became a nervous little girl. In a softer voice, she added, 'I want to build a solid life with Cade, but I don't want to limit myself sexually. Does that make any sense at all?'

'Believe it or not, it does make sense to me,' Hailey said. 'In fact, it seems perfectly natural. More natural than limiting yourself to one partner for the rest of your life.'

'Does it? Sometimes I think I'm crazy. They used to lock up women like me, or medicate us until our brains turned to mush, so we couldn't think about sex any more.'

Hailey struggled into a sitting position, found the damp towel on the floor and pulled it over her body.

'How many lovers do you have? Besides Cade, I mean.'

'Three, right now. Paul's the one I was talking to on the phone. He showers about once a month, and he doesn't know the first thing about making love, but he's got this brutal energy that I crave. Then there's Todd; he's nineteen years old, serves drinks at my club and plays lead guitar in an up-and-coming rock band. He's irresistible, and I love playing teacher once in a while. And now and then, when I'm in the mood, I see Sylvie. I used to take a yoga class from her, until it became pretty clear that she wanted to get more intimate. Now all our lessons are strictly one-on-one.'

'Wow,' Hailey said. 'Are you sure there's no one else hiding under a bed or in a closet somewhere?'

'Well,' Belinda leaned forwards and gave Hailey a confidential smile. 'When I come up to the lodge, I try to stop by the cat park once or twice, just to get a taste of Rick.'

'Somehow that doesn't surprise me,' Hailey said. She thought for a moment, then continued cautiously, 'Have you ever considered telling Cade about this?'

Belinda's eyes widened. 'God, no. Are you kidding? Cade wants his bride to be a near-virgin. I told him I'd had three lovers. I just didn't tell him that I'd had them all within the past week.'

'That's four lovers, counting me,' Hailey reminded her.

The front door slammed. The two women stiffened. Cade and Noah's voices drifted up the stairs, then died away as the men walked towards the kitchen.

Belinda got up and gave herself another once-over in the mirror. When she turned back to Hailey, her attitude had cooled again. She was the successful modern bride-to-be, brisk, professional and efficient.

'I meant everything I said this morning, Hailey,' she said. 'I'm serious about protecting what I love.'

Belinda had gotten Hailey's name right this time, a sure sign that she meant business.

'You know, Belinda, you really don't have anything to feel bad about,' Hailey said, as the other woman unlocked the door.

Belinda glanced over her shoulder. 'What do you mean?'

'The female leopard can mate up to a hundred times a day. What modern career woman can compete with that?' Hailey asked.

Belinda laughed – not a country-club laugh, but a rich, husky, dirty laugh. The spun-gold princess definitely wasn't as much of a tight-ass as Hailey had thought.

Belinda had to rush back to the city that morning for a 'meeting' with her hot new creative discovery, Paul. Hailey watched from the kitchen window as Cade and Belinda stood in the driveway. From the way Cade was saying goodbye to Belinda, it looked like she was heading off to war.

If he only knew, Hailey thought, remembering Belinda's phone conversation with the man she now thought of as the bruiser. One of these days, Belinda's secret sex life was going to smash head-on into Cade's. But for now, they were the picture of romantic devotion. Cade leaned Belinda against the driver's door of her Lexus and kissed her with a lavish passion that made Hailey light-headed. She was so caught up in watching the motions of Cade's lips and tongue that she didn't hear Noah come up behind her.

'I wonder if he'll still be kissing her that way ten years from now,' Noah said.

Hailey jumped. 'Don't scare me like that, or I'll have to tie a bell around your neck.'

'Sorry. I didn't mean to sneak up on you.'

'That's OK,' Hailey said. 'Voyeurs are a sneaky breed. I should know.'

Hailey turned away from the window, expecting to find Noah staring at the couple outside. Instead, he was watching her with a hungry, focused expression.

'I don't want to be a voyeur,' Noah said. 'The last thing I want to do is spend my life watching Cade kiss Belinda.'

'I doubt he'll go on kissing her for that long. She's got a lunch appointment in the city,' Hailey joked.

'That's not what I meant,' Noah said.

She wasn't sure how she felt about the way Noah was acting. He was standing so close to her that she could feel the raised temperature of his skin, and it made her own tingle. The softcore porn scene in the driveway didn't help, either; Cade had eased his hand under Belinda's tight black top and was kneading her breast as he kissed her. His fingers moved lovingly over her flesh, sculpting the mound, and Belinda's long waist undulated in response, like an instrument responding to an expert musician.

Noah set his elbows on the window-sill next to Hailey's, so that his upper arm brushed hers. Fields of fine hairs rose all along Hailey's body, like hundreds of antennae. Her belly tightened into a knot, with a hot stone of longing inside. She was amazed at the way she was reacting to the simple contact; Noah might as well have stroked her from throat to crotch with the palm of his hand.

We should just fuck and get this tension out of the way, Hailey said to herself. But she knew Noah wouldn't be that crude, and he wouldn't let her go that easily. They'd have sex once or twice, but Noah wouldn't be content to move on. He'd want to snarl things up with angst and emotion; plans would be broken, lives would veer off course.

I'm just a catalyst in this house, Hailey reminded herself. I can make changes happen, but I can't be changed in the process.

'I need caffeine,' Hailey said, in a too-bright voice. 'Come and show me how to work that fancy espresso machine of yours. You'd have to be an astronaut to operate that thing.'

She gave Noah a playful slap on the shoulder. He grabbed her wrist and, before she knew it, his mouth was on hers. No shy peck, either, but a hard, raw kiss that pulled all kinds of longing to the surface. He kissed her until her chin burned from his beard stubble, and her lungs ached as if she'd been swimming underwater. When he finally let her come up for air, she had to lean against him to keep from falling down. Her breasts chafed against his chest as she half-slid down his body. He caught her by the elbows and dragged her upright. They stumbled and almost lost their balance.

'Let's go upstairs,' Hailey begged.

The hardness that nudged her lower belly seconded the motion but, before Noah could answer, the sound of Cade's vigorous footsteps broke the spell.

'Wow, what a morning!' he boomed. 'Clear as a bell out there. Hailey, you've got to come and see the park when there's no fog. You never know when we'll get another day like this.'

Noah backed away from Hailey. He turned to the counter and began to fuss with the space-age coffee maker, conveniently hiding his erection. Hailey's blood was still humming, her cheeks burned and her swollen lips probably looked like they'd been through a food processor. Cade's eyes registered all this, and he smiled. Hailey had never tried to kill another human being, but that knowing smile brought her pretty damn close.

'Well? Are you here to work this summer, or not?' he asked. 'Half the morning's gone already.'

'I haven't had my coffee yet,' Hailey said through clenched teeth. 'I'm not human till there's caffeine in my bloodstream.'

'The cats might like you better that way,' Cade said. 'Come on.'

'Noah? Are you coming with us?' Hailey asked.

Noah glanced over his shoulder, but he wouldn't meet her eyes.

'Not today. I'll hang out here,' he mumbled.

So much for sloppy pre-adolescent kisses by the kitchen sink, Hailey thought. At times like this she sympathised with people like her room-mate Jack, who thought that human sexuality was woefully overrated. Equally furious with Cade and Noah, she decided that Cade would be the best bet. At least he knew what he wanted.

'All right. Let's go see some cats,' Hailey said. She went to get her backpack, then followed Cade out of the lodge without giving Noah a second look.

Hailey's temper cooled down on the drive to the park. Cade was right, the morning was glorious. The evergreens were seamed with sunlight, and skeins of mist floated across the road. Through the tree trunks and underbrush, Hailey saw patches of blue water as Cade's car drove alongside the lake where Cade's grandfather used to fish.

Cade let Hailey enjoy the scenery in silence. He drove without saying a word until they pulled up at the gate to the park. A sign on the freshly painted green gate announced that they were about to enter the Sasquanatee Zoological Park, and warned them not to feed, pet, taunt, tease or look cross-eyed at the animals.

'Not very welcoming,' Hailey remarked. 'I hope I don't accidentally sneeze or anything.'

'Rick's the author of that masterpiece,' Cade said. 'We tried to get him to tone it down, but he insisted. He practically makes everyone sign a waiver before they go in.'

'What's his problem?'

'Professional paranoia. It's hard to believe, but Rick used to be an attorney.' Cade laughed, enjoying a private joke. 'A divorce attorney.'

'What's so funny?'

'You'll find out,' Cade said. 'Probably a lot sooner than you think.'

He jumped out of the car to open the gate, then got back in and drove them through, taking them down an unpaved trail that opened onto a gravel-covered visitors' lot. Cade stopped for a while and let Hailey take in the sweeping view of the park.

It was love at first sight when Hailey saw the little zoo. If she could have designed a place to live, work and study, this would be it: a cosy arrangement of modest buildings, cages and corrals arranged in a clearing that rolled gently out to the woods. Behind the open space rose the treetops, and then the magnificent mountains. Abundant spring rains had left everything brilliantly green.

'This is it,' Cade said. 'Noah's paradise. When we first got involved with the park, it was exclusively wildlife rehabilitation: a few bobcats, a bear cub and a lynx. Now it's more of a commercial operation, with a zoo and a gift shop, but we're still heavily involved in rehabilitation and conservation. We get funding from a lot of different local and federal sources, but he's the heart and soul of the place. What do you think?'

'I love it. I absolutely love it.'

Admiring the scene in front of her, Hailey almost forgave Noah for his behaviour earlier. There were much worse crimes than being confused about sex. Humans made it so complicated and loaded with meaning that it was a miracle the species had made it this far.

For the next two hours Cade gave Hailey a thorough tour of the park, introducing her to each of the animals. Though most of the park's residents were felines – including a male and female white tiger, a Bengal tiger, an African serval, a bobcat, an American mountain lion and a rare clouded leopard that made Hailey shriek with joy – there was also a small reptile house, an aviary filled with birds and an assortment of domestic dogs patrolling the property.

By the time Cade had finished recounting each animal's history, the zoo had opened for business. A bus packed with children from a nearby summer camp had unloaded its cargo into the park, and kids were running everywhere, happily ignoring the mandates of Rick's sign. Hailey wanted to spend more time with the clouded leopard, so Cade took her back to see the cat. The endangered leopard's habitat was located some way from the rest of the animals. Cade and Hailey sat down on a bench across from the leopard's cage. Hailey couldn't take her eyes off the cat. Clouded leopards were thought to be descendants of the father of all cats, the sabre-tooth tiger.

The leopard reminded Hailey of why she had started studying cats in the first place. As an evolutionist, she was preoccupied with the way animals changed, yet she was fascinated by the characteristics that cats had retained over time: the predators' jaws, the flattened skull, the powerful hind limbs, the brutally efficient claws. The design worked so beautifully that it had allowed the animals to hunt, kill and devour meat for thousands of years. But the same traits that made them so efficient at killing put them at a disadvantage when it came to mating. When the male clouded leopard mounted a female, he held her by the scruff of the neck with his long fangs, sometimes killing her in the process.

Sex could be just as dangerous for the human female, Hailey thought, glancing at Cade, if you let the wrong male get hold of you.

The leopard watched Hailey impassively from behind a curtain of leaves, his elegant body stretched along a rock. After the racket in the central part of the park, Hailey was grateful for the silence.

'Popular place,' she commented. 'Do you get this much traffic all year round?'

'No. Summer's our peak season; we're pretty quiet the rest of the year, and we're closed for part of the winter. I think Noah prefers it that way. He'll come out here and spend hours sketching the cats. He gets a lot of ideas for his characters by watching the animals. No one knows these cats like Noah.'

'I was surprised he didn't want to come along this

morning,' Hailey said. 'I thought he'd want to show off the animals himself.'

She still had a bitter taste in her mouth from the scene in the kitchen. Sexual frustration wasn't her favourite breakfast dish.

'Noah's unpredictable,' Cade said. 'He's an artist; he has his moods.'

'Well, he was in a strange one this morning.' Hailey shook her head. 'Sometimes I can't figure him out. He's engaged to Val, but he keeps sending me signals that he wants me, too. I could understand if he were a man like you, but Noah's different.'

'Thanks,' Cade said. 'You make me sound like a real prince.'

'You know what I mean. Noah's not an explorer. I can't imagine him having a casual encounter and chalking it up to a need for sexual diversity. From the first time I met him, I knew he was a pair-bonder.'

'You might be surprised. Next time he sends you one of those signals, why don't you pick it up and see what happens?'

'I did, this morning,' Hailey admitted. 'Against my better judgment. I let him kiss me in the kitchen.'

'In the kitchen? You tramp!' Cade said, slapping his forehead in mock surprise. 'I'm going to tell all the girls in my homeroom class!'

'Shut up. It wasn't just a kiss. He wanted to fuck me. We were about to go upstairs when you walked in, bellowing about the weather.'

'Sorry about that,' Cade said, not sounding sorry at all. 'He left you feeling raw and randy, didn't he?'

'You could say that. Not that it's any concern of yours.'

'But it *is* a concern of mine.' Cade had edged closer

to her on the bench, close enough for her to see the green and gold flecks in his blue eyes. 'You're my guest for the summer. I want you to be satisfied.'

'Don't worry about me. I can take care of myself.'

'Can you? Prove it.'

'What?'

'Prove it to me. There's nothing I like to watch more than an independent woman taking care of herself.'

'No way,' Hailey laughed. 'I'm not Belinda. I don't play with myself in public.'

'You're right,' Cade sighed. 'Belinda's wild, adventurous, daring. You're nothing like her.'

'Hah!' Hailey scoffed. 'I'm as adventurous as any other woman; I just don't want to get the leopard all riled up. He doesn't need to see any adult performances this morning.'

'Fair enough, adventure girl. I've got the perfect place for you to give a private performance – no feline audience whatsoever. What do you think? Are you up for it?'

Cade stood up and held out his hand. He looked down at Hailey, a challenge in his boyish grin. She looked around. In the distance she could see a group of kids racing down the hill towards the clouded leopard's cage. A couple of camp counsellors straggled after them, doing their best to keep up.

'Come on. We might as well get out of here, before we get stormed by the troops,' Cade said. 'Or would you rather go back to the lodge and play with Noah in the kitchen?'

'Fuck you, Cade.' Hailey jumped to her feet. 'Let's go.'

Cade led her through a grove of pines to a small, enclosed clearing. The clearing was surrounded by rows of green bleachers, which faced a raised wooden stage.

There was a microphone standing in the centre of the platform, along with an assortment of props.

'There's an exotic-bird show scheduled in half an hour,' Cade said, with a glance at his watch. 'Until then, we have the place to ourselves.'

He sat down on one of the front-row bleachers and looked at Hailey expectantly.

'Wait a second. Are you saying that this place is going to be overrun with kids in thirty minutes?'

'Kids, parrots, cockatiels and an ostrich,' Cade said. 'But we've got plenty of time.'

'Says you! When it comes to pleasuring myself, I don't like to rush things.'

'I don't think you have a choice. The longer we sit here chatting, the more risk you run of getting caught. I'd get to it, if I were you. Belinda would be doing a striptease by now.'

Cade's words were playful, but his voice had changed. He sounded like a CEO again, giving orders to a dawdling secretary. Who did he think he was, talking to her like one of his underlings? That was the problem with these corporate overlords: it wasn't enough for them to dominate their employees, or their girlfriends. They had to be the boss of the whole world.

But his attitude excited Hailey all the same. Cade knew how to take charge, and he wasn't afraid to do it. His arrogance had kickstarted her libido.

'Fine. You want a show – you've got it,' Hailey said.

She stomped onto the platform. At first she didn't know where to start, or what to do. Visions of lithe strippers gyrating in bamboo cages in the Amazon Room filled her head. But this backwoods zoo was a far cry from the hip downtown nightclub. Instead of being engulfed by an overheated, oversexed crowd, she was standing in front of one oversexed man, and instead of being assaulted by the beat of dance music, all she could hear was the twittering of wild native birds and the occasional screech from a cockatoo or a parrot in the aviary. Still, sexual instincts were the same, wherever you went.

Hailey closed her eyes and imagined that the beat of hot, slow jazz was making the floorboards vibrate and giving her a rhythm to work with. Swaying from side to side, she unbuttoned her shorts and pulled them halfway down her hips.

She opened her eyes and found Cade watching her. His cocky stare provoked her, made her bold. She slid her hand under the waistband of her panties and found the warm, furred groove, but fondling her sex wasn't comforting and familiar, the way it was when she was alone. She almost felt like she was toying with another woman's flesh as she dug through the folds to find a well of wetness, then lubed her slit with her own cream. Her clitoris rose into a mini-erection under her fingertips, and she experimented with different ways of stroking and tweaking it, pretending that she was touching herself for the first time.

'Use the tree,' Cade ordered. 'Rub yourself against it. Drop the shorts first.'

Hailey shoved down her shorts and panties. They fell to the floor, and she kicked them aside, then gave Cade a glare that told him she was doing this for her own entertainment, not his.

On one side of the stage stood a bare-branched potted tree, a prop for the bird show. Hailey stood beside it, facing Cade, and bent over with her hands on her knees. She arched her back and rubbed her bottom against the tree, letting the trunk nudge her cheeks apart until the wood was wedged snugly against her pussy lips. Rotating her hips, she let herself enjoy the texture of the polished wood against the most sensitive skin on her body. She found a knot in the tree that protruded enough to penetrate her, and leaned back against it with all her weight. By bucking her hips up and down, she was able to stimulate her greasy hole and her clit at the same time.

I'm going to have to take this tree home with me, Hailey thought. I think I'm in love.

She was so lost in the sensations of the wood and the tempo of her grinding that she didn't know Cade had stepped up onto the stage until she opened her eyes and saw him standing in front of her. He'd made a cat's cradle out of her white thong panties, winding them around his fingers.

'Stand up straight,' he said. 'Put your back against the tree. Hands behind the trunk, wrists together.'

'What are you saying? I thought this was *my* show.'

'You thought wrong. Do what I tell you.'

Hailey obeyed. She didn't want to be Cade's sex toy, but she was eager to see where he'd take this. As soon as she'd assumed the position he wanted, he slipped behind her and wrapped her panties around her wrists.

'I could leave you here all day,' he mused. 'Wouldn't that be a riot?'

'No! It wouldn't. You said you wanted a quick performance – a solo performance, by the way. I was doing just fine.'

Hailey flopped her bound wrists against the trunk. She'd never have thought that a pair of cotton panties could serve as such an effective restraint. Cade must have been a great Boy Scout.

'I've never been very good at watching from the sidelines,' Cade said. 'I'm too impatient, and too greedy.'

He pushed Hailey's tank top up to her collar-bone, then tugged down the cups of her bra. She was embarrassed at how hard her nipples were. They got even harder when Cade began to tweak them between his thumbs and index fingers. He pushed her breasts together and ran his tongue along the valley between them, then sucked on the dark tips, one after the other. Hailey moaned. Her pussy, after receiving so much attention, throbbed painfully now that it was being neglected.

Hailey widened her stance, thrust her hips out as far as she could and tilted her pelvis in an invitation that only a blind man could fail to read.

'Horny, aren't you?' Cade said, with a self-satisfied smile. He checked his watch. 'Oops, looks like you're going to have to wind up your act. There's only ten minutes till they start setting up the bird show.'

'Hey, no fair!' Hailey wailed.

She writhed and twisted, scraping her arms against the tree, but she couldn't work the panties off her wrists. Cade was right – she was horny as hell, but she was also starting to panic. Here she was, tied up and naked below the waist, with her shorts lying seven feet away on the platform. People could start wandering over there at any minute. There was always at least one obsessive punctuality freak in the crowd, someone who had to get his seat early, even if it was only to watch a bunch of trained parrots.

'Is there anything sexier than a captive woman?' Cade asked himself softly. He wasn't touching Hailey's pussy yet, but she knew he was considering it. He was gazing at the swathe of dusky blonde fur between her legs like a dieter staring longingly at a 600-calorie dessert.

What was wrong with Cade and Noah? Hailey wondered. They both seemed like healthy, red-blooded males, but when it came to her, they might as well have taken a vow of celibacy. Though they couldn't stop coming on to Hailey – or in Cade's case, even making her come – neither one of them seemed willing to take things to their natural conclusion.

At this point, Hailey would take what she could get.

'You can't leave me here like this,' Hailey said. 'You wanted to see me come; if you won't let me go, you're going to have to do it yourself.'

'Bossy little slut,' Cade chuckled.

Hailey gave him a defiant glare. 'You call this bossy? Wait till you're married.'

'Believe me, I know what I'm in for with Belinda.'

Hailey doubted that very much, but she didn't say a word. Cade would find out eventually what a sex fiend his oh-so-perfect fiancée was, probably after the wedding band was safely on her finger.

'I guess I should have mercy on you,' Cade relented. 'Poor thing, you look like you're about to burst.'

He slid two fingers into Hailey's pussy, then, when he felt how overripe she was, he inserted a third. She gasped. He looked her straight in the eye while he fingered her, first at a sensual pace, then faster as her breathing became ragged. She moved her hips to meet his thrusts, pushing her mound against the heel of his hand so that her clit got extra stimulation. Meanwhile, his hard knuckles gave her inner flesh a brutal massage.

Cade's breathing was uneven too. He gritted his teeth and drove his fingers into her as if he were trying to pay her back for the fact that he couldn't fuck her.

'Harder,' she hissed. 'You can do better than that.'

'Not without splitting you in half.'

Cade's forehead glistened with sweat. He closed his eyes, and his face muscles grew tense, like a man in pain. Watching him in that kind of agony took Hailey to the edge, and when he drove his hand into her one more time, she went all the way over.

Hailey came hard. Too hard – she almost fell to her knees from the force of the waves, and when she became aware of her surroundings again, she realised that her throat hurt from screaming. But Cade wasn't done with her yet. Instead of letting her orgasm die away, he revved her up a second time with a few more gentle thrusts, then tickled her clit with feather-light strokes until she climaxed again.

Hailey collapsed against the tree, threw her head back and looked at the sky. Delicate nimbus clouds floated in a blue sea. Hailey felt as light and free as the clouds. God, it felt good to come like that: with a man instead of a vibrator. She'd spent way too much time watching sex lately, and too little time having it.

All that was going to change, starting today.

'We've got to go,' Cade said. Unlike Hailey, he didn't seem happy at all. When he untied her and handed her the panties, Hailey grabbed the belt buckle on his shorts.

'Not yet. It's your turn,' she said.

'I can't,' he said, sounding like he might cry with disappointment.

'Oh, I think you can. It's easy.' Hailey unbuttoned the fly of his shorts and furrowed through the folds of his boxers to grab his cock. The hot, moist rod wasn't hard to find; the head was so slick with pre-come that Hailey almost lost her grip on his oiled-up member. She opened Cade's fly, and set his hard-on free.

'Today's your lucky day,' she said in a sexy whisper. 'In high school they used to call me Handjob Hailey.'

Hailey pulled her hand out of Cade's shorts just long enough to lick her palm, then set to work. A gravelly moan came from Cade's throat as she began to pump his erection. As she stroked the shaft, she stopped every now and then to bury her thumb in the notch where his cock met his balls. She really did feel like she was back in high school, rushing to bring her latest boyfriend to a quick and dirty orgasm behind the gymnasium before the bell rang for fourth period.

Hailey must have conveyed that old excitement to Cade, because he was giving her the same look that the boys used to give her back then: a look of stunned lust mixed with admiration, disbelief and a touch of fear. She felt a flow of urgency run through his body, then he trembled. She covered the tip of his cock just in time with her balled-up panties, and he came with sharp jerks into the cotton.

There wasn't much time to savour the afterglow. Cade leaned against Hailey, his face buried in her shoulder, but as he was catching his breath they heard the sound of a bird squawking in the grove. Cade hastily buttoned his fly, and Hailey whipped her shorts on in record time.

'Hey, Cade. Come to see the show?'

A tall, auburn-haired man stood in the clearing. A brilliant scarlet macaw was perched on his shoulder. Hailey recognised him as the sexy but serious nature lover from the woods. She could feel her face turning the same colour as the bird. How long had Rick been standing in the pines?

'I was just showing Hailey the performance area,' Cade said. 'We'll be on our way.'

Hailey sensed a competitive aggression running between the two men, as obvious as though they'd been joined by a tightrope.

'Seems like a shame to show her an empty stage, then run away when the show's about to start.'

'We've got things to do. Drop it,' Cade said.

Rick shrugged. 'Suit yourself.'

He smiled at Hailey. The sarcastic twist of his upper lip told her three things. One, he thought Cade was a fool. Two, he thought Hailey had gotten the raw end of the deal by spending the morning with him.

Three, he had seen everything that had just happened between Hailey and Cade, and he didn't think it would be too hard to get a piece of her for himself.

6 Feeding Time

Belinda was supposed to meet Paul for lunch but, as she guided BELSBABY through the warehouse district where he had his loft, she changed her mind. Far from curbing her appetite, the encounter with Hailey had left her hungrier than ever, but she wasn't in the mood for Paul's rough-edged, animal energy. Today she wanted to be the one in charge.

Belinda smiled to herself as she thought about the encounter back at the lodge. Hailey's lithe, sinuous form had felt as compliant as a silk ribbon under Belinda's masterful hands. Belinda could tell that Hailey was anything but passive by nature, but the new arrival had known when to submit to a stronger, more influential woman.

The car's rear-view mirror showed a satisfying reflection of Belinda's face. Under her smoked sunglasses, with her hair billowing back from her forehead and her lips pursed in pleasure, she looked expensive, high-maintenance and dangerous in the wrong hands, a lot like the high-powered car she was driving.

Driving aroused Belinda almost as much as sexual contact. She loved speeding down the highway in her brand new baby, feeling the engine's power at her fingertips, effortlessly gliding in and out of traffic to put distance between herself and the economy clunkers that most people drove. Belinda was always ahead of the pack, and she worked hard to stay that way.

She squeezed her inner thighs together to the beat

of the sultry rock music that came from her CD player. When that stimulation wasn't enough, she focused on her pussy muscles, making them pulse in and out like a hot pink fist. Sylvie, her yoga instructor, had taught her how to contract her inner core like a pro. A visit to Sylvie's studio might be just what Belinda needed right now.

Or maybe a piece of *that* was what she needed. Belinda stepped on the brakes, bringing her Lexus to an abrupt halt in front of a drive-through espresso stand. On the sidewalk stood a boy and a girl, posed in the classic tableau of young, brand-new love. She was leaning against the wall of the coffee shack; he was standing next to her, one arm raised, his hand braced against the wall as he leaned in close, just a bit too shy to kiss her.

Belinda recognised the boy. He was one of the new programmers Cade had hired to work on his most recent game, *Monster Fest*, or whatever the hell it was called. Belinda could never remember the titles of Cade's products, but she remembered this young man's name: Tuan. He had actually been Belinda's discovery; his mother was her manicurist and, when she told Belinda that her son was graduating summa cum laude with a degree in computer science, Belinda had snapped him up for Cade.

Now it was time to snap him up for herself. Tuan was half Vietnamese, half German-American, and the blend of his parents' genes had resulted in a work of art. In his T-shirt and baggy jeans, he was slender and long-waisted, with elongated muscles that paid tribute to the hours he spent studying martial arts. His skin was the colour of latte, and his thick, straight hair was streaked by the sun. But his most striking feature was his eyes – they had his mother's almond shape, and his father's light-green colour. Amazing. Too bad he was wasting his attention on a flat-chested girl who bore an alarming resemblance to Barbie's virginal little sister, Skipper. She was sweet, slender, angelic in a white sun-dress, and she couldn't be a minute over eighteen.

'Time to grow up, Skipper,' Belinda said under her breath. 'Mama lion's hungry, and she eats first.'

She swerved into the parking lot and pulled up next to the sweethearts. They stopped giving each other syrupy looks and gaped at Belinda instead. Good thing she'd decided to drive with the top down this morning. She knew exactly what she looked like as she smiled up at Tuan: an expensive, mature blonde in an expensive new convertible, the kind of woman who would demand sex in seven different positions and still be ready for more.

Belinda shook back her fragrant mane, pulled off her sunglasses and gave Tuan a thousand-watt smile that broadcast her desire like a beacon. There was no way a male his age could miss the signals she was sending out, especially when she ran her finger down the plunging neckline of her black body suit. She 'accidentally' let her finger brush across her breast as she lowered her hand, and her nipple sprang to attention under the shiny black fabric.

'Gorgeous day, isn't it, Tuan?' she said, in her throatiest purr. 'It's way too warm for coffee on a day like this. Come for a ride with me.'

She rubbed the passenger seat with the flat of her hand, making slow, sensuous circles, as if his taut behind were already sitting there.

Tuan's face was a study in confusion. Belinda could hear the conflicting thoughts ricocheting through his brain like cartoon gunfire: God, she's hot ... but she's **engaged to my boss ... I'd do anything to fuck her ...**

If I leave with this babe, I'll blow my chance with the other chick . . .

'Um . . . I dunno. I've kinda got plans.' He glanced at Skipper, who suddenly looked like she'd been hit by a truck. 'But I guess I could go, I mean, I think I've got some time –'

'Let me make it easy on you,' Belinda said, using a voice guaranteed to turn a man's balls to acorns. 'Get in the car. Now.'

She revved the engine and opened the passenger-side door. Tuan scurried around the car like a schoolboy in serious danger of getting a spanking. He slid into the passenger seat and, before he had even closed the door, Belinda was backing out of the lot, leaving the girl in the sun-dress far behind.

'I'm really supposed to be at the office,' Tuan said nervously, as Belinda took an exit onto the freeway. 'The guys sent me out to get lattes. They're gonna think I flaked.'

'Don't worry about it. You've officially been kidnapped by your boss's future wife. If anyone complains, they'll have to answer to me. There's not a damn thing you can do, so sit back and enjoy the ride.' Belinda emphasised the statement with a sharp turn of the steering wheel.

They were on the highway now, heading into the clear, breezy morning. Driving without a destination made Belinda feel liberated; in fact, it was the only time she didn't feel hopelessly schedule-bound. The convertible felt like an extension of her body, a high-octane animal with streamlined contours, soaring through space.

'Where are we going?' Tuan had to shout to make himself heard over the wind that buffeted the convertible.

'I don't have a clue!' Belinda shouted back.

Tuan grinned. He was settling down, leaning back and spreading his arms along the back of the seat. The sunlight turned his biceps into golden ropes. He pulled a pair of sunglasses out of his front pocket and put them on. With the dark lenses on, and his streaked hair blowing straight back, he looked like an up-and-coming rock star.

Belinda hadn't felt so free in weeks. Between the stress of opening a new gallery and the trials and tribulations of planning a double wedding, she'd been living in a pressure cooker. Cade had been acting like a typical man, letting Belinda do all the work of arranging the ceremony, the reception and the catering, while reserving the right to throw a monkey-wrench into the plans whenever he felt like it. Just the other day, he had suddenly decided to cancel the minimalist Japanese banquet that Belinda had ordered for the wedding dinner, in favour of a *hofbrau* buffet.

'I want meat at my wedding,' he had demanded. 'Red meat. I don't want to see a flock of your campy friends prancing around serving cat food; I want to have a busty chick in lederhosen slicing a side of bloody roast beef.'

So Belinda had played along, pretending to let Cade have his way, but she hadn't cancelled her plans for the sushi and sashimi. Cade was going to have to learn that he couldn't always get what he wanted. She strongly suspected that he had his eye on other women; he hadn't invited Hailey to the lodge to play Chinese Checkers. Within a year, he'd be sleeping around, if he wasn't already. She might have been willing to accommodate his extra-curricular activities, if it weren't for his old-fashioned double standards.

Belinda laid a proprietary hand on Tuan's thigh. She

thought he'd jerk away, but he didn't. He slid deeper into the seat, spread his legs wide and leaned his head against the headrest.

'Are you sure this is OK?' he said. 'Cade won't mind?'

'Cade won't mind what he doesn't know,' Belinda assured him. 'And he's not going to know, is he?'

'No way!'

His earnest reply made her smile. Younger men were so . . . enthusiastic. She kept her left hand on the wheel and let her right hand continue its adventures along Tuan's thigh. She didn't care much for the baggy jeans that kids wore these days – it didn't make sense to hide a pair of prime young male buns under floppy folds of denim – but the loose waistbands came in handy when your hands felt like roving. Traffic was light that morning and, with a stretch of open road lying ahead of her, Belinda could easily drive and explore at the same time.

Below the jeans, below the boxers, crept Belinda's fingers. It didn't take her long to find what she was looking for; Tuan's erection leaped up to meet her hand like a puppy jumping at its mistress's knees. The shaft was slender, but what it lacked in width it made up for in length. Belinda loved learning the contours of a new penis. Every man's was different; they all had their unique textures, dimensions and quirks. She couldn't imagine giving up the excitement of making those discoveries. Touching an unfamiliar cock was as thrilling as finding a new artist. Belinda would be the first to admit that she was a size queen; Cade's big, bullying prick was her favourite of all time. But the infinite variations in other men's penises would never stop arousing her curiosity.

Belinda maintained a light grasp on her latest discovery while she sped up to pass a Mercedes. Tuan's muscles stiffened as she swerved around the other car, but when she cleared the Mercedes, he laughed, and his cock swelled with a fresh surge of blood. Belinda tightened her grip, then put on another burst of speed. She manipulated Tuan's shaft as if it were her gear-shift, guiding her car into the right lane, then the left. Three-way sex at its best: a woman, a man and a car, all operating as a single high-powered unit. The speedometer said that she was going impossibly, dangerously fast, but she still felt unsatisfied.

So did her driving partner.

'Faster!' Tuan shouted. 'Step on it!'

Tense with excitement, he pushed his pelvis forwards, shoving himself into her hand. She turned her fingers into a sheath for him to fuck, with his pre-come fluids providing a natural lubricant. As he thrust, his groans blended with the cry of the wind, and when she pushed the gas pedal all the way to the floor he exploded.

Tuan collapsed against the seat, gasping, as Belinda regained control of the car. She'd almost lost it for a second, when the boy came. Males that age were like live wires; just touching the source of those vibrant young nerves charged her with energy. She desperately needed to come, and she wasn't in any condition to keep driving.

Belinda pulled off the highway at the next rest area. They'd left the city behind, and had reached a scenic stretch of the Pacific coastline. Belinda parked near an outcropping of rocks that overlooked the sea. In the distance, they could see the ferry crossing the water, leaving silver streamers in its wake.

'That was awesome,' Tuan said. 'That was better than the time I got the high score on *Speed Demons III*!'

Belinda cringed. 'Let me give you a bit of advice

about women, darling. Don't compare sex with a computer game. Save that for your buddies at work.'

'Sorry,' Tuan said, looking crushed. He probably figured he'd blown his chances to get laid again.

'Well, I might forgive you, if you can prove that you're a man and not just another boy.'

'I can prove it,' Tuan said, with a formal sincerity that made Belinda laugh.

Belinda touched his wind-blown hair. She let the coarse, glossy strands sift through her fingers, then she pulled off his sunglasses so that she could enjoy the contrast of his olive skin with his pale-green eyes. He had exquisite, high cheekbones that sloped down to a full cupid's-bow mouth. His lips were a shade or two darker than his skin, and she traced their outline with the tip of her tongue. When he tried to kiss her, she sank her fingernails into the scruff of his neck and held his head so that he couldn't move.

'No kissing,' she said gently. Some part of the sex act had to be exclusive. Kissing was saved for Cade. 'But you can do anything else. Why don't you start here?'

Belinda pulled her stretchy black body suit down over her shoulders. Thanks to hours of working out at the weight machine, her breasts didn't require a bra. The air was warm, and slightly astringent from the sea. The sun felt fantastic on her firm, heavy breasts. She'd forgotten how much she loved being naked outdoors – sunbathing, fucking, it didn't matter what she was doing, as long as she was exposed to fresh air, and to the eyes of total strangers. If she'd been born into a different world, Belinda would have made her living as a stripper. She loved being the object of lustful male attention; exhibitionism was more intoxicating than 100-proof booze.

'Go ahead,' she said. 'You can touch them.'

Tuan reached for her breasts as if they were a couple of porcelain figurines in a hoity-toity gift shop. The cherry tips were rock-hard before his fingers made contact.

'You're a man, remember?' Belinda said. 'Don't be shy. Take control. You can squeeze, bite, suck. Do the things you've only seen on those sleazy internet porn sites. You can do whatever you want, but don't be a baby.'

She leaned back against the driver's-side door and folded her arms behind her head. The position looked either regal or submissive, depending on how you looked at her. When Cade made her put her arms in this position, it usually meant that he wanted her to play slave girl while he subjected her to a little tit torture. With Tuan, she felt more like the queen of Sheba, reclining in her private barge while a young warrior paid tribute to her beauty.

A semi-truck rumbled by on the highway. Belinda caught sight of a slack-jawed trucker's face before the rig disappeared up the coastline. Belinda tipped her head back, closed her eyes and smiled. As the light caressed her eyelids, her lips, her throat, Tuan began to caress her breasts. His hands were still tentative at first, but soon he was handling her flesh the way it was meant to be handled, with mastery and purpose. She opened her eyes and watched his lips find her nipple, then gasped when he tugged her breast into his mouth, and looked up at her with a sly light in his incredible eyes.

'This is what you wanted, isn't it?'

'That's a bit better,' Belinda said. She liked to dole out praise at her own pace. No sense in tossing men her approval as if it were a dog-biscuit.

'How about this?' He stroked the undersides of her

breasts with his palms, first one, then the other, flipping his hands up at the nipple. Crouching over Belinda, he pushed his knee into the V between her legs.

'That's good. Very good,' Belinda murmured.

'Is it OK if I touch you down there?'

'It's more than OK, Tuan. It's mandatory.'

Tuan reached under the waistband of her pants. He fumbled around for a few moments, looking confused, while he tried to figure out the mysteries of her body suit. When his fingers made it past the gusset and sank into her cleft, he beamed in triumph. Belinda loved the way his expression changed as he explored the textures of her pussy – the coarse velvet of the outer lips, the moist satin inside, the well of wetness at the centre. When he found her little knot under its hood of skin, she rewarded him with a throaty moan.

'Stay there,' she said. 'You just struck gold.'

But Tuan didn't spend much time on Belinda's clit. His hand soon returned to her sex, then followed the groove all the way to her anus. He popped one slick finger into the tight opening and pushed it in well past the knuckle, then rotated the digit in a way she'd never experienced before. Belinda's eyes widened. She'd never liked anal intercourse – Cade's cock was too thick for that narrow passage – but this was different. The gentle, probing motion was stimulating pleasure zones she didn't know she had.

'Where did you learn to do that?' she asked.

'I saw it on the web,' Tuan said proudly.

'Of course. Kids don't learn about sex in the back seats of cars any more; it's all being demonstrated on a webcam somewhere.'

Belinda's voice faded as Tuan increased the speed and depth of the circular motion. He was creating unfamiliar sensations in unfamiliar places; instead of the sharp, distinct pleasure that came from her clit, these surges rose from the pit of her belly and spread through her entire body. A warm, earthy feeling, tinged with shame, grew inside her. Distant memories rose in her imagination – the excitement and humiliation of toilet training – and then her head was bursting with the force of her orgasm. It brought harsh, bestial sounds from her mouth and, when she came to her senses, she felt embarrassed by the noises she'd made.

'Did you enjoy that?' Tuan asked smugly.

'To say I liked it would be an understatement. That was incredible.'

'I knew you'd like having an anal orgasm. Everyone knows you're a slut.'

'*What* did you say?' Belinda struggled to sit up, but Tuan held her down. He wasn't muscle-bound, but thanks to his martial-arts training he knew how to balance his body weight against Belinda's to keep her in place.

'You heard me. All the guys at Shiva Systems know you're wild.' Tuan's voice had turned husky, raw. 'We know you want us to take you in a million different ways. We've seen the way you look at us when you come to the office.'

Suddenly Belinda wondered if she'd created a monster, possibly a whole army of them. How many times had she been to Cade's office, flaunting her body in Lycra work-out clothes, or sexy business suits? It didn't take much to arouse the imaginations of twenty-something computer programmers, and Belinda had taken full advantage of their awestruck gazes to boost her ego.

On one memorable night, when everyone was working late, Belinda had asked Tuan and one of his friends to teach her how to play pinball. She had lapped up their attention, thrusting out her bottom as she played and arching her back as if she were begging to be taken from behind. By midnight, the game room was heavy with testosterone, and Belinda was flying high on the lust of two shy young men.

'I never meant to lead you on,' Belinda lied.

'Yes you did. Now it's payback time.'

Tuan's threat came straight out of a cheesy action flick, but his physical prowess was amply convincing. In fact, his sudden coarseness was turning Belinda's sex to jelly. She shrieked as he unceremoniously yanked down her black tights and tore apart the snaps on the crotch of her body suit. He sniggered to himself when he saw how wet she was; her blonde bush sparkled with dew. He unzipped his fly and released his penis but, instead of sinking into her, he sat back.

'Turn around,' he ordered. 'I want you on your knees, with your elbows on the door. We're going to do it doggie style.'

Belinda obeyed. It wasn't easy to manoeuvre her tall body in the space between the car seat and the steering wheel. She wasn't used to feeling clumsy and graceless. Having her ass in the air for all to see wasn't as glamorous as lying around topless. She felt big and awkward and thoroughly humiliated. She tried not to think about what her bottom must look like, with her pink pussy lips puffing through the cleft between her cheeks.

'Who's in control now?' Tuan asked.

Then the juvenile delinquent actually slapped her rump – not once but twice, once on each cheek. No man had ever spanked her before Cade, and she had sworn that no man ever would. Spanking was right up there with kissing, an act that should be saved for her future husband.

'Hey!' Belinda looked over her shoulder indignantly. 'Do that one more time, you little bastard, and I'll scream.'

Tuan laughed, and smacked her again. 'Go for it. Who's gonna hear you, a couple of seagulls?'

He was right. The rest stop was deserted apart from Belinda's car, and the vehicles shooting by on the freeway were going too fast to hear any calls for help.

'Look, you might as well relax,' Tuan said. 'I'm not going to hurt you. I'm just going to take what you've been promising me for so long.'

He held onto Belinda's hips and used the tip of his penis to part her honeyed outer lips. She assumed that he would act like a typical kid, following his impulses and delivering a fifteen-second fuck, but it seemed that Tuan had a lot more artistry and self-restraint than he'd let on. The evil brat probably used this strategy all the time to seduce older women: pretending to be the naïve innocent, then unleashing his expertise at the last minute. Right now he was practising a form of torture on Belinda, penetrating her with an inch or two of cock then moving back and forth and round and round in minuscule motions that were driving her crazy.

Her pussy was so famished that when he fed her another inch of flesh, her inner muscles gulped at his shaft. She made her lower back concave and raised her tailbone, exposing more of her velvety wet pinkness. He kept an authoritative grip on her hips, so that she couldn't force him inside her before he was ready, but he didn't try to stop her when she reached between her legs to rub her own clit.

When she touched the engorged button, it sent sparks through her body, from deep inside her core all the way to her nerve endings. She wasn't about to wait around for some punk to make her come, not when he'd already had his turn. Belinda started to rub herself in earnest. Her self-stimulation, combined with the heavenly friction of Tuan's cock, was too much to take.

Tuan must have sensed that she was cresting, because he chose that moment to slide into her with his full length, all the way to the hilt. When the head of his cock hit her cervix, she felt herself reach the peak, but she wasn't prepared for the force of her climax. The spasms knocked the wind out of her lungs. She hadn't felt so overwhelmed since she was a little girl, when she had waded too far into the ocean and been engulfed by a giant swell.

But Tuan wasn't finished with her. He kept going, with his post-pubescent battering-ram, until she had come again, making it three times. She'd always thought she was insatiable, but this was getting ridiculous. Not even an orgasm could stop her crazed lover; he was a medical miracle, a male with no need for recovery time. By the time he slowed down, then stopped, she was as limp and wet as a strand of seaweed plastered to a rock.

'I think I'm still coming,' she gasped. 'Are you done with me?'

'For now,' he said happily.

'Look, Tuan, this isn't the start of some big affair,' Belinda warned. 'I'm getting married in a few months.'

Tuan's full lips drooped into a pout. 'So what? That hasn't stopped Cade.'

In the balmy summer morning, Belinda felt a chill. 'What are you trying to tell me?'

'Uh, nothing.' Tuan was trying to back-pedal, but it was too late. He busied himself with rearranging his boxer shorts and stared down at his jeans as he yanked at the zipper. Belinda grabbed his chin and lifted his face so that he couldn't avoid her scrutiny.

'Tell me,' Belinda insisted.

Tuan looked miserable. He hunched his shoulders, making a self-protective shell. 'Cade likes women in general. That's all I meant.'

'No, it's not. You were trying to tell me that Cade's been cheating on me. How do you know?'

'I've seen him meeting women down at his car, when he didn't think anyone was watching. And I've heard him on the phone. And there was this one time in the freight elevator –'

'OK, that's enough. That's all the proof I need. It's not as if you're telling me anything I didn't know.'

'Are you going to dump him because of what I said? Shit! I am *so* fired!' Tuan wailed.

'Oh, stop it. I'm not about to dump Cade. I'm stuck with him, for better or worse.'

'What are you going to do?'

Belinda pulled on her body suit and tights, ran a comb through her hair and slicked on some lipgloss. She tilted the rear-view mirror so that she could see herself. Perfect. She looked healthy, happy and well-fucked, the way a beautiful woman should look every day.

'I'm going to go back to the gallery, fix myself a stiff Bloody Mary and rewrite the rules for our marriage,' she said.

Belinda turned the key in the ignition, and BELS-BABY purred into action.

From the way Cade had rushed Hailey out of the outdoor theatre, she could tell he wanted to get her away from Rick. That only whetted her appetite to see the cat handler again.

Cade spent another hour helping her get her bearings and taking her round the staff. He introduced her as a visiting scientist, which was a lot more flattering than being called a volunteer, and he even showed her a cubby-hole in the administrators' trailer that she could use as a temporary office. He seemed to be doing everything he could to avoid leaving her alone, but he couldn't hang around the park all day. As soon as he left, Hailey went searching for the forbidden fruit.

She found Rick at the tiger compound, mixing a bone-meal supplement into a tray of horseflesh. He was bent over, so she couldn't see his face, but she recognised his plaid flannel shirt-tails, and the ass that filled out the seat of his Levi's to perfection.

'Feeding time?' Hailey asked.

Rick glanced up when he saw her coming. She couldn't read the expression on his face.

'Just making lunch for the love of my life.' He nodded at Seka, the white tiger.

'Lucky girl,' Hailey said.

He reached into the tray and mixed the meat with a gloved hand. Watching his thick forearm rotate back and forth in the raw red mass, Hailey's throat went dry.

'Why? Do you have a taste for raw meat?'

'If it's served at the right temperature. I tend to like it at about 37 degrees Celsius.'

Rick grinned. 'Isn't that roughly the body temperature of a live human?'

'That's right.'

'Never knew a female who didn't like warm meat.'

'Sounds like you've known a few.'

'You could say that. But Seka's the only one who's won my heart,' he said, pointing to the white tiger. The elegant cat had roused herself at the promise of being fed. She walked up to Rick, her shoulders shifting with each step. Watching the fluid motions of her muscles under her fur, her beautiful carriage and the commanding swing of her tail, Hailey could understand why Rick was so devoted to her.

'You don't care much for females of your own species, do you?' Hailey asked.

'I'm not a misogynist, if that's what you mean. I like women.'

'Cade says you can't get enough of them.'

'Actually, it's the other way around. Women can't get enough of *me*.'

Rick winked, taking some of the air out of his boastful statement. So he did have a sense of humour, after all. Hailey didn't mind cocky men, as long as they weren't so stuck on themselves that they couldn't see the humour in their own arrogance.

'Think your reputation would hold up with a woman from the city?' Hailey asked. 'It's easy to be the most sought-after man in town, when your town has a population of 57.'

'I'll have you know that Sasquanatee has a population of 442,' Rick said. 'And if you want to know how a small-town zookeeper measures up to the city boys, you'll have to formulate a hypothesis and test it for yourself.'

'As a matter of fact, I've already got one,' Hailey said. 'Based on what I've observed in the animal kingdom, a male has the most sexual success when he's subject to the least amount of competition. In a population this small, the odds are overwhelmingly in your favour. From what I've seen of the local men, you don't have a lot to worry about. My guess is that Cade's your biggest competitor for female attention, and he's only here for a month or two out of the year.'

'So what's your hypothesis?'

'My hypothesis is that if you and I were to have sex,

you'd expend less effort than the average urban male of your age and degree of physical attractiveness. As a result, I'd be less satisfied than I would be with a man like Cade, who's had a lot of experience trying to outperform other males.'

Rick mixed the meat thoughtfully.

'Let's look at your theory from another angle,' he said. 'If a man like Cade spends all his energy trying to outdo other males, what's he got left to offer his lovers? Your average urban professional is so worn-out from wondering what a woman thinks of his car, what she thinks of his income, where to take her to dinner, how to approach her sexually – all without being sued, I might add – that he doesn't have much left to give when the clothes come off. He's so worried about how his performance compares to everyone else's that he can't be himself.'

'And you?' Hailey asked.

'I'm myself 24 hours a day. I don't have to work at it. I own four shirts, three pairs of jeans and an old pair of boots. I drive a beat-up truck that breaks down once a month. I only earn enough money to live on, and any woman who dines with me is going to be served something out of a can.'

'Sounds like my idea of heaven,' Hailey said dryly.

'What can I say? I channel all my energy into sex,' Rick said. 'If you think it's easy providing sensual gratification to an entire county of women, you're wrong. Small-town women get bored easily. They're like Seka. It's not enough for me to toss her some processed meat once a day. I have to keep her interested, and I have to make sure her diet has plenty of variety. One day I feed her a moderate amount of meat mixed with a calcium supplement, and the next day I give her a whole leg to tear into. Then she'll have a day or two of fasting, to break up the monotony and sharpen her appetite. Since she's no longer living in the wild, I have to keep her on edge.'

'I know how she feels.'

Rick folded his arms over his chest. He looked Hailey up and down. 'Doesn't seem like you need much help staying on the edge. I caught your performance this morning.'

Hailey tried to hang on to her composure, but it was tough when Rick was so obviously stripping off her clothes in his mind.

'Did you like what you saw?' she asked.

'You and Cade put on quite a show. Definitely caught my attention. Not really appropriate for a family park, though. I could arrest both of you for indecent exposure, and possibly for corrupting minors.'

'*You* could arrest me?' Hailey laughed. 'What are you, a cop?'

'County sheriff.'

'You're kidding. Aren't you?'

Rick looked her straight in the eye. He wasn't kidding.

'Nope. It's an elected position. I was elected. Of course, we don't have a lot of crime in this county, so it's only a part-time post.'

'Then I guess you're only authorised to give me a part-time sentence.'

'You seem to think you deserve to be punished,' Rick said. 'You must have a guilty conscience.'

Hailey trailed the toe of her sneaker along the ground. 'I guess do have a lot to feel guilty about.'

'Such as?'

'Voyeurism, for one thing. Sexual acts in public

places, for another. Then there's the kicker: sex in public places with men who are engaged to be married.'

'What do you think your punishment should be?'

Hailey tipped her head to one side as she considered his question. 'You're the one with the legal background. Why don't you choose?'

'I could make you pick up scat all day, for a start. There's plenty of that to go around.'

'Good idea, but it wouldn't be very effective as a punishment for someone like me. Animal scat is a great biological resource. I could learn all kinds of things from a cat's droppings.'

Rick stripped off his gloves, peeling them off slowly, so that Hailey couldn't help noting the contour of every long, thick, well-shaped finger. She looked at the jagged white scar that ran along his right hand and imagined tracing it with the very tip of her tongue. Hailey usually followed the dictates of science rather than folklore, but she was a firm believer in the old wives' tale that a man's fingers reflected the size and shape of an entirely different organ. Hailey could already feel one of those fingers sunk deep in her mouth, its salty flavour just a prelude to the wilder, muskier taste of his cock.

'Tell you what,' Rick said, after he'd made Hailey endure an agonising wait. 'I'll put you to work in the gift shop tomorrow. How's that for torture?'

'You can't be serious!' Hailey cried, her body sagging with disappointment. 'The gift shop?'

'You asked me to choose, and we need help behind the cash register. One of the summer girls just walked out this morning. Had a falling-out with some guy she'd been sleeping with and decided to quit.' Rick sighed. 'Too bad. She was a hottie.'

So the gift-shop 'hottie' had a falling-out with 'some

guy'. Hailey didn't have to wrack her brain to figure out who the guy was in that combination. She wasn't exactly thrilled about punching a cash register all afternoon, but she did want to stay on Rick's good side. He was the keeper of the cats, after all, and the cats were Hailey's reason for being here.

'Fine. I'll play along,' Hailey said. 'You need another hottie to work in your shop, then I'll fill in for you. But it's only for tomorrow. I'm a scientist, not a cashier.'

'Fair enough,' Rick said. 'That's your punishment. For now.'

For now. Those two words were enough to keep Hailey simmering, in spite of the cold water that Rick had splashed on her libido. As she watched Seka relishing her meal of raw flesh, Hailey felt a burst of envy for the big cat. The white tiger didn't know how lucky she was, to have a stud like Rick treat her with such care and consideration. He sure as hell didn't know how to treat a human woman with respect – or if he did, he didn't care enough to try.

But who needed respect from a stud like Rick? All Hailey needed was a taste of what was under those tight faded jeans. She had a strong suspicion that he would be worth the wait.

'What do you think you're doing, Hailey? Trying to kill your career?'

Hailey ground her teeth to keep from telling her friend Parker to mind her own fucking business. She slammed the phone receiver into her pillow a few times, but it didn't do much to relieve her frustration.

'Hailey? Are you still there? Answer me.' Parker's imperious voice rang out through the wires.

'I'm still here,' Hailey sighed.

She was sitting on her bed in the guest-room at the

lodge. Until she'd decided to call Parker, she'd been having a blissful evening, lying on a pile of quilts and sipping warm cocoa laced with Kahlua. Her notebook computer sat open on her lap, and she'd been typing up some ideas that had occurred to her late in the afternoon. A chapter on captive breeding of felines might be the perfect juxtaposition to her Costa Rican research on reproduction and propagation in the wild. Hailey had been so excited about the idea that she'd had to share her thoughts with someone.

She'd made the mistake of calling her die-hard feminist friend, Parker. The conversation had gone well at first, the anthrologist enthused about the new turn Hailey's research was taking. But as soon as the two friends stopped talking about cats and started talking about men, the conversation had been derailed.

'The last thing you need right now is a man,' Parker declared. 'If you absolutely have to bond with someone, wait till you've finished your thesis. This situation you're in sounds like a brain drain to me. What are you doing, getting involved with a married man?'

'First of all, I'm not "involved" with Noah,' Hailey said. 'Second, he's not married; he's engaged.'

'Same difference. The point is, if he got engaged in the first place, he's a reactionary. You need to be with someone who's enlightened, someone who's free of all that crap. You've said it yourself a thousand times – the human pair-bond is an anachronism.'

Hailey twisted the telephone cord around her finger. The phone was an old-fashioned rotary machine. Another anachronism, but did that make it worthless?

'That was before I met Noah,' Hailey said.

'So fuck him, then get on with your life. Better yet, fuck that other guy you told me about, the lion-tamer, or whatever he is. Get your libido under control, then go back to work. What's so special about Noah, anyway?'

Hailey thought this over. 'Well,' she said slowly, 'He has this fierce, quiet passion that I love. He's dedicated to his art. He's committed to the cats. He's sincere, he's direct, he's gentle, and he seems like he could really care about me. Besides, he has the most gorgeous dark eyes ...'

'Oh, god,' Parker groaned. 'You're lost. Next thing you know, you'll be up to your elbows in Betty Crocker cookbooks, and your degree will go right out the window.'

'What about you?' Hailey shot back. 'You've been living with Alicia for five years, and it hasn't hurt your work in any way. In fact, you're always gushing about how supportive she is. You attack other people for wanting to have committed relationships, but you've been monogamous since the day you fell in love with her.'

'Alicia's different,' Parker said archly.

'How?' Hailey demanded.

She could hear her friend floundering.

'She just is,' Parker sputtered.

'Mmm, hmm. I thought so. You're no different from anyone else.'

'All right,' Parker said. 'I give in. But you're wrong about one thing – I didn't commit to Alicia as soon as I knew I was in love with her. Before we moved in together, I had one of the hottest flings of my life.'

'With who?'

'If I tell you, you've got to promise not to tell anyone else. Ever.'

'I'll never tell a soul. Do I know her?'

Parker hesitated. 'It wasn't a her. It was Jack.'

'Jack?' Hailey cried. 'My room-mate Jack, the bacteria freak? Excuse me, but didn't you say this was a "hot" fling?'

'Jack's a very sensual man, once you drag him away from his microscope,' Parker said defensively. 'I'd have to say he was one of the best lovers I've ever had. Not good enough to make up for the fact that he's male, but he was damn gifted in bed.'

'That's why you attacked his poor little girlfriend that night, isn't it?' Hailey crowed. 'You were jealous!'

'Don't try to change the subject,' Parker snapped. 'The point is, I didn't jump into monogamy. I waded in one step at a time, with hip-high boots on. I suggest you do the same. Get the sex out of your system so you can think this over with your brain, not your cunt.'

Parker was right, Hailey thought as she hung up the phone. Aside from the erotic games she'd been playing with Cade, she hadn't done anything lately but observe as other people had mad, feverish sex. Maybe her attraction to Noah was a by-product of her sexual frustration, masked as romantic love. Hailey was an intelligent, educated woman, but she wasn't immune to self-deception.

On the opposite wall hung an old black-and-white photo of Cade's grandfather, displaying a giant salmon: the big hunter showing off his catch. His handsome face was a study in masculine pride. He wore the same expression in a wedding portrait that Hailey had seen downstairs. Hailey had seen that look in Cade's eyes as well, when he talked about dominating Belinda; the grandfather's genes expressed themselves beautifully in the grandson. Were people condemned to live according to their chromosomes, or could they alter themselves to fit society's demands?

Hailey didn't think they could. Of course, that didn't

mean that a person's needs couldn't change with age, experience or the natural reshaping of their desires.

She shut her computer down with a firm click, set it aside and got out of bed. Noah's room was down the hall. The door was half closed, but Hailey could see the flickering blue light of his computer. With a soft push, she opened the door all the way. Noah sat at his desk, working on a 3D model of another female figure.

'Don't you ever take a break?' Hailey asked.

Noah looked over his shoulder. Surprise, pleasure and a touch of guilt flickered across his face. 'This *is* my break,' he said sheepishly. 'I'm working on a private project.'

'Can I see?'

'Not much to see yet, but go ahead.'

Noah scooted his chair away from the monitor to let Hailey have a look. So far, the woman he was designing was nothing but a web of lines, a grid with a lean, feminine shape. Hailey thought she saw something familiar in its proportions: the smallish breasts, the long legs, the narrow waist and hips.

'That doesn't look like your usual 3D goddess,' Hailey remarked. 'She actually has figure flaws.'

'Like I said, it's my own project. She doesn't have to fit any ideal but the one in my mind.'

Before Hailey could get him to elaborate, Noah clicked his mouse and closed the file. The figure was replaced by a screensaver showing Noah's jungle background from *Mutant Quest*. Otherworldly animals, lurking in masses of dark-green leaves, peered out from a magical wilderness. Once again, Hailey marvelled at how much sensual detail Noah had been able to convey on a computer screen.

'You're very gifted,' she said.

The comment made her think of a phrase Parker had

used: *He's damn gifted in bed.* She looked down at Noah's well-shaped, competent hands and remembered how he'd touched her that morning. In the short time she'd known him, he'd used those hands with her in so many different ways. He'd cleaned up her scrapes, helped her pull her top off, cooked for her and kept her from falling down when he'd turned her legs to jelly. There was so much more he could do with those fine instruments, if only he'd let go of his fears, his inhibitions, his plans to get married . . . all those not-so-minor obstacles that were holding him back.

'Thanks.' Noah sounded dubious. 'I'd love to be able to do more of my own artwork, but game design eats up most of my creative energy.'

'Who's the woman you were drawing?'

Noah didn't answer.

'Is she someone you know? Someone you're attracted to?'

Noah still didn't say anything, but this time he smiled.

'I'm attracted to you, too,' Hailey said. 'Maybe you don't know how much.'

Hailey lowered herself to the floor and knelt in front of his chair. She pushed his knees apart and slid into the nook between his thighs. The room hummed with the currents of attraction that ran between them. Noah wasn't touching her yet, but he wasn't stopping her from touching him either. He was wearing shorts, and she could feel the hard, steady pulse of his femoral arteries as she ran her fingers over his legs. Hailey pressed her cheek against the warm skin and felt that faint beat as if it were her own. If she moved up just a few inches more, she'd be close enough to tug the edge of his shorts with her teeth.

The chime of a Swiss cuckoo-clock, another one of

Cade's grandfather's bizarre knick-knacks, broke the promising tension.

Noah released a long, shuddering breath. 'Eight o'clock. I have to make a phone call.'

'What?' Hailey backed away, stunned.

'I have to call Val. I call her every night at eight.'

'You call her every night? Sounds like you're marrying your mother.'

Hailey couldn't keep that remark from popping out. She dug her nails into her palms as she tried to get her anger under control. She thought Noah would have the decency to act guilty, but he seemed as angry as she was.

'Some men are considerate and reliable,' he said. 'But they're probably not the kind of jerks you go for. Would you excuse me?'

He got up and led Hailey to the door, then shut it behind her. She stood in the hallway, her heart thudding as she waited to eavesdrop on his conversation with Val. She never heard him make the call. After a few minutes, she walked back to her room. She was still seething.

A long, warm bath in water scented with almond oil calmed Hailey's emotions. After she'd gone to bed, she lay awake thinking about Noah, and the image he'd been working on when she interrupted him earlier. She wasn't sure, but Hailey could have sworn that the woman he'd been rendering on his computer monitor was the spitting image of her.

Hailey fell asleep that night wondering who Noah had been drawing, and whether he had ever gotten around to calling his fiancée.

7 The Rules of Variation

Working in the gift shop the next day was worse than she could have dreamed. Hailey couldn't stand small, enclosed spaces, and the shop was little more than a sweat shack. She spent her afternoon ringing up postcards, T-shirts and junk food for what seemed like ten thousand rambunctious brats. None of the kids had any patience with her clumsiness at the cash register; one of the brats from hell called her a 'dork' when she gave him the wrong change; and, since there was no one to cover for her over a lunch break, she had to gobble a bag of salted peanuts behind the counter. By closing time, she was exhausted, starving and more humiliated than she'd ever been in her life.

At five o'clock, as she was gratefully locking the register, a male silhouette filled the doorway. Hailey didn't notice Noah standing there until he cleared his throat.

'Thank god it's you! I thought you were another customer,' Hailey said. 'How long have you been watching me?'

'Only a couple of minutes. I didn't mean to stare. It's just that you look so –'

'Defeated?' Hailey offered. 'Beaten down? Belittled?'

'You look beautiful,' Noah said.

'Give me a break.' Hailey felt her cheeks getting warm at Noah's simple compliment. She ducked her head so he couldn't see how sweaty and dishevelled she was. 'I've looked better after a day of crawling through the jungle on my belly.'

'I came to rescue you. I couldn't believe it when Rick told me you were working here. What was he thinking?'

'It's part of a deal we worked out. A very temporary deal,' she said with distaste.

'I wouldn't have let you work here at all, if I'd known. Rick's good with the animals, but he's a sadist with women. You should stay away from that fucker.'

Hailey looked up, startled at the anger in Noah's statement. 'How am I supposed to stay away from Rick? He runs the zoo.'

'Just don't get involved with him in any way that's not professional. He can be a bona fide jerk.'

'I appreciate the warning, but I'm a grown woman, Noah. No one chooses my sex partners but me.' She straightened up and faced Noah dead-on. 'Besides, you had your chance last night. You blew it. Why should you care if I have some fun with Rick?'

'Because *I* want you. I don't want to use you for fun, either. I want you for a lot more than that.'

Noah's voice was strained and hoarse, as if he'd had to tear those words out of his throat. Hailey was suddenly aware of the shop's claustrophobic dimensions. It was impossible to move in such a cramped space, and Noah was blocking the only exit. There was no way to escape from a confrontation. He seemed to be waiting for Hailey to say something, but she couldn't take a full breath, much less talk.

'Had enough, Hailey? It's quitting time.'

Another male voice broke the tension. Rick shouldered his way past Noah into the shop. Next to Noah, he seemed huge, dynamic, almost brutal in his energy. Just what Hailey needed – a big, sexy bastard who had zero interest in romantic commitments of any kind. She darted out from behind the counter and sank her fingers into one of Rick's meaty biceps.

'Let's go,' she said, dragging him out of the shop and towards his pick-up truck, which was idling outside. Rick got behind the wheel, and Hailey jumped into the passenger seat. She felt a pang when she saw Noah's face as the truck pulled out of the lot. He looked exactly the way Hailey had felt when Alessandro dumped her for the Norwegian ecologist.

It had felt a lot like being punched in the stomach.

'I was planning to kidnap you this afternoon,' Rick said, 'but now I'm not sure who's kidnapping whom. Are you still feeling guilty?'

Hailey was feeling more guilty than ever. She was trying to wipe Noah's face from her memory, but it was next to impossible to forget the way he'd looked at her. She wished she could replay that awkward encounter in the shop, analyse it frame by frame, like a videotape, so that she could understand what Noah had been trying to say. She had wanted to help him figure out what he wanted from this vacation – what he wanted from sex in general – but she'd just blown a chance to learn more about his desires.

'Actually, I do have a few regrets right now,' Hailey said.

'Good.'

'Why? Got any more cruel and unusual torments in mind?'

'As a matter of fact,' Rick said, steering the truck up a steep trail that led into the woods, 'I do.'

Rick flexed his fingers on the steering wheel. He gave Hailey a strange, sidelong look that made her go hot, then cold, then hot again. He might have something truly kinky in store for her. On the other hand, he might drive her up to some ramshackle, secluded cabin and make her scrub his toilet and wash a mountain of crusty dishes. After the gift shop, anything was possible.

Rick's cabin wasn't dilapidated, but it was secluded enough to keep a screaming woman from being heard by anyone within a three-mile radius. The modest log structure was set back in a stand of trees that looked like they'd been guarding the same spot for a thousand years. On the postage-stamp porch sat a freezer, a rocking-chair and a balding, one-eyed cat. The whole cabin was covered with a layer of moss, so vibrantly green that it looked radioactive. Even the cat had a greenish tinge to his sparse fur.

A single chain hung from the roof of the porch, with a rusty hook dangling from it. The links of the chain were mossy too. Noah had called Rick a sadist. Hailey was starting to wonder if she was about to become the star performer in some twisted mountain sex scene with the small-town sheriff: Andy Griffith meets the Marquis de Sade.

'Here we are.' Rick brought the truck to a stop. The engine sputtered, then died. The silence was as dense and heavy as a thick woollen blanket.

'It's quiet up here,' Hailey said. 'Too quiet.'

'Yep. That's just how I like it.'

Before Hailey had time to register what Rick was doing, he had pulled a pair of handcuffs out of his pocket. With brisk, no-nonsense motions, he snapped them on her wrists.

'Hey! What are those for?' Hailey protested. 'I thought you were only into law enforcement part-time. Why are you carrying handcuffs?'

'The handcuffs have nothing to do with my position as county sheriff,' Rick said. 'I brought them just for you.'

'Wow. I'm flattered.'

'You should be. I only use them on special occasions, for women who need correction.'

Rick got out of the truck, slammed the door and walked around to Hailey's side. He opened the door for her, then helped her hop down from the high seat. As she followed him up the gravel path that led to his cabin, she heard nothing but the crunch-crunch of tiny rocks under their feet.

'Help?' Hailey called experimentally.

The forest swallowed her voice.

Rick turned and gave her a curious look. 'Something wrong?'

'Um, no. I'm totally comfortable with the idea of being handcuffed by a near-stranger and led into an isolated cabin that has a rusty hook hanging from the porch.'

'Here. I'll fix that for you.' Rick covered the rest of the distance to the cabin in a few long strides. He stepped onto the porch, lifted a mass of hairy green vegetation off the floor, and hung it on the hook. Rick adjusted the plant's fronds, like a hairdresser fussing with a client's new style, then turned to Hailey.

'The hook is for my Boston fern. What did you think I hung on it, human carcasses?'

'Something like that,' Hailey said. Rick wasn't sick or twisted, she decided. He was just weird.

Weird, but oh so attractive. Seeing him at home, with his plant and his cat and his broken-down rocking-chair, made his rough edges seem softer. Sure, he had an authority complex, but it wasn't *so* bad being bossed around by a tall, broad-shouldered cat handler with long auburn hair and long, thick fingers.

'Let me ask you something,' Hailey said as she approached the cabin. 'Cade says you used to be an attorney. What kind of house did you give up for a place like this?'

'A mansion, compared to what I'm living in now. Four bedrooms. Six bathrooms, for crying out loud. Two-car garage, swimming pool.'

Hailey laughed in disbelief. 'And you don't miss it?'

'Not at all. Come on in, I'll show you my new palace.'

Rick pulled open the front door. The frame was warped, like everything else around here. The rainy climate was great for plants, but it left all human structures in a state of slow disintegration. Even indoors, things were perpetually damp – furniture, books, clothes, towels. Hailey didn't mind the excess moisture. She was pretty moist herself. The handcuffs were starting to grow on her. She'd never been the type of woman who liked to give up control to a man, but now that she was on Rick's turf, restrained by his cuffs, she was starting to enjoy her submissive state.

The one-room cabin was shabby but cosy inside. A desk, an old-fashioned gas stove, a sink (with no dirty dishes, Hailey was pleased to note) and a butcher-block table with two chairs occupied over half the room, but the big bed, with its four-poster maple frame, dominated her attention. Covered with a thick blue comforter and a heap of multicoloured velveteen pillows, it looked like a bed made for erotic bliss.

'Is this where you incarcerate all your prisoners?' she asked.

'Only the ones who need to be locked away for a long time,' Rick replied.

Hailey felt a prickle of worry. 'What do you consider a long time? Days? Weeks? I have to finish a draft of my thesis by the end of the month.'

Rick laughed. 'Do you really think a man like me would keep the same woman under his roof for more than 24 hours? I'm a strictly short-term lover – no ties, no regrets. I have a feeling that you and I are two of a kind.'

Hailey considered this. A week or two ago, she wouldn't have hesitated to agree with Rick. But today, for some reason, she wasn't so sure. She couldn't see herself ever developing a taste for monogamy, but would she always be, as Rick put it, a short-term lover? Hailey had a sudden vision of herself getting old and crablike, skittering away from intimate contact with anyone.

'Have you ever been married?' Hailey asked.

'You ask a lot of questions, for a woman in handcuffs.'

'I'm curious. It's a trait I picked up from hanging out with cats.'

'Never been married,' Rick said. 'I came close once, but I didn't get caught.'

'So you had a house with six bathrooms all to yourself?'

'Six bathrooms, two cars. The day I gave it all up was the happiest day of my life. The only things I took with me when I left the city were a couple of keepsakes, a few of my favourite books and Cyclops.'

'Cyclops?'

'He's the scrawny, one-eyed fleabag you saw outside.'

'Do you ever wish you weren't alone? Alone except for Cyclops, I mean.'

Rick rolled his eyes. 'I'm not alone. You're here. And I'm going to have to add a muzzle to those cuffs if you don't get your curiosity under control.'

He switched on a small lamp on a table next to the bed. Light pooled across the blue comforter. Though the sun hadn't set on this early summer evening, it was already twilight in Rick's cabin under the trees. The lamplight caught the copper glints in Rick's wavy hair, and made his suntanned skin seem to glow like burnished white pine. Hailey swallowed hard when he pulled his T-shirt over his head, revealing a torso that could have belonged to a large jungle cat. The way he moved – sinuously purposeful, never taking his unblinking gaze off Hailey – he might as well have been a predatory beast.

Which made Hailey his prey.

Rick smoothed the blue comforter with his hand, up and down the length of the bed, making a hollow that was wide enough for Hailey's body.

'Welcome to captivity,' he said. 'Lie down.'

'Are you going to take the cuffs off? They're starting to chafe.'

'I'll take them off when I want you to use your hands. Stop trying to run the show. While you're here, you'll do as I say.'

Hailey took a step backwards, as if she were thinking of bolting. 'What if I leave?'

Rick didn't miss a beat. 'That would be your loss.'

'And yours.'

'And mine,' he agreed. 'But I'm not the one with the guilty conscience. You wanted me to punish you. Come over here and take what you deserve.'

Hailey's legs trembled as she walked across the wooden floorboards. She didn't want Rick to see how excited she was; his ego was bloated enough already. Staring at the wall ahead of her, she lowered herself gingerly onto the very edge of the mattress. Sitting so close to the shirtless Rick, she could pretend to be indifferent, but her whole body was in an erotic uproar. Although he wasn't physically touching her, he was driving her crazy with his proximity. She felt frozen, not with fear, but with something just as powerful, an instinct that ordered her not to move until she was sure it was safe.

Rick set his hands on her shoulders and turned her around, easing her onto her back. Her head sank into a pile of soft pillows, and her cuffed wrists came to rest in the groove between her thighs.

There weren't many signs of sensual indulgence in Rick's cabin, but his bed was an exception. The blue comforter was made of silk, which felt cool and smooth as water against Hailey's bare legs. Under the comforter, she could feel the airy mass of a goose-down blanket. The mattress was firm and resilient, yielding in exactly the right places. Rick might have given up his taste for most luxuries, but he hadn't sacrificed anything when it came to the place where he slept, dreamed, and fucked.

'Are you comfortable?' Rick asked.

'I'd be more comfortable if I knew what you were going to do to me next,' Hailey said.

'That's the whole point, to keep you in suspense. Now you're going to have to exercise some patience while I find the right instrument to handle you with.'

Rick got up and walked over to the other side of the cabin. Hailey couldn't see what he was doing, but from the sounds he made she could tell he was looking for something. He took his sweet time, making her wait while he rummaged through his things. When she heard him laughing to himself under his breath, she started to worry. Laughter could be a sign of solitude-induced psychosis. Hailey turned her wrists in the handcuffs, testing their durability. The cuffs felt like the real thing, and the bed frame was solid. She was going to have to take whatever Rick dished out. She only hoped he didn't burst out of the shadows wielding a machete.

Rick reappeared with his hands behind his back. Hailey felt numb with the awareness of being trapped, yet she'd never experienced such keen anticipation in her life. Her heart was beating so hard that she was afraid it might pound its way out of her ribcage. Her nipples were on high alert, and every inch of her skin tingled.

'I thought a lot about how I would handle a woman like you,' Rick said. 'I doubt that any of the classic sexual punishments would have much effect. If I wanted to train you to do what I wanted, I'd use pleasure, not pain. That's how I've always handled the cats.'

'I'm not a cat.'

'No, but you're highly independent, and deeply sensual. You respond well to tactile stimulation, as I've seen for myself. And I can tell by the way you're glaring at me that you're not all that civilised, under that sexy skin of yours. If I let you go right now you'd try to claw me to ribbons.'

'You're right about that.'

'That's why I have no intention of letting you loose until I know I can deal with you.'

Rick sat down on the edge of the bed again.

'What have you got behind your back?' Hailey asked.

When Rick showed her what he'd been holding, Hailey burst out laughing. She'd been expecting something sinister and menacing – a whip or a cattle prod. What Rick held in his hand was a slim, graceful wand topped by a cluster of feathers. It was either a cat toy or a house-cleaning implement; either way, it was clear proof that Rick was out of his mind.

'Do you use that on a lot of women?' Hailey gasped, when she was able to talk.

'Only the ones who can't be handled any other way,' Rick said calmly. 'This is my favorite tickler. Believe me, by the time I'm done with it, you won't be laughing. Unless you're a woman who laughs in mid-orgasm.'

He was absolutely serious.

'All right. Do with me what you will, Master.' Hailey lay back. Since she wasn't going anywhere anytime soon, she might as well enjoy herself.

Rick put the feather tickler down on the mattress. His abdominal muscles moved in a deliberate tempo with each slow, deep breath as he pulled up Hailey's T-shirt. She could tell he was a pro by the skilful way he unclasped her bra: one quick motion, and her breasts were exposed. He unbuttoned her shorts and pulled them part of the way down, just far enough to bare her lower belly and show the top of her panties.

Rick picked up the tickler again. He dangled the feathers at the edge of Hailey's face, barely brushing her cheek, flirting with her peripheral vision. The flickering motion evoked a primitive response, the good old hunting instinct that she'd seen a thousand times in every feline she'd ever observed. With cruel delicacy, Rick ran the tickler lightly down her neck, letting it dance across her nipples, her ribs, her half-uncovered hips. Then swoosh, swoosh, back and forth along her abdomen, all the way up to her throat and the soft swelling under her chin. The sensation was maddening and provocative at the same time; if Hailey really were a feline, she'd be psychotic by now. She wanted to bat the feathers away, but the handcuffs held her wrists firmly in place.

'This isn't as amusing as you thought it would be, is

it?' Rick asked. He trailed the very tips of the feathers along her jaw and down the midline of her throat. She'd never realised that feathers could create such sharp, precise sensations, like the tips of dry paint-brushes. But when he held the wand at a different angle and whisked the feathers across her clavicle, they felt smooth and slick, more like a swathe of satin.

'You're getting excited.'

'Maybe,' said Hailey. It was hard to fake indifference when those feathers were igniting sparks all over her skin, but she wasn't going to melt for Rick like one of his summer gift-shop cashiers. When Rick began to lash her breasts gently, she bit her lip and caught her breath.

'You're turned on. I can see a pulse beating.' The feathers etched their way down Hailey's neck.

Hailey shook her head. 'It always does that.'

Rick painted her abdomen with the smooth side of the tickler, then edged down her panties and dusted her lower belly. The breath Hailey had been holding seeped out of her mouth in a long, husky moan. Rick replaced the tickler with his palm. His hand felt warm and firm on her belly. He kneaded the flesh with his fingers, moving lower, until he touched the humid heat under her shorts.

'Admit it,' Rick said. 'You're mine.'

'Not yet,' she whispered.

Rick set the tickler on the bed beside him, and Hailey released the breath she'd been holding. He lowered his head to Hailey's breast and kissed the dark pink ridges that rimmed her nipple. Her areolae tightened into rosy rings. He ran his tongue around the nub until the corresponding ripples in her sex and belly made her whimper, then he licked the nubs with his warm, coarse tongue.

Hailey's moan rose into a wail. Rick picked up her wrists and lifted her arms over her head, resting her hands on the backboard of the bed. She shivered. Every nerve in her body was alight. Even though she was still half-dressed, she felt more naked than she ever had in her life – she felt like she'd been skinned.

'I know you want to move,' Rick said, 'but you're not going to. You're going to close your eyes, and you're going to hold absolutely still until I give you permission to let go.'

Hailey kept her eyes closed as Rick pulled down her shorts, lingering over her thighs and calves as he moved down her legs. Then he eased down her panties. When she felt the air on her sex-lips, Hailey opened her eyes again. She loved the look of concentration on Rick's face, the vertical line that formed between his eyebrows as he worked her over, learning her body's contours. He looked like a sculptor who was trying to capture the line of a model just right. Men rarely focused so thoroughly on her. The only man who'd done that in her recent memory was Noah.

Noah. Where the hell did he come from? Hailey tried to push him out of her mind. As sexy as Rick was, he wasn't distracting Hailey from the image of Noah's dark, intense eyes.

Rick frowned. 'You're not focusing. I want all your attention.'

'I'm sorry. Please don't stop.'

'Are you sure? You looked like you were somewhere else for a moment.'

'I'm focused. I promise.'

Hailey kept her eyes fixed on Rick's hands. He was massaging her pubis now, combing the borders of her tawny bush. He parted her legs and worked his way in between them, then picked up the tickler again and swished it in circular motions along her inner thighs. The feeling was sheer torture; if Hailey had been a captured spy, she would have given up all of her country's secrets by now.

Though he kept his cool, Rick was as aroused as she was. The ridge of his cock snaked along his groin, almost reaching his waist. When he parted her outer labia, the bulge shifted and twitched. He drew his index finger along the slash that nature had given her, splitting her slick lips like two halves of a ripe seed pod. He held her pussy open while he brushed the swollen flesh with his torture tool.

Rick's breathing was getting heavy. The whisk of the feathers was shattering in its intense precision, but what Hailey really craved was a hard, blunt cock. Her muscles ached from the tension of holding still, and her wrists were starting to go numb.

'I think I've learned my lesson,' Hailey said. 'Can I let go now?'

He put the tickler down and took the key to the handcuffs out of his pocket.

'You can let go.'

He unlocked the cuffs and rubbed Hailey's wrists to restore her circulation. Then he lifted her body so that she was perched on top of the headboard, and crouched between her thighs. She gripped handfuls of his long hair, using it to guide his head as his tongue wended its way through her channel. He was taking his time, skirting her hot spots. He laughed softly to himself when she got impatient and tugged his hair, trying to make him lick her where it would pleasure her most.

But Hailey wasn't in the mood to be tortured anymore. After all that time spent lying as still as a statue while she submitted to Rick's torments, she was ready to go wild. She wanted to tear Rick apart like a tiger ripping into a fresh chunk of horseflesh. She braced her hands on Rick's shoulders and pushed him with all her might, so that he rolled backwards and landed flat on his back on the mattress.

'Now you're mine, Mr Control Freak,' she announced, sitting squarely on his upper thighs.

'I guess I know when I'm defeated,' Rick said with a grin. 'Do with me what you will.'

Without a second's hesitation, Hailey unzipped Rick's jeans and reached into the pile of damp auburn curls. He wasn't wearing any underwear, so it was easy to pull out his cock. She was torn for a moment between her desire to cram the long, meaty member into her mouth, and needing to feel it inside her pussy. His prick was a rosy violet colour, streaked with vessels that carried his rich blood.

A pearl of pre-come was cresting the slit. Hailey couldn't miss out on that creamy treat. As she leaned down to catch the droplet with her tongue, Rick pushed her head down. Out of practice with fellatio, Hailey sucked Rick's penis with more hunger than skill, but he didn't seem to mind her lack of technique. He grunted when she gobbled at the glans, and threw his head back and moaned when she throated the entire shaft.

Hailey had forgotten how much she loved the ripe, musky, slightly bitter flavour of cock; it reminded her of the wild taste of unfiltered honey. This was the first time in over a year that she'd been able to let go with a man, without being limited or restrained in any way. She felt like she could eat Rick alive, tear him apart with her claws, and still not get enough of him.

Hailey let Rick's cock slip out of her mouth. The stalk swayed in mid-air until she sat down on top of it, landing with all her weight on Rick's groin. She didn't care whether he minded the change of venue; all she cared about was getting her fill of a strong, healthy, unattached male. She dug her nails into Rick's pecs and threw all her energy into riding him. Through her pre-orgasmic haze, she was vaguely aware of his hands on her breasts, then on her waist, but all she knew for sure was that the rough rhythm of his hips matched perfectly with hers, and that his cock and her pussy were interlocking like the gears of a well-lubed machine.

Rick's hand slipped into the hot gap under her pubic bone. Though he didn't have much room to manipulate her pussy, he was able to use his fingers as an accompaniment to his motions, so that her clit wasn't left out in the heat of all that thrusting.

'How did I go so long without this?' Hailey asked out loud.

She couldn't answer her own question, because her climax was coming on and she couldn't think clearly enough to speak. First there was that still, floating moment, when her whole body hummed with the hope of release. Then the orgasm unfurled at the heart of her pussy and spread outwards. Rick stopped thrusting and she sank onto his shaft, little by little, while the spasms shimmered through her.

When she went limp, Rick rolled her over onto her back. She tilted her hips and wrapped her thighs around his waist. He took his sweet time reaching his own peak, thrusting at a measured pace that Hailey, in her worn-out state, was happy to match. The muscles of his arms and chest, oiled by sweat, worked smoothly as he held himself over her. Hailey lay back and played the passive partner, admiring Rick's physical prowess.

She could see why he was considered the stud of the county – he had strength, stamina and no shortage of masculine beauty.

But when she looked up at his face, Hailey saw Noah.

Rick's climax blew the vision away. His moan started with a low rumble behind his sternum, and rose in volume to a near howl. At the last moment, he pulled out of Hailey, turned her on her stomach, and pushed her legs apart with his knee. He re-entered her from behind, then lowered his body onto hers, driving her into the bed. His body tensed, trembling. When he came, he sank his teeth into the back of her neck and ground her face into the comforter. Hailey was so shocked that she came a second time, just as Rick was finishing. After the last of his thrusts, he rolled onto his side. His sweaty skin parted from hers with a kissing suction.

'You learned that grand finale from the clouded leopard, didn't you?' Hailey asked, rubbing the tooth marks on her neck.

'I've always done that, long before I started working with cats. It seemed to come naturally to me. Did you like it?'

'Loved it,' Hailey said, stretching contentedly.

Flesh, claws, teeth – sex with Rick had been just what Hailey needed. But she couldn't help wondering what Noah was doing tonight. He was probably in his room back at the lodge, staring at his monitor, making minor adjustments to Yulana's voluptuous figure on his computer. Men were so misguided when it came to love. Noah was infatuated with a pixelated virgin warrior. Rick had given his heart to a female tiger. And Cade adored Belinda, but he couldn't keep his dick in his pants to save his life.

In the end, a woman could only count on herself, Hailey thought. In unspoken agreement, the stud of Sasquanatee County began to snore. Hailey trailed her fingers along the planes and curves of Rick's back. His musculature was so well defined that he could serve as a model for an anatomy lesson. She smoothed his thick hair away from his face, fascinated by the way the light brought out a gradient of colours, from mahogany to copper. The coppery glints continued in the fur that lightly covered his chest and nipples. The hair formed a sleek arrow at his abdomen, then flared out again at his groin. In the nest of damp pubic curls, his cock slumbered in a dusky pink coil.

No doubt about it, Hailey had a spectacular male specimen at her fingertips. She thought about sliding down Rick's body and slipping his cock into her mouth, sucking at the head until the snake uncoiled and hardened. He'd be at her service for the rest of the night, if she wanted him.

But gorgeous though he was, Rick wasn't the man Hailey wanted.

Belinda was biding her time. Most women made the mistake of acting on impulse when they got concrete proof that their man was cheating. They threw fits, tore up photos, smashed anniversary gifts, gouged big chunks of flesh out of their mate's body. Belinda was too smart to go psycho on Cade. She phoned him every night, reporting the news of their wedding plans, and during those half-hour conversations she was his good little girl. For the remaining 23½ hours, all bets were off.

Once a week, Belinda and Val met to discuss their double ceremony over cocktails. They usually went to the country club and sipped white-wine spritzers on the balcony overlooking the golf course. Each woman brought her laptop computer, so that they could compare spreadsheets of wedding costs, discuss layouts for the invitations or revise their ideas for the food and flowers. After the shoptalk was out of the way, they accessed the internet via their wireless modems, logged onto their wedding registry website and gloated over the gifts that people were buying for them.

This week, Belinda announced a change in plans. Instead of going to the country club to hang out with the mummified wives and pouty toy-boys of the city's wealthy population, Belinda arranged for Val to meet her at a dive called the Tarantula. It was one of Cade's favourite hangouts, a male sanctuary where the boys got down and dirty over pool and beer. He'd always refused to take Belinda there. With Cade safely tucked away at the lodge, Belinda couldn't wait to violate his sacred space.

'I think you'll like what I have in mind,' Belinda told Val on the cellphone. 'I thought we'd let our hair down, go wild for once. Call it a pre-bachelorette party.'

'I'm not going to take my 4000-dollar laptop into a place called the Tarantula,' Val said. Belinda could visualise the sour face she was making. 'And I don't believe in pre-wedding flings – for either partner. Too much of a liability. If you want to be decadent, why not meet for latte and tiramisu at the Mezzanine?'

Right. A heaped helping of tiramisu was just what Val's figure needed, when she was hoping to squeeze into a size-eight wedding-dress.

'I don't want to go to the Mezzanine,' Belinda said. 'I can go to the Mezzanine and nibble pastries when I'm 75 years old. I'm in a hunting mood.'

'Hunting?' Val asked, with an exasperated snort. 'Belinda, you're getting married. If you're not faithful now, how on earth are you going to be faithful after the ceremony?'

'Cade and I are going to define fidelity for ourselves,' Belinda said.

'You mean Cade knows that you're sleeping with other men? And he approves?'

'He doesn't know yet, but I'll make sure he approves.'

'What if he doesn't? What if he calls off the wedding?'

'Then he'll call off the wedding. It won't be the end of *my* world.'

Belinda heard an alarmed silence on the other end of the cellphone. She could imagine how the gears in Val's brain must be churning as she calculated the risks. If Cade and Belinda broke up, the double ceremony would be called off. Val and Noah could get married by themselves, but without his best friend, Noah might have second thoughts.

Did Noah really want to get married? The question hovered on the airwaves between the two women. Val had to be feeling the deep-freeze of doubt.

'Belinda, let's discuss this reasonably. Meet me at my office in an hour.' Val's words took on a commanding edge as she shifted into her lawyer persona, trying to regain control.

'I'm not one of your clients, Val. You can't order me to be anywhere I don't want to be. To tell you the truth, I feel sorry for Noah. I wouldn't want to be led around by the balls for the rest of my life.'

Belinda snapped her cellphone shut, ending the conversation with a satisfying click. The phone started trilling immediately. Belinda shut it off and tossed it into her shoulder bag. Then she steered BELSBABY towards home. She did agree with Val on one point:

the neighbourhood where the Tarantula was located was no place to leave a valuable possession. If she was going to spend a steamy evening in hell, Belinda would take a cab.

Besides, she needed to take a shower, change her clothes and apply some serious make-up. Tonight she was going to shed her professional skin and unleash her inner slut for all to see.

The pool hall was already crowded when Belinda arrived. The din of drunken laughter and jukebox rock filled the dim, smoky room. Belinda struck a slinky pose in the doorway of the bar to let the patrons acknowledge her presence. Her figure was framed in a rectangle of red neon light from the rent-by-the-hour motel across the street, and she knew the impact would be devastating.

The way the crowd responded, Belinda might as well have been a purple unicorn stepping into the dive. Pool sticks and beer mugs were warily lowered as a roomful of blue-collar men, and their disgruntled girlfriends, gaped at the stunning vision. Belinda had dressed for maximum impact. She had squeezed her curves into a black fishnet catsuit, a garment she'd bought from a sleazy lingerie catalogue but had never dared to wear before. The catsuit sheathed her skin in a see-through layer of netting, with two skimpy black satin cups that barely covered her nipples. Over the catsuit she wore a black leather micro-mini that was little more than a nod to minimal standards of public decency. She wore black stiletto heels – fuck-me-twice pumps – and a bolero jacket made of synthetic leopard's fur with a black velvet collar. The jacket was too warm for the season, but Belinda couldn't resist. She was on the prowl tonight. Might as well give the men fair warning.

nd who wasn't, by now?) could
se of the shadowed paradise

came over Belinda. Something
ed up and saw a man standing
er. She couldn't see his features
igarette smoke, but his angular,
dressed in a casual but expen-
akis, was unmistakable.
whispered.

ut of her fingers and clattered on
p and frantically straightened her
't do anything about her whorish
ke-up, or the circle of males who'd
r peep-show. She'd wanted to give
tonight, but she hadn't expected
to be in the audience.
ter? See someone you recognise?'
as a knowing gleam in his eye.
ancé?' Belinda hissed. 'You son of a

rty laugh, coarsened by years of
o. Belinda should have known she
an with a gold fang. She tried to
the bar, but Nick seized her upper
and flailed, but his fingers held her
e couldn't tear herself out of his grip.
f that sweet ass of yours before the
aid.
etime. Cade!' Belinda cried. 'Get me

over to the pool table. He didn't seem
ry to rescue Belinda. In fact, his smile

The men had been warned, perhaps too effectively. They stood stone-still, like a roomful of statues, and watched Belinda stroll over to the bar. She resisted the urge to wipe the bar stool with a tissue before she sat down. She could play the princess with Cade, but these guys were made of tougher stuff.

'What'll you have?' asked the bartender. He was a burly, bearded fellow, a concrete slab of a man who looked like he wouldn't blink if you shot a flame-thrower under his nose. But when Belinda leaned forwards on her elbows, pressing her breasts between her upper arms to form a sweet gulch of cleavage, the giant blinked.

'I'll have an Old-Fashioned,' Belinda purred.

The bartender gulped. Someone in the bar sniggered. Belinda saw a maroon flush spreading along the frayed collar of his plaid workshirt.

'Never made one of those,' he admitted. 'Can't say as I'd know how.'

Belinda smiled. She flicked her tongue lightly across her upper lip. The bartender looked like he might faint.

'Give me your specialty, then,' she said. 'Whatever you do best.'

'Mort's specialty is a boilermaker,' said a male voice. 'Are you sure you're in the right place, sweetheart?'

Belinda turned on her barstool. She raised one exquisite leg and crossed it over the other, then leaned back against the bar, resting her arms against the scarred wood. From the blur of male faces, she singled out the wiseass who had spoken. He had the build of a construction worker, the face of a professional boxer and more tattoos than an entire fleet of merchant marines. He looked like he'd had his nose broken at least twice and, from the way he held his pool cue, Belinda would guess that he'd bashed a few noses himself.

'Trust me, "sweetheart",' Belinda said, 'I'm *always* in the right place.'

She slid off the barstool, sashayed up to the boxer and plucked the cue out of his hands. The boxer gave a long, low whistle.

'You play eight ball?' he asked.

Belinda gave him her patented sex-siren stare, a look that was guaranteed to divert a man's blood flow straight to his cock. 'I can play any game you want.'

'Well, Miss Game-Player, my name's Nick.'

'I'm Belinda.'

'Sure you want to play me?'

'Absolutely.'

'I call my shots,' Nick warned.

'So do I,' said Belinda. She pulled off her leopard-skin jacket and tossed it over a chair. 'Rack 'em.'

Belinda prayed she wasn't too rusty. She hadn't played the game since college, when she'd dated a clean-cut law student who was moonlighting as a pool shark. Pool was all about geometry, he had told her; winning the game required identifying the right lines and angles. But when Belinda played, winning required showing the right curves. When her opponent gained an advantage, all she had to do was bend way over the table, arching her lower back and tilting her bottom just enough to show a flash of panties or the hint of a garter belt, and he'd be too bedazzled to sink his next shot.

The boxer racked the balls while Belinda chalked the cue. She let him break, so she could check out his package as he leaned over to shoot. Men weren't the only ones who liked to gaze at a shapely pair of buns. This guy had a broad, meaty pair of glutes, a double slab of grade-A beef that looked solid enough to take

was looking carefully (a
have caught a glimp
between her thighs.

An uneasy feeling
wasn't right. She glan
at the bar, watching h
through the cloud of
well-tended physique
sive polo shirt and kh

'Oh, fuck,' Belinda

It was Cade.

The cue slipped o
the table. She stood u
skirt, but she couldn
outfit, her heavy ma
gathered to watch h
a killer performanc
her future husband

'What's the mat
Nick asked. There w

'You know my fi
bitch.'

Nick gave a d
whisky and tobac
couldn't trust a r
make a break for
arm. She twisted
like a vice, and sh

'I'll see more
night's over,' he s

'Not in this li
out of here!'

Cade strolled
to be in any hu

suggested that he was amused by her struggle with the pumped-up macho thug.

'Good job, Nick,' Cade said. 'Thanks for keeping an eye on her.'

'Wasn't hard, with her dressed like that.' Nick gave that filthy laugh again. The sound caused a twinge in Belinda's pussy. She hated her body for responding that way, but her shame only sharpened the tingling sensation.

'She looks like a real tart, doesn't she?' Cade asked. He crossed his arms and tapped his finger on his lip as he assessed his fiancée's appearance. 'You'd never know what a spoiled princess she is.'

'Spoiled, is she? I could take her down a peg.'

Nick was standing behind Belinda, holding her by both elbows now. His torso felt like a wall – a prison wall. His breath was hot on the back of her neck. Belinda had talked and teased and fucked her way out of a lot of messes in her lifetime, but she'd never gotten herself into anything like this.

'You're going to have to,' Cade agreed. 'I've given her lots of discipline, but she's obviously not afraid of anything I might do to her. She needs a firmer hand.'

'How did you know I was going to be here tonight?' Belinda demanded.

'Val called me. She told me what you had in mind, and I knew I had to intervene. You can't handle yourself at the Tarantula, princess.'

'I was doing fine until you showed up,' Belinda retorted. 'You were supposed to be up at the lodge all week.'

'I came back to the city to have dinner with a new investor. Good thing, too; I might have missed your little show. I called Nick and asked him to look out for you until I could get here. Nick, why don't we take Belinda back to the poker room?'

'Can't we go home and talk this over, Cade?' Belinda pleaded.

She didn't like the way this scene was unfolding. Cade had an unfamiliar hunger in his eyes. She knew he craved edgy sexual experiences, and that he loved to dominate her, but in the back of her mind she'd always secretly known that she held the reins. Tonight she wasn't so sure.

'I'm not in the mood for talking,' Cade said. 'Nick, do you feel like talking?'

'Nope.'

The men exchanged a comradely smile. Cade led his fiancée and her captor past a gauntlet of leering males. Every one of them wished he were Nick right now, and most of them would have given Belinda exactly the same treatment. Nick was shoving her along as if she were an inmate at a women's penitentiary. He held her close, so that her bottom kept bumping against his crotch, providing rock-hard evidence of how much he was enjoying his role.

The poker room was a smoky hole. A group of men sat hunched over a table, playing cards. Cade was the first to go in, then Nick pushed Belinda into the gloom.

'Get lost, guys. Game's over for now,' Nick announced. 'Go out and get a life. And clear off the table – we're going to be using it.'

Grumbling, the men scooped up their ashtrays, highball glasses, poker chips and grimy bills. Belinda was amazed that they were willing to clear out, much less clean up their mess. They looked like they'd been stuck to those chairs for years, like fungi growing on the walls of a cave. Nick must have a lot of clout in this dive.

The thought of Nick having any kind of power sent

chills up Belinda's spine, but it also added a knife-like edge to her desire. She could barely admit to herself that she was looking forward to what was going to happen to her, much less allow Cade and his tattooed henchman to see her enthusiasm.

Cade pulled up a chair and sat down. He leaned back, clasped his hands behind his head and propped up his heels on the poker table. With her arms restrained behind her back, Belinda felt like a juvenile delinquent standing up in court to be sentenced.

'OK, Belinda,' he said. 'It's time for your future husband to lay down some rules.'

Belinda fought the impulse to look down at her feet like a child being scolded. 'If we're going to have rules in our marriage, we should be making them together,' she said.

Nick sniggered. Belinda wished she could drive her stiletto heel into his toe, but she didn't dare.

'Fair enough,' Cade said. 'Give me your version.'

'First of all, I think we should be straightforward with each other about sex. If we're going to have other lovers, we should tell each other about them, not run around behind each other's backs.'

'That sounds like a man's rule to me,' Nick remarked.

Cade had the decency to look guilty for a second, but the guilt was soon replaced by an accusing glare. 'Are you saying you've already been having sex with other people, Belinda?'

'I follow my sexual impulses, Cade. I've always been that way. Sorry if you had a false image of me, but this is who I am.'

'Is that kind of freedom really what you want?' Cade asked.

'I want it for both of us,' Belinda said. 'But I want us to be open about what we do.'

Cade considered this for a moment. 'We wouldn't exactly have a traditional marriage, then.'

'Traditional means that the man fucks around to his heart's content, while the woman stays home,' Nick said.

'You're right,' Cade said with a chuckle. 'And that's not a bad deal, in my opinion. But I'd like to propose a compromise.'

'What kind of compromise?' Belinda asked suspiciously.

'Well, I agree that you should be able to have other lovers, but only on the condition that you accept punishment from me every time you look for sex outside the marriage.'

'How lame,' Belinda scoffed. 'That's no compromise; it's just a variation on the same tired old theme.'

'That's my final offer,' Cade said. 'Take it or leave it.'

'What if I leave it?'

'Then the wedding's off. I'll let you play your games, have your fun, but if you don't agree to my terms, you can go get a spineless sap to marry you. That shouldn't be hard. The world is full of men who can't stand up to their women.'

Cade and Belinda stared each other down. In their professional lives, both of them were tough negotiators, but they'd never faced off with each other. A current of fear shook Belinda from head to toe. She'd always been confident that Cade would do anything she wanted. Now, as he watched her with cold, impassive blue eyes and waited for her response, she saw how ruthless he could be.

'Well?' he pressed. 'What's it going to be? Do you agree to my terms?'

Belinda lowered her head. She let her tensed muscles go soft.

'Yes,' she said.

'Excellent. We'll start tonight. Nick, will you do the honours of punishing my fiancée?'

'Wait,' Belinda broke in. 'What am I being punished for? I didn't have sex with anyone tonight.'

'No, but you had a fling with one of my junior programmers. He confessed everything. The poor kid tried to resign over it, but I wouldn't let him; I knew the whole incident was your idea. And only a few hours before you seduced Tuan, you made love to Hailey at the lodge.'

'How did you know about Hailey and me?' Belinda cried.

'I tasted her on you, when you kissed me by the car. I know you now, Belinda. I used to hold you up on a pedestal, like some kind of plaster virgin, but I like you much better as a slut in designer clothing.'

'Cade, listen, I –'

'Nick, could we get on with it, before she talks her way out of this?' Cade interrupted.

'Sure thing, boss,' Nick said with relish. 'I've been waiting for this all night.'

The brute pushed Belinda over. She landed face-down on the poker table, her backside in the air. Without warning, Nick rucked up her leather skirt, bunching it around her waist. She knew he was giving her a thorough inspection, loving the way the black threads criss-crossed her bottom and thighs. She could hear him licking his chapped lips as he spread her legs apart. He tugged at the fabric of her catsuit, then let it snap back against her skin.

'Go ahead and rip that thing off her,' Cade said. 'I don't want to see her wearing that cheap outfit again.'

Eager as a kid at Christmas, Nick tore open the patch of netting that covered Belinda's bottom. The fishnet hadn't given Belinda much coverage, but she distinctly felt the shame of having her cheeks bared to the air. She gnawed her lower lip to keep from crying in humiliation.

'Can I feel her?' Nick asked Cade. His voice was thick with lust.

'For now, you'll only touch her to punish her,' Cade said. 'If you do a good job, we'll see about giving you some special privileges.'

What special privileges? Belinda wondered. Her heart hammered with terror as she thought of what a man like Nick might do to her. He could do things to a woman that sophisticated, well-educated, civilised men like Cade wouldn't even know about.

'Cade, please don't let him sodomise me,' Belinda whispered. From her prone position she looked up at her fiancé, letting her tears spill liberally down her cheeks.

'No one said anything about sodomy – yet,' Cade said, as he settled in to watch Belinda's ordeal. His tone was soothing, but his words didn't provide much reassurance. 'Be a good girl and follow the rules of our agreement, and I'll make sure you get exactly what's coming to you. No more, no less.'

Belinda's 'medicine' came sooner than she expected. She thought she'd get some kind of warm-up to her punishment, but Nick's hard, heavy palm struck her bottom before she knew what was happening. Cade had been right: he had a much firmer stroke, probably from years of rugged manual labour.

Belinda clung to the edge of the round table with all her might, squeezed her eyes shut and told herself that she was doing this for Cade. There was no romance or ceremony to Nick's spanking, just one masterful smack after another. With each blow, the tingling burn spread from her cheeks to her pussy. She found herself grinding her sex against the table in the aftermath of every swat, giving herself a sweet burst of pleasure to compensate for the pain.

'You like that treatment, don't you, you little tart?' Nick muttered between swats.

The truth was, Belinda did like it, much more than she'd ever admit. The catsuit, the bar, the pool table – everything about the evening had been leading her to this mortifying position. She'd never realised that she craved this kind of manhandling, but her body knew. Her pussy gave testimony to her enjoyment by sending a runnel of sap down her inner thigh. She prayed that Nick wouldn't see the evidence, but Belinda knew she was done for when he suddenly stopped spanking her.

'Your woman is dripping wet,' Nick reported to Cade. 'It's not my fault; I caught her rubbing herself on the table. She's trying to make herself come without you knowing it.'

Cade stood up. His crotch was level with Belinda's eyes. His erection strained against the fly of his trousers.

'Thanks for telling me,' Cade said. 'If my princess is going to have an orgasm, I don't want us to miss out. Why don't you finish her off? Take your time. I want her to service me while you're fondling her.'

Cade unzipped his khakis and freed his penis. The ruddy stalk jutted away from his body, towards Belinda's face. She tongued the head hungrily, anxious for the familiar taste of him. He didn't disappoint her. As soon as his cock met her lips, a warm liquid seeped into her mouth, filling it with a sour-sweet flavour that was unique to Cade. He pushed his hips forwards until his shaft was lodged deep in Belinda's throat, and she inhaled his musk through her nostrils. He kept a loving grip on the back of her neck as she sucked.

'You can feel her now, Nick,' Cade said huskily. 'Make my princess come.'

Nick slid his paw into the crevice between Belinda's thighs. He began to rub her pussy with bear-like motions, giving her a coarse stimulation she'd never felt before. His knuckles ground against her outer lips as his fingers worked at the inner folds. While he diddled her, he rubbed his denim-covered cock against the back of her thigh. The friction of the long, warm bulge intensified her pleasure. Though she didn't want Nick to enter her, she enjoyed the thought that she was turning him on.

Belinda pushed back against Nick's broad hand. He was fingering her at a brisk pace, and she closed her eyes, loosened her mouth on Cade's cock and focused on the swelling warmth in her pussy. Soon the warmth reached fever heat. Belinda clutched the table as hard as she could, bracing herself for the explosion. Cade stepped back to let her come, and Belinda cried out as her pussy filled Nick's palm with its juices.

'Switch places with me,' Cade ordered Nick.

The two men traded positions. Cade stepped between Belinda's legs, took hold of her hips and slid into her from behind. It felt so good to be ridden by the man she loved, instead of a dangerous stranger. Cade was pumping her so hard she knew he wouldn't last long. Though she couldn't see his face, Belinda knew how Cade would look when he came: how his forehead would form a furrow down the middle, and how his teeth would clench. She waited for the familiar hissing sound, like steam escaping from a kettle, that meant his last spasm had ended, and then she turned around to smile at him.

'Thank you, my love,' she said.

'Hey,' Nick protested. 'Don't I get to come too?'

Nick's lower lip quivered. He looked like a kid who'd missed his own birthday party. Belinda felt sorry for the thug who'd punished her, especially after that gratifying spanking.

Belinda turned to Cade. 'May I?' she asked.

'Go ahead,' Cade said. 'He deserves a reward.'

Belinda got off the table, stood up and yanked down her skirt.

'Take out your cock,' she said to Nick. 'It's your turn.'

Belinda knelt in front of Nick and watched him try to work the buttons on his fly. With such big, clumsy fingers, it was a wonder he could put on his own pants at all. His excitement didn't help him, either. Belinda had to do most of the work herself, but the effort was worth it. The more of his body she uncovered, the more she wanted to see, and by the time she was done, Nick's jeans were crumpled around his ankles. His thighs could have been sculpted by a master artist, and his engorged penis, arching out at a splendid angle, was a priceless specimen.

I should collect cocks, not art, Belinda said to herself. She wanted to do something special for Nick, a gesture that would thank him for the orgasm he'd given her, while making Cade just the slightest bit jealous.

Belinda lay back on the floor, propping herself up on her elbows. While Nick stared down at her, his cock bobbing expectantly, she brought her knees to her chest, then raised her legs in a languid motion. Bending her knees, she lowered her calves until they were level with Nick's groin. Then she arched her long feet, encircling Nick's prick, and began to slide them back and forth along the shaft.

Belinda's yoga instructor had taught her that feet, often considered little more than shoehorns by a lot of Westerners, were precious tools for aligning and stabilising the body. Belinda had also learned, through her own research, that feet could be used as instruments of pleasure. Keeping her knees parted, so that Nick could look down into the shiny pink cleft between her thighs, Belinda went to work. While she massaged the shaft of his penis with her soles, she tickled the upper ridge with her toes. He rewarded her with a groan of disbelief.

'What are you doing to me?' he asked.

'Giving you the first foot-job of your life,' she said.

'Please don't stop,' he begged.

'Don't worry,' Belinda laughed. 'I won't. I'm just getting the knack of this.'

Belinda moved her feet like a dancer, manipulating Nick's penis, catching the head between her big toe and second toe and nudging at the groove between his balls. He was rocking back and forth on his heels, whimpering in ecstasy. Belinda tightened her grip on the root of his cock and pulled aggressively, using her strong thighs to intensify the pressure. Cade had always told her that a woman could never stroke a man's cock as hard as he wanted her to; maybe this technique was the answer.

It was the answer for Nick. He threw his head back, gave a mighty grunt and held onto Belinda's ankles as he rained over her legs in copious bursts.

'You've never done that to me before,' Cade said accusingly after Nick had left the two of them alone. Belinda was trying to pull herself together, but it wasn't easy to look decent when you were wearing nothing but a scrap of fishnet that couldn't have held a single fish. Belinda only hoped that there weren't any undercover vice cops at the Tarantula tonight.

'I was saving it for our honeymoon,' Belinda said.

'And you tried out this new move on Nick instead?' Cade looked wounded.

'Nick has a very firm hand. You said so yourself,' said Belinda with a shrug. 'I thought he deserved something unique. Besides, we're operating under new rules now, remember?'

'I remember the rules, all right.' Cade clutched Belinda's bottom and squeezed so hard she could feel bruises forming under his fingers. 'Wait till I get you home, missy.'

'I'm shaking with excitement,' Belinda quipped.

She meant it.

8 Breeding in Captivity

Hailey stayed away from Noah for the next two weeks. It wasn't hard to avoid him. He stayed in his room at the lodge for hours on end, working on the preliminary art for Shiva Systems' next release, and Hailey spent most of her time at the zoo, trying to hammer out a draft of her thesis while working on a research protocol for the summer. When she wasn't working in her borrowed cubby-hole in the administrative trailer, Hailey was out in the park, observing the cats and helping out wherever she could.

Since the evening at Rick's cabin, Hailey had kept the cat handler at arm's length. He invited her to go hiking one weekend, then asked her if she'd like to drive into town to see a movie. Hailey refused. After she'd turned him down the second time, he gave up and went in search of more accommodating females.

Hailey wasn't the only female who lacked interest in sex these days. Seka was indifferent to the mate that had been selected for her and transported with great care from a metropolitan zoo. Rick had been meticulous about tracking Seka's oestrus. He had arranged her introduction to the male with all the paternal pride of a father preparing for his daughter's first formal dance, going so far as to design a special 'mixing enclosure' for the first copulation. He had logged all of Seka's responses to the male, and had been vigilant about tracking positive vocalisations and other cues of interest.

In spite of all his efforts, he couldn't convince Seka that sex was on her list of top priorities. The white feline seemed far more interested in eating and self-grooming than in making herself accessible to her would-be mate. Her first introduction to the male had been promising: the two cats had made visual contact between the bars, and had seemed interested in getting to know each other. But their first physical intro had taken a hostile turn, and Rick had had to separate the cats with a hose before their aggression exploded into a full-blown fight.

'I don't know what's wrong with her,' Rick complained. 'We've gone by the book at every step. We've invested so much time, hope and money in breeding Seka, it's unbelievable. If it doesn't work out, it'll be a disaster.'

'A disaster for you, not for her,' Hailey snapped. 'If she's anything like human females, she doesn't enjoy sex under pressure.'

Rick narrowed his eyes. 'Are you trying to tell me something?'

'No. Well, maybe.'

'You and Seka seem to have a lot in common lately.'

'So you've noticed,' Hailey said.

'How could I not? Something's going on with you. What's wrong?'

It was a warm, clear day, and Hailey was taking advantage of the sunshine. Rick had found her sunbathing beside an ornamental pond at the zoo. She was wearing a white string bikini top and her faded denim cut-offs, and she could tell by the light in Rick's eyes that she looked appetising. Unfortunately, Rick didn't stir her desire any more.

'I don't feel like talking about it,' Hailey said. She flopped down on her towel and closed her eyes.

'Fair enough,' Rick said. 'I'll be around if you change your mind.'

He stood over her for a few seconds, then she heard the soles of his work boots crunching across the grass. Though Hailey had lost her lust for Rick, she had come to appreciate him in other ways. He was great with the cats, he could fix anything with duct tape and, most importantly for Hailey, he was an expert at balancing concern for his friends with a respect for their privacy.

Hailey dozed off in the sun's mellow warmth. She woke up to the sound of footsteps circling her towel.

'I still don't want to talk about it,' she warned. 'Go away.'

'Rick said you wanted to see me.'

Hailey sat up. She shielded her eyes with her hand and squinted up at the man standing over her. Deep in her belly, where all her desires lived, a flame flared back into life.

'Noah! I never said –'

Hailey stopped herself from finishing the sentence. What was Rick doing? Trying to play matchmaker with Hailey, since his efforts with Seka had been a flop? Hailey didn't know whether to feel mad at Rick for interfering, or grateful that he'd sent Noah out to talk to her. As Noah lowered himself down onto the towel beside her, she decided that she definitely felt grateful. Seeing his dark eyes set so intently on her face was like breathing in a fresh breeze off the ocean after months of being landlocked.

'I wanted to talk to you anyway,' Noah said. 'I have to apologise.'

'For what?'

'For being antisocial. You're my guest, and I've been ignoring you. No, that's not right. I haven't been ignoring you.' He looked down at Hailey's brown legs, stretched out on the green towel. 'That would be impossible. I've been holed up in my room because I needed to make a decision.'

'If it takes that long for you to make a decision, I'd never let you order a pizza for me,' Hailey said with a laugh.

'This was a lot more serious than a pizza. It's about me and you.'

A swarm of bees seemed to have invaded Hailey's stomach. She couldn't wait to hear what Noah had to say, but at the same time she was dreading it.

'We keep missing each other,' Noah began. 'It seems that whenever one of us is ready to talk about this, the other finds an excuse to run away. We're both scared, for different reasons. You know what I'm talking about, don't you?'

Hailey swallowed. She tried to answer, but her throat was too dry.

'When you came to my office the other night, I acted like an idiot,' Noah went on. 'I wanted more than anything to just get down on the floor and fuck you, but I couldn't. I'm not a man who gives up easily when he makes a commitment. That night, I was still committed to Val.'

'And you're not any more?' Hailey managed to say.

Noah shook his head. His pitch-black eyes were more serious than she'd ever seen them. 'When I finally got around to calling her, I told her that I didn't want to marry her.'

Hailey looked down at the grass. She plucked at the blades nervously. 'What's going to happen next?'

'I'm claiming what I want,' Noah said.

He stood up and held out his hand. Still dazed from her nap, the warmth of the sun and the shock of what Noah had said, Hailey took a while to collect herself, and Noah had to drag her to her feet. The strength and determination in his grip surprised her.

'Come on,' he urged. 'I've been waiting for this for a long time.'

'Waiting for what?'

'You'll find out soon enough.'

Twilight was setting over the park, cloaking the animal compounds in a mild summer dusk. The zoo was closed, but there were still a few employees closing up. Hailey wondered what they must think, seeing the zoo's major benefactor forcibly dragging a woman across the park. If he'd only been pulling Hailey by her hair, they would have looked like the perfect Neanderthal couple.

'Can't you at least tell me where we're going?' Hailey asked.

'We're going to fulfil one of my oldest fantasies,' Noah said mysteriously.

He was leading her towards a cinder-block building at the distant end of the park, a place that was out of earshot of any of the departing employees. Hailey had never been inside the building, but she knew that it served as storage for extra feed and supplies. Noah unlocked the door and led Hailey inside. He pulled on a long chain that dangled from the ceiling, and a hanging lamp went on, illuminating a broad wooden table. On top of the table sat something that took Hailey's breath away – not because it was an unusual object to see at a zoo, but because Noah's evil plan was starting to take shape before her eyes.

'So *this* is your fantasy?' she asked.

The cage, designed for transporting large animals, was just big enough for a woman Hailey's size. If anyone had asked her to describe herself sexually, she would have said that she was hip, free-spirited, open to experimentation. But then, no one had ever asked her to do anything like this.

'I've had this fantasy since I was thirteen,' Noah said. 'All you have to do is sit inside and let me watch you . . . and touch you.'

Noah stood behind her, easing her closer to the cage. His fingers played up and down her ribs, and his breath tickled the hairs on the back of her neck. In the small of her back, she felt hard proof of how excited he was by the image of a naked Hailey sitting behind bars. The more she thought about it, the more she caught on to his excitement. But she couldn't let Noah have his way so fast.

'Noah, cages are for animals,' Hailey said, trying to sound stern and disapproving.

'That's why I thought of you when I bought this one,' Noah replied.

'You bought this just for me?'

'It arrived this morning. Look, it's perfect for you.'

Noah demonstrated how the simple design worked. The cage had a door that opened in the back, and a feeding slot in the front. The floor was covered with foam padding, to protect Hailey's hands and knees. Best of all, he explained, the bars were spaced wide enough to give him easy access to Hailey's body.

'Is this really an animal-transport cage?' Hailey asked suspiciously. 'The bars are too far apart for a pet. I'd be willing to bet my entire fall stipend that you ordered this from a bondage outlet somewhere.'

'It's from a company in San Francisco. They build slave equipment,' he said, with shy pleasure. 'What do you think?'

Hailey's physical reaction to the cage was about as politically incorrect as it was possible to get. Her nerves were buzzing, and the inner folds of her pussy were already feeling slick and moist. Parker, a militant feminist, would die if she saw this contraption. And if she knew how Hailey was responding to it, she'd disown her friend, and probably kill her for good measure.

'I hope you don't think this means I'm going to be your slave,' Hailey said. 'I'm not that kind of woman at all.'

'I know you're not.' Noah laughed. 'That's why I haven't stopped thinking about doing this to you since the day we met.'

'You've had this in mind for me all along?'

'I told you it was one of my oldest fantasies. I just haven't found the right woman to help me live it out, until you.'

Hailey and Noah had unconsciously moved closer together as they talked, and now they were all but touching. Without asking permission, Noah put his arms around Hailey and untied her white bikini top. He pushed the shoulder straps down her shoulders, pulled off the scrap of fabric, and let it fall to the floor. She thought back to the first time he had undressed her, in the Shiva Systems building, and how tentative he had been. She liked both sides of him, but the assertive version was much more exciting.

'So you *do* know how to be dominant,' Hailey said.

'Of course I do. Take your shorts and shoes off,' he ordered.

Hailey's legs wobbled as she unbuttoned her shorts and unlaced her sneakers. After she'd pushed off her shorts, she stood naked in front of Noah and let him look her up and down. Hailey didn't usually feel self-conscious without her clothes on; her body was fit and supple, and she liked the way she felt inside it. But tonight she was unnaturally aware of how she must look to the man who was checking her out. Did he think her breasts were too small? Her hips too narrow? Her legs were spangled with scars, and she hadn't waxed her bikini line in so long that she was starting to look as untamed as some of the animals around here. Noah was an artist, and the women he designed were way beyond any human ideal.

'Well?' Hailey said, with a nervous laugh. 'What do you think? Can an ex-tomboy measure up to a goddess like Yulana?'

Noah didn't say anything for so long that Hailey was afraid she'd flunked his visual inspection.

'I'm only an artist,' he finally said. 'Not even a great one. Do you think I could design anything half as hot as you?'

For once in her life, Hailey didn't know what to say. She just stood there, speechless, while Noah opened the cage.

'Get in,' he said. 'You're mine for the night.'

He had set a footstool next to the table so that Hailey could step up into the cage. Climbing into the structure was awkward but, once she was inside, Hailey found that she fitted comfortably, as long as she didn't try to stand up or stretch out.

'Now I know how the animals feel,' she said.

'That's the whole idea,' said Noah with a sly grin. 'Confinement is going to bring out the beast in you.'

He locked the latch on the cage. Now Hailey couldn't get out, even if she wanted to. She was surprised at how she reacted to the click of metal on metal. The sound made her captivity real; she was truly trapped. If Noah decided to leave, she'd be stuck here for the night. At this hour, there was no one left in the park to hear her if she screamed.

She'd have to work extra hard to please her captor.

Hailey shifted onto all fours, then lowered herself

onto her elbows and raised her bottom. She gave Noah her sultriest stare, the one that could ignite a four-alarm fire below a man's belt line.

'What do you want me to do?' she purred.

'Hold still, just the way you are.'

Noah walked around the cage, studying Hailey from all angles. He took slow, careful steps, as if the vision in front of him might disappear if he made the wrong move.

'I remember the day we got the clouded leopard,' Noah said. 'I couldn't believe he was real. How could a guy like me be responsible for such a rare, magnificent creature? That's how I feel tonight.'

Standing behind Hailey, he reached through the bars of the cage and lightly rubbed the back of her neck. The soothing caress took the edge off Hailey's fear of being closed in, and she began to relax into her new role. She lengthened her spine and realised that there was room to stretch out a little, if she arched her back. Noah's fingers ran along her vertebrae, from her neck to her tailbone and back again. Each time he made the sweep along her lumbar curve, she raised her hips a bit more, until her bottom was almost pressed against the upper crossbars of the cage.

Now that he'd sent Hailey into a trance, Noah turned his attention from her back to her flanks. His touch was assertive, soothing and sensual, all at the same time. Hailey deepened the curve in her spine, giving him full access to anything he wanted to explore. He ran the flat of his hand along the backs of her thighs, then up and down the toned inner muscles. Just when Hailey was about to growl with impatience for him to touch her between her legs, Noah slid his hand under her buttocks and gripped her entire sex. He gave a sigh of satisfaction when her legs began to quake.

'You like that, don't you?' he asked.

That question could only be rhetorical; a man would have to be missing all five senses not to perceive how aroused Hailey was. He was inspecting her like a prized pet, and she was loving every second of it. When he parted her outer lips and tickled her clit with his middle finger, she pushed her bottom all the way against the bars and made an imploring noise deep in her throat. Noah rubbed her erect button until the friction was almost unbearable, but before Hailey could lose herself in the sensation he pulled away.

'Not yet,' Noah said. 'I've got you all night, and I'm going to make the most of it.'

He came around to the front of the cage. Hailey lifted herself onto her hands and knees again. Noah reached between the bars to cup her face in his hands, and she could smell her own scent on his fingers – a fierce musk, more potent than usual. When he bent down to kiss her through the bars, she thought she'd go out of her mind. His tongue, pushing forcefully into her mouth, was a sweet violation. The kiss he'd given her in the kitchen was child's play compared to the powerful lip-lock he delivered tonight.

Noah ended the kiss with her wanting more. He straightened up and pulled his shirt over his head, then unzipped his jeans and got out of those too. For the first time, Hailey got to feast her eyes on his naked body. Without his clothes, there was nothing to hide his physique, and Hailey could admire the athletic economy of his torso, hips and thighs. Smooth hair etched his abdominal muscles, thickening into a sleek black pelt around his cock, which rose away from his body at a proud angle, broadcasting his desire.

Hailey had never experienced such a keen contrast of emotions: an impatience with being confined, combined with a feeling of being freed from the constraints of her human self. Underlying this intoxicating mix was a sense of being wanted more than she'd ever been wanted in her life.

'Does this mean you're going to let me out?' Hailey pushed her breasts against the bars and rubbed them up and down, the tips hardening as they made contact with the steel.

'No such luck. We're just getting to the good part.' Noah stepped up to the cage and opened the feeding slot. The table was just high enough for him to ease his cock into the opening.

Hailey didn't have to be told what he wanted her to do next. She lowered her mouth onto Noah's cock and swept its circumference with her tongue, savouring his taste. Closing her eyes, she let her other senses guide her as she stroked his shaft with her fingertips, getting to know its unique contours, anticipating how it would feel when it was filling her pussy. For once she didn't have to rush through the smells, sounds or flavours of sex. She was trapped in the cage, and secure in the knowledge that this was only the first of many times that she and Noah would be together.

Noah gripped the bars of the cage and groaned when Hailey swallowed him halfway. She rolled his erect penis around in her mouth, teasing him the way he'd teased her earlier, until his hips began to move back and forth of their own accord. She kept up with his rhythm, lifting her head up and down in time to his thrusts. When she opened her eyes, she saw his hard abdomen moving in and out like a bellows with his deepening breaths.

'Suck harder,' he ordered, his voice rough and guttural.

That crude command, coming from a man like Noah, drove Hailey into a frenzy. She held on tight to the root of Noah's cock and picked up the pace, using her hips to propel herself back and forth. She threw her whole body into the act, intensifying Noah's pleasure with her momentum. Soon she was rewarded with a harsh cry, a series of sharp thrusts and a surge of warm jism in her mouth.

'Mmmm,' she said.

The sounds of pleasure that she made as she cleaned his cock with her tongue sounded rich, rumbling and unfamiliar. Noah smoothed her hair in a grateful grooming gesture that made her feel like she was being petted. Hailey rolled over onto her side, then onto her back. Noah came up beside her and took advantage of her prone position to rub her belly. After a moment or two of that, Hailey was purring in earnest. She spread her legs and lifted her bottom in a frank request for pleasure.

'All right,' Noah said, laughing softly. 'You've earned it.'

He stood at the foot of the cage and massaged her muff, which was soaking wet by now, until Hailey's purr turned into a high crooning. While he was touching her, Noah never stopped watching Hailey; his dark eyes registered every move she made under his hand. An artist to the core, Noah seemed to love watching the effects of his fingers on Hailey's body, the responses she made when he touched her at different angles and applied pressure in different degrees.

'How do you like this?' he asked.

Hailey couldn't come up with a decent answer. 'Fuck me,' was all she could say.

'Not yet.'

'Now!'

She didn't recognise the coarse, crude growl that came out of her mouth. It came from some primal, alternate identity that she'd never met before. This new being wanted to tear its way out of that cage, to get free and do what she was meant to do. She grabbed the bars above her head and shook them with all her might, until the steel cage rattled like a flimsy crate in a hurricane. When Noah tried to calm her by stroking her belly again, she lashed out and tried to bite his hand.

Noah stepped back from the cage. 'Settle down,' he warned. 'Or I'll have to leave you in there until you're calm again.'

Hailey gave the bars one last shake, then fell back. Currents of agitation still coursed through her muscles, but she forced herself to relax. It was warm inside the warehouse, and she'd only made herself hotter by fighting. Her thighs were jewelled with sweat, and she was flushed all over from exertion.

'Are you going to behave?' Noah asked.

Hailey nodded. Moving cautiously, Noah slid his hand back into the cage and caressed her throat. When he was confident that she wasn't going to attack him, he ran his fingers along her collar-bone, then down the damp groove between her breasts.

'That's a good girl,' he said in a low, soothing voice. 'Now, if you can behave yourself, I'll let you out of the cage. Are you ready?'

'Way past ready,' Hailey whispered.

Noah opened the door of the cage. Hailey had to roll

over onto her stomach and crawl out backwards. Being trapped in such a small space for so long had left her stiff and sore. Noah watched her stretch. She knew he was getting turned on again by the sight of her naked body, so she played it up for him, standing against a wall with her hands flat against the cinder block and extending herself as far as she could.

'Stay like that,' Noah said. 'Don't move.'

Hailey felt him come up behind her. He pressed down on the small of her back, making her bottom rise to the level of his groin. He circled one arm around her waist, then took hold of the scruff of her neck with his free hand. He nudged his knee between her thighs to open her legs.

Hailey had always thought that when Noah fucked her for the first time, he'd enter her slowly, romantically, while gazing into her eyes and whispering something sweet and profound. She gasped when he drove himself into her without the least bit of warning. He held onto her with a steady grip while he pounded her from behind, thrusting so ferociously that she wondered if Noah had disappeared and let some other guy step in. Soon his pace got so fast and furious that Hailey had to lean into the wall to keep from falling, her fingernails clawing at the cinder block. This was the kind of crude, nasty fucking that she'd always craved, the kind that men who loved you never wanted to deliver. The fact that she was getting this brutal treatment from Noah drove her crazy.

The rapid percussion of Noah's cock against her hyper-aroused sex drove her to a quick, fierce climax. As the tide overwhelmed her, Noah ground his fist into her cunt, turning her orgasm into a rough, tumbling river ride that didn't seem to have an end. Somewhere in the midst of it she felt Noah's grip on her tighten, and she could tell by the way his body was heaving that he was coming along with her.

After the storm passed, Hailey and Noah eased their damp, steaming bodies to the floor. They lay down together on a pile of canvas – not exactly a bed of roses, but Hailey had already been so wracked by sensation that the fabric's rough texture didn't bother her. She thought they'd curl up in each other's arms and go to sleep, but Noah wasn't in a napping mood. He lay down on his back and rolled Hailey over so that she was lying on top of him, then pushed her into a sitting position. Unbelievably, she could already feel his penis stirring underneath her.

'You can't be ready again,' Hailey said. 'You'd think you were sixteen!'

Noah grinned. 'Blame it on the cage. I've never seen anything like that. You were incredible.'

'Was it as good as all your fantasies?'

'It was way, way better.'

Hailey slid Noah's cock, now fully hard, back into her pussy. Her bruised inner flesh protested at first, but soon her juices began to flow again, easing the motions. She rocked back and forth, riding Noah's cock, with her hands planted in the centre of his chest. His heart beat steadily under her palms. When she came again – this time in a softer succession of ripples – he never took his eyes off her.

'This has never happened to me before,' Hailey gasped.

'What's never happened?'

'I've never come that way with a guy like you,' Hailey said, sinking back down onto his chest. She lay against his side and nuzzled against his arm, inhaling his tangy, masculine scent.

'You mean a nice guy?' There was a sad note in his voice.

'No. I mean with a man I was in love with.'

The rise and fall of Noah's chest stopped abruptly. For a few seconds, he didn't breathe. 'Did you just say you're in love with me?'

Hailey never heard Noah's question. He tried to shake her awake, but she had fallen into a blissfully heavy sleep. She slept like an animal after a satisfying feed, without a single dream.

When Noah called Cade on his cellphone and told him that he needed to cut his business short and drive back to Sasquanatee County the next day, Cade knew something was wrong. When Noah said that he wanted to meet Cade at the Wagon Wheel Tavern instead of at the lodge, Cade knew something was seriously wrong.

Fond memories of debauchery filled Cade's mind as he stepped through the door of the roadhouse. He had spent many an evening at the Wheel back in the old days, getting smashed while he listened to local bands and tried to pick up women. The place used to rock with the sounds of grunge music, the lights were lurid and low, and after midnight the liquor and the women were so easy to obtain that you were all but swimming in booze and female flesh.

At two o'clock on a weekday afternoon, the Wheel had only one customer. Noah sat at a table in the corner, a pitcher of beer and a bottle of liquor in front of him. A smarmy country song was playing on the jukebox and, as Cade watched, Noah slammed down a shot, then poured another from the bottle.

Noah never drank hard liquor. He never listened to country music.

Cade's best friend was in love.

'What's the matter, buddy?' Cade asked, sliding onto the bench across from Noah. They had shared a lot of drinks at this roadhouse but, now that Cade thought about it, they had only come here to get plastered when one of them was going through a heavy emotional ordeal.

'I have a confession to make,' Noah said.

Noah's speech wasn't slurred yet, which meant that they could still have a rational discussion. In fact, the alcohol didn't seem to be affecting him at all. He looked serious, determined and completely in control.

'What's that?' Cade poured himself a beer.

Noah took a deep breath. 'The game's over. I took Hailey for myself.'

Cade, who'd been lifting the mug to his lips, coughed into his foam. He spluttered for a few seconds while he tried to gather his thoughts. He knew he shouldn't feel betrayed – he was in his thirties, a successful CEO and about to get married to an incredible woman – but for some reason Noah's words hit him hard. When he'd said the game was over, he'd meant that it was over for good. Cade had never been able to swallow the idea that this phase of their lives was going to end; now the reality of it was being shoved in his face.

'That's hard to believe,' Cade said. 'In all the time we've been friends, you've never let me down. The game only had one rule, and you broke it. Do you know how hard it's been for me, holding back with every girl so you and I could take her together?'

'You're talking like we're still in college,' Noah said. 'Hailey's not a girl; she's a full-grown woman. I wanted her, and I took her. What's wrong with me taking something that I want? When have I ever stood up to you, or anyone else, and gone after what I need?'

'Nothing's wrong with that at all. About time you grew a back-bone, Noah.'

The two men glanced up to see who had broken into their argument. Rick was standing over their table, looking pleased with himself.

'What the hell are you smiling about?' Cade grumbled. 'You look like you just got laid again.'

'Not me,' Rick said. 'Seka. She finally accepted the male. They mated twelve times this afternoon. That beats all my personal records.'

'That's terrific!' Noah beamed. He gave Rick a congratulatory slap on the shoulder. 'Sit down and have a drink with us. This calls for a celebration.'

'Be glad to.'

Rick sat down next to Noah, who called the waitress to bring them a fresh mug and shot glass.

'Hold on, Noah,' Cade interrupted. 'We were having an important conversation. You had me rush all the way out here because you needed to tell me something. If you want to spill your guts in front of Mr Wild Kingdom, that's fine, but I'm not leaving until I find out what's wrong.'

'Sounds like Noah's finally standing up for himself,' Rick said, unruffled by Cade's jab. 'My guess is that he wanted to make it official.'

'Stay out of this, Rick. We don't need a mediator,' Cade said.

'I disagree,' said Noah. 'I think that's exactly what we need. Rick used to do this professionally. He's probably the best mediator we could ask for.'

'Rick's no good to us. He used to dedicate his life to breaking up marriages.'

'You're wrong, Cade,' Rick said. 'I never broke up a marriage; I helped people end their relationships without killing each other. Believe it or not, I spent a hell of a lot of time trying to reconcile couples. It never worked, not once. That's one of the big reasons I gave it up. Too much pain, especially when there were kids involved. I'd rather work with wild animals than a fighting human couple any day.'

'Give me some advice, then,' Noah said. 'Am I better off ending my marriage before it starts?'

Rick gave Noah a curious look. 'You need a divorce attorney to answer that question?'

'He knows the answer to the question,' Cade said. 'He just needs someone else to tell him he's right.'

'Listen, if there's one thing I tried to do for my clients, it was to try to get their hearts and brains to work in tandem. I've always believed that humans would be much smarter if we followed our instincts. If you don't love this woman, don't marry her. It'll be the smartest decision you ever make.'

Cade smacked his forehead in fake disbelief. 'I never thought this day would come. I agree with Rick. Did you hear the man, Noah? Follow your instincts.'

'It's always worked for me,' Rick said with a shrug.

'I think we need another round.' Noah poured three more shots from the bottle. 'I'd like to propose a toast – to getting divorced before I get married.'

'How about to not getting divorced *or* married?' Rick suggested. 'Personally, I'd rather drink to fucking around.'

'And I'll drink to getting married, and still getting to fuck around,' Cade put in.

The three men solemnly raised their glasses. A joyous buzz was spreading through Cade's being. Noah's break-up with Val was the best news he'd heard since Belinda told him she wanted an open marriage. Rick was turning out to be a decent guy. Life was good.

'OK, Noah,' Cade said. He folded his arms and rested them on the table. 'Let's get down to business. When are you going to break the news to Val that the wedding's off?'

Noah reddened. 'I already told her. Last night. I was going to wait to talk it over with you, but I couldn't do it. You and Belinda are going to have to get married alone.'

'You told her?' Cade laughed. 'And she hasn't come up here for a final showdown?'

'That showdown's going to happen in the city,' Noah said, his face turning grim. 'I'm going to need some legal counsel, since Val and I own property together.'

'Don't look at me,' said Rick. 'I'm out of that life. All I can do is give you a referral and another piece of advice – let her take what she wants. Whatever it is, it's not a fraction of what it'll cost if you fight with her. The lawyers will eat you alive, then pick your bones and leave them out to dry.'

'You're probably right,' Noah admitted. 'She's got it in for me. I thought she'd cry, get upset about me leaving her, but all she did was scream about all the money she'd spent on the wedding.'

'Good riddance.' Rick shuddered.

'You didn't arrange this little party just so you could tell me about Val,' Cade said to Noah. 'You've got something else brewing. Spit it out.'

'Well,' said Noah, 'my other big announcement is that I'm in love with Hailey. The best part is, it goes both ways. She loves me too.'

Rick gave Cade an inscrutable smile. 'Guess you're officially out of the running, Cade. This must be a first for you.'

'Hey, I could've had Hailey if I'd wanted her,' Cade

blustered. 'You should know; you saw us together at the park.'

'How far did you go?' Noah asked accusingly.

'Don't give me that look,' Cade protested. 'Hailey and I fooled around a little, but it was nothing serious. I was saving the grande finale for you.'

'Ah. So all the stories are true,' Rick said. 'I thought they were just local legends.'

'What stories?'

'People around here say that the two of you are a tag team. You chase the same women, then you engage them in a little three-way action.'

Noah avoided looking at Cade. 'Rumours,' he muttered.

'Nope. Those tales are true,' said Cade. He poured himself another shot and knocked it back, then chased it with a satisfying gulp of cold beer. 'We've been playing our game for years, since we were room-mates in college.'

'I'm all for a threesome now and then,' Rick said. 'But Hailey deserves better than to be the prize in some male-bonding competition. You both know it.'

Noah hung his head. Cade didn't flinch from Rick's stare, but an unfamiliar emotion was welling in his gut. It took him a few moments to recognise the queasiness as shame. He'd always taken pride in his sexual conquests, especially the ones he'd made with Noah. With Rick giving him the evil eye, and Noah staring down at the table like a chastised schoolboy, those exploits seemed cheap and easy.

'Do what you want, but if Hailey gets hurt, I'm going to be one furious son of a bitch,' Rick said. He finished his beer, then got up from the table. 'Gentlemen, thanks for the drink. I've got to go see to my one and only.'

Cade and Noah sat at the table, sipping their beer.

After Rick had roared off in his truck to check on the tigers, Cade broke the silence.

'You're serious about Hailey, aren't you?'

Noah nodded. He was starting to get misty-eyed. Cade hoped it was just the whisky. He was willing to give Noah a bit of leeway for being an artist, but he wasn't prepared for an afternoon of sentimental boozing.

'She's the one I want,' Noah said. 'For once I'm in love with a woman that I didn't design myself. I could stay here with her forever, never go back to civilisation. We'd live in a state of nature, walking around nude and making love in the woods ...'

'Wait one red-hot minute.' Cade broke into Noah's reverie. 'We've got another product deadline coming up early next year. I'll let you have your little honeymoon, but you're going to have to come back to the city soon. You're the head of the creative team. Without you, our graphics department is useless.'

'I know. But I'm crazy about Hailey,' said Noah.

He was painting designs on the table-top with his fingertip, using the condensation from his beer mug. The shapes he was drawing looked suspiciously like a female body. Noah must have sex on the brain.

'If you feel that way about her, she's yours,' Cade said. 'The game's over, like you said.'

'It's the end of an era,' Noah sighed in agreement.

Cade sipped his beer reflectively. He found his eyes wandering over to the plump, heart-shaped bottom of the Wagon Wheel's copper-haired waitress, who was leaning over the bar as she polished the brass fixtures. At one time, the voluptuous beauty would have made a fine afternoon's sport for him and Noah.

'Go ahead,' said Noah. 'I know what's going through that primal brain of yours. I'll be fine on my own.'

'You sure?' Cade asked. 'Don't want to join me for one last –'

'No,' Noah said. 'It's never going to happen again. I mean it this time.'

'Fair enough.'

Cade pushed away from the table and sauntered over to the bar to pursue his instincts on his own. The redhead tossed her hair and watched him approach. Cade winked at her, and her lily-white skin turned as pink as a freshly spanked ass. The end of the game might be bittersweet, but it didn't have to kill him.

9 Triple Play

Hailey was a fixture at the park now. The animals knew her, the employees and volunteers knew her, and no one looked twice any more when she strolled around in a bikini top and barely-there cut-offs on warm days.

Well, almost no one. Noah definitely noticed, and Rick still gave her a lustful once-over now and then. But Rick's interest had mellowed into an abstract appreciation; he knew she wasn't interested in him.

'You've really settled down, haven't you?' Rick commented one day, as she was helping him out on the feeding rounds.

Hailey narrowed her eyes at him. 'Are you saying I'm getting stodgy and boring?'

'Not exactly,' Rick said, eyeing her cleavage. 'You're as hot as ever, but you don't give the impression of being on the prowl any more.'

'I guess I'm not. You know, it's been at least two months since I went out.'

'Sounds like you miss it.'

'I do.'

Hailey thought longingly of her club days – slinking like a lynx through the urban jungle, watching lithe young bodies gyrate to the thump of house music. Noah was a homebody. If their relationship turned permanent, Hailey would have to do her prowling alone.

'There's not much nightlife here in Sasquanatee

County,' Rick said. 'Not much that's out in the open, anyway. Folks keep their secret proclivities to themselves.'

'Secret proclivities? Tell me more.'

'Well, take Cade and Noah and their infamous threesomes. It doesn't take a genius to figure out that these female "guests" they invite to the lodge aren't there to help them redecorate.'

'Ah. So the two of them are into threesomes. No one let me in on that.'

Rick looked sheepish. 'Sorry. I thought Noah would have told you.'

'He hasn't told me anything. Not yet, anyway.'

Hailey set down the pail of meat she'd been carrying. They'd been walking towards the tiger compound, but the cats were going to have to wait. Hailey sat down on a large flat rock, crossed her arms over her chest and waited for Rick to talk.

'Go ahead, Rick. Might as well let the cat out of the bag, so to speak.'

Rick sat down next to her. 'They'll kill me if they find out I told you this, but I believe you deserve to know. Cade and Noah have been playing this game together for years. Here's how it goes – they find a woman they both like, then they play her off each other until they finally convince her to go to bed with both of them. It always made me jealous as hell.'

'A game. How interesting,' Hailey mused. 'I knew they had something going on, but I didn't know it was so organised. It's all clear to me now. They practice symbiotic mating. That's unusual in males, but somehow it makes sense for those two.'

'They're not practising it any more. They've given up on the game,' Rick said. 'Noah called it off.'

'Called it off? You mean there was a game in progress?'

'Definitely.'

'Who was the prize?'

'Guess.' Rick grinned.

'Oh, I don't have to guess. I've known from the very beginning that something was brewing between Noah and Cade.'

Hailey got up, brushed off her seat and picked up her pail again. She set off briskly towards the tiger compound. Rick had to take long strides to catch up.

'I thought it was only fair that you knew what was going on,' Rick said. 'You have to give the guys some credit. They've both changed, especially Noah. I've never seen him like this.'

'The boys might have changed,' Hailey said with a sly smile, 'but I haven't. I'm a highly competitive girl. When it comes to games, I always have to win.'

'The game's been called off,' Rick reminded her.

'That's what *they* think,' said Hailey.

Hailey wasn't much of a cook, but she was planning a feast for three on Friday afternoon. Since the weather had been so co-operative lately, she decided to organise a picnic in a secluded grove near the lake. The hardest part would be luring both men out to the woods without either of them knowing that the other had been invited too. Cade was coming to the lodge on Friday morning, but Belinda would be joining him on Saturday afternoon. Hailey had a narrow window to work with, and the stress of trying to arrange everything in secret was killing her.

By Thursday, the stage was set. French bread, fresh fruit, ham and cheese had been packed in a basket and hidden away. Three bottles of champagne were chilling in the fridge. Hailey had visited the picnic site and checked that the grove was secluded enough for no one to hear a woman and two men screaming like animals.

Convincing Noah to join her was easy. On Thursday night, as he was lying on Hailey's bed with his face buried between her thighs, she whispered a few suggestions about primal sex in the great outdoors, and he was raring to go. Hailey hadn't said a word to Cade about the picnic, but she was confident that, with the proper coaxing, she could get him to come.

On Friday morning, Hailey's best-laid plans went to hell. She woke to the dismal plunk-plunk of rain dripping from the eaves. The rain didn't do anything to dampen Noah's libido. When he felt her stirring, he woke up hard as a rock and slid straight into her pussy without so much as a 'good morning'. For the next half hour Hailey lost herself in the pleasure of getting fucked, but after two orgasms the rain was coming down harder than ever.

'Looks like we'll have to postpone that picnic you were talking about,' Noah said, nuzzling the back of Hailey's neck.

'Not if I can help it,' Hailey said darkly.

But the rain wasn't the worst of it. She might have moved the picnic indoors, but Cade didn't show up at the expected time. The day passed, grey and dreary, with no sign of Cade's car. Finally, close to dinner-time, he showed up.

To top it all off, Cade wasn't alone. Belinda, looking as perfect as ever in a candy-apple-red rain slicker, followed him through the front door of the lodge. As soon as she saw Hailey, she dragged her into the kitchen for a cup of hot chai and some girl-girl chat.

'Too bad about Noah and Val, isn't it?' Belinda said,

handing Hailey a steaming mug of the spicy, milky drink. 'Cade told me everything. But you know, I never could stand that bitch. You'll make a much better sister-in-law.'

'Sister-in-law?' Hailey froze, holding her mug in mid-air.

'Cade and Noah are closer than most brothers. I'll be spending a lot of time with the woman Noah marries.' She gave Hailey a suggestive stare and licked the corner of her mouth with the pointed tip of her tongue. 'I'd rather that woman be you than Val. You have a much sexier body.'

Hailey gave Belina a wan smile. 'Noah and I haven't talked about getting married. We're taking it slowly. I'm not even used to exclusive dating.'

Belinda waved a manicured hand. 'Oh, you'll end up together. Cade says Noah's crazy about you, and Cade knows Noah like a brother.'

'Maybe,' said Hailey. 'That's the best I can do for now.'

'Well, marriage definitely works for me,' Belinda said. 'Since we got engaged, sex with Cade has been better than ever. All I had to do was lay down a few ground rules. You know, you should join us sometime.'

Belinda sidled up to Hailey. Under Belinda's ice-blue silk blouse, Hailey could see that she wasn't wearing a bra. Her nipples rose dark and hard under the sheer fabric. 'How about tonight?'

Hailey edged away from the insatiable blonde. 'I'd love to – some other time. I'll be turning in early. It's this rain. Makes me so sleepy.' She faked a yawn to prove her point.

'Fine,' Belinda sniffed, flipping her hair. 'Some other time.'

She left Hailey alone in the kitchen and went

upstairs. Cade had already gone up there and, within a few minutes, the vigorous creaking of floorboards told Hailey that Belinda and Cade were enjoying some of that fantastic sex that Belinda had told her about.

Hailey sighed. Maybe this was all for the best. She should curb her competitive impulses and be satisfied with what she had with Noah. The fragrant chai she'd been drinking suddenly tasted like cardboard, as she realised how disappointed she was at missing out on a threesome with Noah and Cade.

You're being unreasonable, she scolded herself. Millions of women were satisfied having sex with a single partner. If Hailey tried very hard, she might be able to change her spots and become monogamous, like them. It would mean transforming her personal life, as well as turning her back on the beliefs about sexuality that she'd developed through her research. Her theory that females needed erotic variety as much as males would be a mere abstraction, an academic idea all neatly wrapped up in a dissertation, not a philosophy she lived by.

That wasn't too much of a sacrifice, for a man she loved.

Or was it?

Hailey went to bed early and alone, but the solitude didn't do her much good. She tossed and turned for a few hours, then decided to give up on sleeping and go downstairs for a snack. The picnic basket she'd tucked away was packed with delicious food; someone might as well enjoy it. She was standing at the kitchen counter, slicing bread for a ham sandwich, when she heard a noise in the shadows and realised that she wasn't alone.

Hailey wheeled around, knife in hand.

'Who's there?' she demanded.

'It's me,' said Noah.

'And me,' said Cade. 'Noah told me about the picnic you were planning. Too bad it got rained out. I've always loved fucking in the woods.'

Cade and Noah stepped out of the darkness into the dim circle of light thrown by the open refrigerator. Hailey's heartbeat accelerated. Both men were wearing nothing but their briefs, and both were watching her intently. She wasn't used to being the centre of such focused attention from two males.

Cade propped his hand against the counter beside her, while Noah blocked her off on the opposite side. This wasn't how she had planned for this scene to go down. She'd seen herself catching the two friends off guard and taking the advantage from the very start. They'd turned the tables on her, and she wasn't sure if she liked it.

'That's not much of a midnight snack,' Cade remarked, nodding at the sandwich Hailey had made. He took the knife out of her hand and placed it in the sink. 'Wouldn't you rather have something more substantial?'

'Like this,' Noah said, taking Hailey's hand and placing it on his crotch. The bulge shifted under her palm. He was standing close enough for her to feel the warmth of his breath against her ear, matching the warmth of his cock under her fingers. Acting on reflex, she kneaded the length of flesh, and he moaned.

'Hey, none of that yet,' Cade scolded. 'You two have already had lots of time together; I'm not going to watch you have a quickie in the kitchen. Let's take this party to the den.'

He put his arm around Hailey's waist. Noah encircled her from the other side. Together they guided her out of the kitchen and into the room that had been Cade's grandfather's favourite place to relax. A fire had already been lit in the flagstone fireplace, and the big leather couch had been covered with a soft feather blanket. Hailey had to admit it – the two men had gotten the best of her.

They manoeuvred her onto the couch, then sat down next to her, one on either side.

'This isn't what you expected, is it?' Cade asked. 'You thought you'd turn the game around by setting up a picnic *à trois*.'

'How did you know what I was planning?' Hailey cried in frustration.

Cade and Noah exchanged a smile. 'A keen mind, a loyal buddy and a lucky guess,' Cade said. 'I had a strong hunch that you'd found out about the game. I've just been waiting for you to make your move.'

'I guess I should have anticipated a counter-play from an alpha male,' Hailey said.

'If I'm the alpha male, that makes Noah the beta,' Cade said. 'The dominant male has the best chance of getting a mate, right?'

'In some species, a beta wouldn't get to mate at all,' Hailey agreed.

'Fortunately, it's not like that with humans,' Noah whispered into Hailey's ear, sliding his arm around her waist.

Sandwiched between the two men on the leather couch, Hailey was having a hard time making her usual snappy comebacks. In fact, she was having a hard time remembering to take air into her lungs. Breathing was easy, she reminded herself – in and out, in and out. But with Cade rubbing his outer thigh against hers, and Noah gently edging his tongue into her mouth, the phrase 'in and out' was loaded with possibilities.

'You thought you could get the better of us, didn't you?' Cade said. 'Thought you could beat us at our own game.'

'You never had a chance,' added Noah. 'We're expert manipulators.'

As four male hands skilfully eased her out of her clothes, Hailey had no grounds for argument. She hadn't been wearing much, just a cotton nightie and a pair of sheer panties, so it didn't take them long to get her the way they wanted her. While Noah seduced her with deep french kisses, Cade slid down onto the oriental rug and wedged himself between her thighs. Soon she was being tongued in two places, and it was hard to tell whether her mouth or pussy were absorbing more of the pleasure. Noah was an exquisite kisser, and Cade was turning out to be remarkably gifted at cunnilingus. The dual stimulation was hypnotising, and before long Hailey was writhing like a snake on the couch. The novelty of the situation, combined with the expert attentions of the two men, was getting her so turned on that she could already feel an orgasm gathering on the horizon.

'Not so fast, greedy girl,' Cade scolded, lifting himself up from the floor. 'You need a lesson in sharing.'

Cade stepped out of his underwear, and Noah moved out of the way. Hailey was face to face with the CEO's cock. She'd held his large member in her hand before, but she'd never seen it up close. At this distance, she could appreciate what a magnificent specimen it was: a stout rod of hardwood crowned by a shiny russet head. He was circumcised, and the fine netting of blood vessels in his penis stood out in relief against the engorged skin.

He didn't give Hailey much time to admire his cock before he cupped the back of her head in his palm and pushed her towards his groin. His erection more than filled her mouth. She had to focus her attention on the head at first, then take in the rest of the meat one mouthful at a time. Finally she found a comfortable tempo, her head bobbing as she manipulated his balls with her hands. His sac was covered with a layer of wiry fuzz, and Hailey tugged at the curly strands and massaged the folds of warm skin until Cade groaned.

That's when Cade and Noah proved the extent of their experience. Cade backed slowly away, while Noah lifted Hailey's body off the slippery couch and moved her onto the rug. The men managed to rearrange themselves so that Hailey was on all fours, with Cade's cock still in her mouth, while Noah mounted her from behind. Together the two friends moved her back and forth between them, using her body to its fullest capacity. She loved the pornographic brutality of it, the sensation of being hammered from both ends. Knowing that Noah loved her, and that Cade cared about her, she was secure enough to let herself go and enjoy being a sex object.

Cade was the first to come. He pulled out of Hailey's lips just before he exploded, then showered her uplifted face with his seed. The sight of his friend climaxing was too much for Noah; he gave a ferocious cry a few seconds later, then gripped Hailey's hips so savagely that she thought he might tear her apart. At his peak, he grabbed a handful of her hair and pulled her head back. That rough gesture was all it took to bring her to her own finish.

'Now that we've got the first one out of the way, we can really take our time and enjoy each other,' Cade said. He pulled the feather blanket off the couch and spread it out on the floor. 'Have you ever seen two men make love?'

Hailey shook her head and took a seat on the couch. Wide-eyed, she watched as Cade and Noah lay down together on the blanket. Now that both men were together, Hailey couldn't resist comparing Noah's cock to Cade's. Cade had the edge on Noah in length and girth, but Noah's penis had a unique beauty, a form and colour all its own. She stared, riveted, as the two friends put their arms around each other and began to rub those cocks together at a leisurely, exploratory pace.

The scene had a aura of rediscovery. Hailey had the sense that while Cade and Noah knew each other's bodies intimately, it had been a while since they were naked together. She was amazed to see Cade kissing Noah's neck with the affection of a true lover, and, when Cade lowered his lips to Noah's nipples, he sucked the twin disks with such loving expertise that Hailey could tell the men had always been more than just friends.

Hailey sank back against the leather and fondled her pussy. She felt like she was back in the jungle in Costa Rica, observing an extraordinary species that she'd read about but never seen. The most intriguing part was that, for once, Noah seemed to be taking the dominant role. He was the one guiding Cade's hands where he wanted them to go, kissing Cade forcefully (more forcefully than he'd kissed Hailey) and finally pushing down on Cade's shoulders and directing him to suck his cock. That, too, was an amazing sight – Cade hungrily throating Noah's penis, pleasuring him with the deep instinct of a man who knows another man through and through. While he sucked, Cade reached up and toyed with Noah's erect nipples. Noah moaned, threw his head back and clung to Cade's short-cropped hair as his hips rose off the rug and he came into his best friend's mouth.

'Let me in,' Hailey begged, scrambling off her perch to join them. 'I can't take this any more.'

'Tired of sex as a spectator sport?' Cade teased.

'Yes,' Hailey said firmly.

Cade and Noah parted, and Hailey lay down between them. Now it was her turn to be the absolute centre of attention. The two men lavished her with caresses, lips and hands roving over her body in artful orchestration, until she lost track of who was stimulating her where. At one point, she felt Noah's silky hair between her thighs, and knew he was down there, delving for her pussy. She opened her legs and rested them on his shoulders, letting him dive in. In contrast to Noah's extravagant lapping, Cade squeezed her breasts roughly, tweaking and pinching the points, snapping at the nubs with his strong teeth. Then Noah lifted her bottom off the ground, moistened his index finger with her fluids, and inserted it into the tight bud between her cheeks.

'Give it to her,' Cade encouraged him. 'Let her see what it feels like.'

Noah plunged his finger into her ass. Hailey cried out in surprise. The feeling was alien, but exciting; she'd had men play around down there before, but none of her lovers had ever fully penetrated her anus.

'Give her your cock,' Cade urged. 'Come on.'

Noah looked up at Hailey from between her thighs. 'Is that OK?'

'Please,' Hailey moaned.

Noah slid upwards, pulling Hailey's legs up with him. He spread her thighs into a wide split, tilting her ass to give himself access to her anus, then shunted into her. It wasn't easy at first. The passage was tight, and his first thrusts felt like he was ripping her open. She could almost feel herself tearing, and the stinging pain brought tears to her eyes.

'Relax,' Noah said, in the same low voice that she'd heard him use with the animals. 'Let me in.'

Hailey exhaled, let her muscles go and closed her eyes. As painful as it was, this reaming seemed right. This was a night of first times. It was the first time she'd had a front-row seat at a male-male sex encounter, and the first time she'd let two men take her at once. It made perfect sense that she should get her first real ass-fucking from the lover who would probably be her mate for the rest of her life.

Noah slid in a few inches deeper, then all the way. After a few thrusts back and forth, the pain subsided into a coarse friction. When he felt Hailey loosen up, Noah sank in further. She moaned. Such a complete penetration: Noah's cock seemed to strike her straight to the heart. Just when she thought she couldn't tolerate the discomfort any more, it transformed into a gut-wrenching pleasure. Her bottom clenched down on Noah's cock as her muscles tensed for orgasm. The pressure of Noah's groin against her mound added a more familiar note, and soon she was reverberating with waves that radiated from her anus, pussy and clit. The symphony crested in a burst of sensations, a blur of moans and wetness. Hailey flooded herself and Noah – and Cade's grandfather's antique rug – with her juices. Luckily, she was too far gone to be embarrassed.

'I think she enjoyed that,' Cade said to Noah.

'Oh, I know she did.' Noah laughed, stroking Hailey's flushed skin.

Through the blur of the afterglow, Hailey heard

Noah and Cade whispering to each other, like two boys at a sleepover party.

'This is absolutely the last time we play this game,' Noah hissed.

'After tonight, I think we should reconsider,' Cade whispered back.

'No! I mean it. We just played our final round. This is the only woman I'll ever want or need.' He laid his hand possessively over Hailey's pussy, as if he could seal it off for himself.

'Right,' Cade chuckled. 'Whatever you say, my friend.'

Still half awake, Hailey smiled.

LOOK OUT FOR THE ALL-NEW BLACK LACE BOOKS – AVAILABLE NOW!

All new books priced £7.99 in the UK. Please note publication dates apply to the UK only. For other territories, please contact your retailer.

FIRE AND ICE
Laura Hamilton
ISBN 0 352 33486 X

Nina, auditor extraordinaire, is known at work as the Ice Queen, where her colleagues joke that her frosty demeanour travels to the bedroom. But what they don't know is that Nina spends her after-work hours locked into fiery games with her boyfriend Andrew, where she acts out her deepest fantasy of being a prostitute. Nina ups the stakes in her anonymous guise, being drawn deeper and deeper into London's seedy underworld – where everything can be bought and sold and no one is to be trusted. **A dark and shocking story of fantasy taken to extremes.**

SLEAZY RIDER
Karen S Smith
ISBN 0 352 33964 0

When newlyweds Emma and Kit speed away on their matching Ducati motorbikes, Emma knows not to expect a conventional honeymoon. From the moment they meet a biker gang and the leader takes a shine to Emma, events take a turn for the bizarre. For the first time in her life, she will be pushed to her limits as the gang's ideas for how to have a good time get more and more outrageous. With hard-drinking rock bands, hunky stuntmen, biker festivals and a whole lot of kinky behaviour on the agenda, Emma's taste for adventure is tested to the max – and Kit's not about to step in and save her from the wild bunch as he's having too much fun himself!

VILLAGE OF SECRETS
Mercedes Kelly
ISBN 0 352 33344 8

A small town hides many secrets and the Cornish village featured in this tale of lust, surfing and fetishism is no exception. When London journalist Laura inherits her grandmother's cottage, her eccentric neighbours waste no time in getting her to join in their bizarre games. Everyone knows each other's business and, when Laura strikes up an affair with a rugged young fisherman, you can be sure that the whole village will soon know her intimate secrets.

Coming in July 05

PAGAN HEAT
Monica Belle
ISBN 0 352 33974 8

For Sophie Page, the job of warden at Elmcote Hall is a dream come true. The beauty of the ruined house and the overgrown grounds speaks to her love of nature. As a venue for weddings, films and exotic parties the Hall draws curious and interesting people, including the handsome Richard Fox and his friends – who are equally alluring and more puzzling still. Her aim is to be with Richard, but it quickly becomes plain that he wants rather more than she had expected to give. She suspects he may have something to do with the sexually charged and strange events taking place by night in the woods around the Hall. Sophie wants to give in to her desires, but the consequences of doing that threaten to take her down a road she hardly dare consider.

NICOLE'S REVENGE
Lisette Allen
ISBN 0 352 32984 X

It is September 1792 and France is in the throes of violent revolution. Nicole Chabrier came to Paris four years earlier to seek fame and fortune with the Paris Opera but now her life is in danger from the hordes who are venting their anger on the decadent aristocracy. Rescued by a handsome stranger who has been badly wronged by the nobility, Nicole soon becomes ruled by her passion for this man. Together they seek a reversal of fortune using their charm, good looks and sexual magnetism. Against an explosive background of turmoil and danger, Nicole and her lover enjoy some explosions of their own!

Black Lace Booklist

Information is correct at time of printing. To avoid disappointment check availability before ordering. Go to www.blacklace-books.co.uk. All books are priced £6.99 unless another price is given.

BLACK LACE BOOKS WITH A CONTEMPORARY SETTING

❑ SHAMELESS	Stella Black	ISBN 0 352 33485 1	£5.99
❑ INTENSE BLUE	Lyn Wood	ISBN 0 352 33496 7	£5.99
❑ A SPORTING CHANCE	Susie Raymond	ISBN 0 352 33501 7	£5.99
❑ TAKING LIBERTIES	Susie Raymond	ISBN 0 352 33357 X	£5.99
❑ ON THE EDGE	Laura Hamilton	ISBN 0 352 33534 3	£5.99
❑ LURED BY LUST	Tania Picarda	ISBN 0 352 33533 5	£5.99
❑ THE NINETY DAYS OF GENEVIEVE	Lucinda Carrington	ISBN 0 352 33070 8	£5.99
❑ DREAMING SPIRES	Juliet Hastings	ISBN 0 352 33584 X	
❑ THE TRANSFORMATION	Natasha Rostova	ISBN 0 352 33311 1	
❑ SIN.NET	Helena Ravenscroft	ISBN 0 352 33598 X	
❑ TWO WEEKS IN TANGIER	Annabel Lee	ISBN 0 352 33599 8	
❑ PLAYING HARD	Tina Troy	ISBN 0 352 33617 X	
❑ SYMPHONY X	Jasmine Stone	ISBN 0 352 33629 3	
❑ SUMMER FEVER	Anna Ricci	ISBN 0 352 33625 0	
❑ CONTINUUM	Portia Da Costa	ISBN 0 352 33120 8	
❑ FULL STEAM AHEAD	Tabitha Flyte	ISBN 0 352 33637 4	
❑ A SECRET PLACE	Ella Broussard	ISBN 0 352 33307 3	
❑ GAME FOR ANYTHING	Lyn Wood	ISBN 0 352 33639 0	
❑ CHEAP TRICK	Astrid Fox	ISBN 0 352 33640 4	
❑ THE GIFT OF SHAME	Sara Hope-Walker	ISBN 0 352 32935 1	
❑ COMING UP ROSES	Crystalle Valentino	ISBN 0 352 33658 7	
❑ GOING TOO FAR	Laura Hamilton	ISBN 0 352 33657 9	
❑ THE STALLION	Georgina Brown	ISBN 0 352 33005 8	
❑ DOWN UNDER	Juliet Hastings	ISBN 0 352 33663 3	
❑ ODALISQUE	Fleur Reynolds	ISBN 0 352 32887 8	
❑ SWEET THING	Alison Tyler	ISBN 0 352 33682 X	
❑ TIGER LILY	Kimberly Dean	ISBN 0 352 33685 4	

- ❑ RELEASE ME Suki Cunningham ISBN 0 352 33671 4
- ❑ KING'S PAWN Ruth Fox ISBN 0 352 33684 6
- ❑ FULL EXPOSURE Robyn Russell ISBN 0 352 33688 9
- ❑ SLAVE TO SUCCESS Kimberley Raines ISBN 0 352 33687 0
- ❑ STRIPPED TO THE BONE Jasmine Stone ISBN 0 352 33463 0
- ❑ SHADOWPLAY Portia Da Costa ISBN 0 352 33313 8
- ❑ I KNOW YOU, JOANNA Ruth Fox ISBN 0 352 33727 3
- ❑ THE HOUSE IN NEW ORLEANS Fleur Reynolds ISBN 0 352 32951 3
- ❑ HEAT OF THE MOMENT Tesni Morgan ISBN 0 352 33742 7
- ❑ THE WICKED STEPDAUGHTER Wendy Harris ISBN 0 352 33777 X
- ❑ DRAWN TOGETHER Robyn Russell ISBN 0 352 33269 7
- ❑ LEARNING THE HARD WAY Jasmine Archer ISBN 0 352 33782 6
- ❑ VELVET GLOVE Emma Holly ISBN 0 352 33448 7
- ❑ UNKNOWN TERRITORY Annie O'Neill ISBN 0 352 33794 X
- ❑ VIRTUOSO Katrina Vincenzi-Thyre ISBN 0 352 32907 6
- ❑ FIGHTING OVER YOU Laura Hamilton ISBN 0 352 33795 8
- ❑ ARIA APPASSIONATA Juliet Hastings ISBN 0 352 33056 2
- ❑ THE RELUCTANT PRINCESS Patty Glenn ISBN 0 352 33809 1
- ❑ ALWAYS THE BRIDEGROOM Tesni Morgan ISBN0 352 33855 5
- ❑ COMING ROUND THE MOUNTAIN Tabitha Flyte ISBN0 352 33873 3
- ❑ FEMININE WILES Karina Moore ISBN0 352 33235 2
- ❑ MIXED SIGNALS Anna Clare ISBN0 352 33889 X
- ❑ BLACK LIPSTICK KISSES Monica Belle ISBN0 352 33885 7
- ❑ HOT GOSSIP Savannah Smythe ISBN0 352 33880 6
- ❑ GOING DEEP Kimberly Dean ISBN0 352 33876 8
- ❑ PACKING HEAT Karina Moore ISBN0 352 33356 1
- ❑ MIXED DOUBLES Zoe le Verdier ISBN0 352 33312 X
- ❑ WILD BY NATURE Monica Belle ISBN0 352 33915 2
- ❑ UP TO NO GOOD Karen S. Smith ISBN0 352 33589 0
- ❑ CLUB CRÈME Primula Bond ISBN0 352 33907 1
- ❑ BONDED Fleur Reynolds ISBN0 352 33192 5
- ❑ SWITCHING HANDS Alaine Hood ISBN0 352 33896 2
- ❑ BEDDING THE BURGLAR Gabrielle Marcola ISBN0 352 33911 X
- ❑ EDEN'S FLESH Robyn Russell ISBN0 352 33923 3
- ❑ CREAM OF THE CROP Savannah Smythe ISBN0 352 33920 9 £7.99
- ❑ PEEP SHOW Mathilde Madden ISBN0 352 33924 1 £7.99

- ❑ RISKY BUSINESS Lisette Allen ISBN 0 352 33280 8 £7.99
- ❑ OFFICE PERKS Monica Belle ISBN 0 352 33939 X £7.99
- ❑ CAMPAIGN HEAT Gabrielle Marcola ISBN 0 352 33941 1 £7.99
- ❑ MS BEHAVIOUR Mini Lee ISBN 0 352 33962 4
- ❑ FIRE AND ICE Laura Hamilton ISBN 0 352 33486 X
- ❑ SLEAZY RIDER Karen S. Smith ISBN 0 352 33964 0
- ❑ VILLAGE OF SECRETS Mercedes Kelly ISBN 0 352 33344 8

BLACK LACE BOOKS WITH AN HISTORICAL SETTING

- ❑ PRIMAL SKIN Leona Benkt Rhys ISBN 0 352 33500 9 £5.99
- ❑ DARKER THAN LOVE Kristina Lloyd ISBN 0 352 33279 4
- ❑ THE CAPTIVATION Natasha Rostova ISBN 0 352 33234 4
- ❑ MINX Megan Blythe ISBN 0 352 33638 2
- ❑ DIVINE TORMENT Janine Ashbless ISBN 0 352 33719 2
- ❑ SATAN'S ANGEL Melissa MacNeal ISBN 0 352 33726 5
- ❑ THE INTIMATE EYE Georgia Angelis ISBN 0 352 33004 X
- ❑ SILKEN CHAINS Jodi Nicol ISBN 0 352 33143 7
- ❑ THE LION LOVER Mercedes Kelly ISBN 0 352 33162 3
- ❑ THE AMULET Lisette Allen ISBN 0 352 33019 8
- ❑ WHITE ROSE ENSNARED Juliet Hastings ISBN 0 352 33052 X
- ❑ UNHALLOWED RITES Martine Marquand ISBN 0 352 33222 0
- ❑ LA BASQUAISE Angel Strand ISBN 0 352 32988 2
- ❑ THE HAND OF AMUN Juliet Hastings ISBN 0 352 33144 5
- ❑ THE SENSES BEJEWELLED Cleo Cordell ISBN 0 352 32904 1
- ❑ UNDRESSING THE DEVIL Angel Strand ISBN 0 352 33938 1
- ❑ THE BARBARIAN GEISHA Charlotte Royal ISBN 0 352 33267 0
- ❑ FRENCH MANNERS Olivia Christie ISBN 0 352 33214 X

BLACK LACE ANTHOLOGIES

- ❑ WICKED WORDS Various ISBN 0 352 33363 4
- ❑ MORE WICKED WORDS Various ISBN 0 352 33487 8
- ❑ WICKED WORDS 3 Various ISBN 0 352 33522 X
- ❑ WICKED WORDS 4 Various ISBN 0 352 33603 X
- ❑ WICKED WORDS 5 Various ISBN 0 352 33642 0
- ❑ WICKED WORDS 6 Various ISBN 0 352 33690 0
- ❑ WICKED WORDS 7 Various ISBN 0 352 33743 5

- ❑ WICKED WORDS 8 Various ISBN 0 352 33787 7
- ❑ WICKED WORDS 9 Various ISBN 0 352 33860 1
- ❑ WICKED WORDS 10 Various ISBN 0 352 33893 8
- ❑ THE BEST OF BLACK LACE 2 Various ISBN 0 352 33718 4
- ❑ WICKED WORDS: SEX IN THE OFFICE Various ISBN 0 352 33944 6
- ❑ WICKED WORDS: SEX ON HOLIDAY Various ISBN 0 352 33961 6

BLACK LACE NON-FICTION

- ❑ THE BLACK LACE BOOK OF WOMEN'S SEXUAL FANTASIES Ed. Kerri Sharp ISBN 0 352 33793 1
- ❑ THE BLACK LACE SEXY QUIZ BOOK Maddie Saxon ISBN 0 352 33884 9

To find out the latest information about Black Lace titles, check out the website: www.blacklace-books.co.uk or send for a booklist with complete synopses by writing to:

Black Lace Booklist, Virgin Books Ltd
Thames Wharf Studios
Rainville Road
London W6 9HA

Please include an SAE of decent size. Please note only British stamps are valid.

Our privacy policy
We will not disclose information you supply us to any other parties. We will not disclose any information which identifies you personally to any person without your express consent.

From time to time we may send out information about Black Lace books and special offers. Please tick here if you do not wish to receive Black Lace information. ❑

Please send me the books I have ticked above.

Name ....

Address ....

....

....

....

Post Code ....

Send to: Virgin Books Cash Sales, Thames Wharf Studios, Rainville Road, London W6 9HA.

US customers: for prices and details of how to order books for delivery by mail, call 1-800-343-4499.

Please enclose a cheque or postal order, made payable to Virgin Books Ltd, to the value of the books you have ordered plus postage and packing costs as follows:

UK and BFPO – £1.00 for the first book, 50p for each subsequent book.

Overseas (including Republic of Ireland) – £2.00 for the first book, £1.00 for each subsequent book.

If you would prefer to pay by VISA, ACCESS/MASTERCARD, DINERS CLUB, AMEX or SWITCH, please write your card number and expiry date here:

....

Signature ....

Please allow up to 28 days for delivery.